Amish Ac...

The Covert Police Detectives Unit Series (Book 6)

Ashley Emma

Copyright © 2022 by Ashley Emma

All rights reserved.

No portion of this book may be reproduced in any form without written permission from the publisher or author, except as permitted by U.S. copyright law.

Contents

GET 4 OF ASHLEY EMMA'S AMISH EBOOKS FOR FREE	v
1. PROLOGUE	1
2. Chapter One	5
3. Chapter Two	10
4. Chapter Three	16
5. Chapter Four	24
6. Chapter Five	33
7. Chapter Six	39
8. Chapter Seven	48
9. Chapter Eight	54
10. Chapter Nine	60
11. Chapter Ten	69
12. Chapter Eleven	74
13. Chapter Twelve	78
14. Chapter Thirteen	86

15. Chapter Fourteen	92
16. Chapter Fifteen	101
17. Chapter Sixteen	105
18. Chapter Seventeen	114
19. Chapter Eighteen	119
20. Chapter Nineteen	125
21. Chapter Twenty	134
22. Chapter Twenty-one	142
23. Chapter Twenty-two	150
24. Chapter Twenty-three	157
25. Chapter Twenty-four	164
26. Chapter Twenty-five	171
27. Chapter Twenty-six	180
28. Chapter Twenty-seven	187
29. Chapter Twenty-eight	197
30. Chapter Twenty-nine	208
31. Chapter Thirty	218
32. Chapter Thirty-one	231
33. Chapter Thirty-two	240
34. EPILOGUE	245
About the Author (Ashley Emma)	249
GET 4 OF ASHLEY EMMA'S AMISH EBOOKS FOR FREE	251
All of Ashley Emma's Books on Amazon	252
Excerpt of Amish Alias (book 5)	260

GET 4 OF ASHLEY EMMA'S AMISH EBOOKS FOR FREE

www.AshleyEmmaAuthor.com

Your free ebook novellas and printable coloring pages

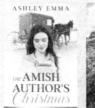   

PROLOGUE

Freya Wilson adjusted her blonde wig as she glanced in the rearview mirror, making sure none of her own red hair was peeking through. She then focused on the long, winding road ahead as she drove through the dark in Unity, Maine.

The never-ending farm fields, barns, and back roads were draped in a soft white blanket, illuminated only by moonlight. The peaceful scenery was the complete opposite of the Boston skyscrapers and bustle that she was so used to.

Normally, she would have enjoyed the picturesque scenery, but right now, she was too preoccupied with just trying to survive.

She rubbed the large bruise on her upper arm hidden by her jacket. The dull ache was just one voice in a chorus of other battle scars from her latest encounter with her ex-fiancé. They marked her ribs, her back, and her arms. There was even one on her face, carefully concealed under makeup.

Hopefully, that was the last time that he would ever hit her—if he didn't find her.

Now she was on the run. Everything she did was in an effort to escape Dean Hamilton, because if he ever found her, Freya was sure he would kill her.

The snow came down heavier on her windshield, and it was getting hard to see, especially since there were no street lights here. Soon, millions of snowflakes obscured her view, and she could barely see a few feet ahead, so she slowed down. She'd never driven in such terrible weather.

The start of her journey had been rough indeed, but it didn't matter as long as the path she was going to drive on would lead her toward freedom and happiness.

She could barely see a few feet ahead of her, so she drove as slowly as possible. The road was covered in snow, and she gripped the steering wheel, which danced in her hands.

Looking around, Freya could not see any other cars on the road. She probably seemed like a madwoman who certainly had a death wish.

But she was used to the fear of death.

Maybe I should pull over somewhere and wait it out, but where? she wondered as she carefully turned a corner.

Suddenly, a horse stood in the middle of her lane, and she yanked on the steering wheel instinctively to avoid it. The car veered off to the left, wheels locking and screeching across a sheet of black ice. As the car careened out of control, her world transformed into a dizzying snow globe of swirling flakes and flashing scenery. Panic gripped her, clouding her thoughts.

Her headlights illuminated something. Was it the horse's foal? A deer? She desperately tried to regain control of the car, but the steering wheel felt like a bucking bronco in her hands, jerking with a will of its own. No matter what she did, the car bore down on the amorphous form, seemingly intent on its target. At the last second, Freya screamed and braced for impact, instinctively attempting to tuck her head and raise her arms.

The vehicle slammed into the victim, and the airbags went off, then the car finally stopped. Tears streamed down her face as steadily as the snowflakes on her windshield. Her ribs and chest ached from the sudden restriction of the airbag and seatbelt, and her head was throbbing.

After several moments, she finally got the nerve to lift her head and look around. *What did I just hit?*

She gingerly opened her door, and the horse whinnied a short distance away. Freya looked up and saw a black buggy with another horse hitched to it, barely visible through the heavily falling snow and the darkness. Where was the driver?

She stepped around to the front of the car, not sure if she wanted to see the damage she had done to the poor animal. Clutching her churning stomach, she walked forward, pulling her jacket up over her chin against the biting cold.

It wasn't a deer or a foal—it was a man. An Amish man.

She felt as though the blood was draining from her body as the horror of what she'd done set in.

She'd hit a man with her car.

"What have I done?" she cried out, falling to her knees beside him.

The man lay lifeless on the road, crushed by the front of her car, surrounded by a puddle of blood that was now mixing with the falling snow. The diluted red liquid began pooling around her knees and feet, and she stifled another scream with her mitten-covered hands.

"I have to do something," she muttered, taking off her white scarf and wrapping it around his head to try to stop the bleeding, but the blood seeped right through the white material as though it was thin paper. She felt for a pulse on his neck and his wrist, but couldn't feel a pulse. She tried CPR, not sure if she was doing it right as she pressed her hands on his chest, then felt for a pulse again.

Nothing.

He was dead.

"I am so, so sorry," she whispered. "I tried to steer the car away from you, I swear..."

The man's black hat sat in a crumpled heap under the fender of her car. She picked it up, dusting the snow off of it. Suddenly overcome with nausea, she scrambled to her feet and hurried to the side of the road as fast as she could without slipping. She retched in a bush twice, her stomach churning with guilt and the shock of what had just happened. She placed her hands on her knees, trying to calm her swirling thoughts. There was nothing she could do to save him.

He was gone.

She'd killed a man. What if someone drove by and saw what she'd done? What if it was reported to the police? He'd find her.

Far off in the distance, the glow of headlights illuminated the powerlines and the trees lining the road. Panic set in once more, and

Freya rushed to her car, fumbling to get inside.

She looked up at the buggy and the two horses.

She had killed an Amish man. An innocent, pure-hearted Amish man.

Certainly, the hottest circle of hell was waiting for her after this miserable life.

No one could know of this. If she was arrested or questioned, her name might come up in the public records or the news, and her ex-fiancé would use his connections to find her.

And he would kill her. In a panic, she dropped the hat onto the passenger seat, threw the gear into reverse, and sped away.

Chapter One

Earlier that day

Dark winter clouds hovered above Freya's Victorian house as if predicting a tragedy. Though Freya had inherited the house, her fiancé, Dean, ruled over it.

"Dean, what happened to all the money?" Freya asked as they sat down at the table to eat breakfast. She'd prepared eggs, bacon, and pancakes cooked to perfection, just the way Dean liked them. The table was set with the fine china that she'd also inherited from her dear friend.

"What money?" Dean asked, slicing into his pancakes. He paused, squinting down at his plate. His black hair was cut into a short, military-style haircut, and he had a carefully trimmed beard. His muscular arms were covered in tattoos, something that had intrigued Freya when she'd first met him.

"The money I inherited from Shirley. Where is it all going? I mean, I know you said you needed some to pay off your dad's medical bills, but it says in the bank statements it's going to the casino. Are you gambling away my inheritance?" she demanded.

Though her voice sounded confident, she tried not to squirm in her seat. Her questions could make him angry, but she couldn't let him squander Shirley's money. She had plans for that money—she wanted to save it for her future children, maybe even buy another property to rent out. Now the money was dwindling away so rapidly she knew those plans would never happen.

Dean set down his fork and knife and stared at her. "Don't question me. It's none of your concern what I decide to do with our money. We have a joint account, remember?"

She almost spat out the drink of water she'd just sipped. "Excuse me? Shirley left me that money when she died. It's actually my money, and it's not meant to be gambled away."

Adding Dean to her bank account had been a huge mistake. She realized that now.

Dean pushed back his chair and came toward her with a raging look in his eyes.

The fear of the pain she knew was coming shivered down her spine. Bruises from the most recent attack still marred her body. Her mind automatically shut down and went into survival mode as she protected her face and vital organs as much as she could with her arms.

Please, God, let him run out of anger before he does any serious or permanent damage, she prayed. *If you spare me, I'll do everything it takes to get away from him and make sure he can never hurt me again.*

He yanked her from the chair she sat in and threw her against the wall. Blood burst out through her nostrils, causing red spots to splatter on Freya's yellow shirt. She fell to the floor.

Dean looked at her as if he wanted to kill her right then and there.

"It's my money now, you understand?" he screamed.

Freya struggled to scream for help as her survival instinct kicked in. He grabbed her throat with both his hands and slammed her head against the wall as if it were a wrecking ball. Freya fell to the floor, her head throbbing with pain. She could not see straight anymore, defenseless in front of a man who looked like he was willing to end her life with his bare hands right then and there.

She still had the signs and bruises on her hands and face from a few nights ago when Dean had attacked her.

"If you dare to say a word to someone about this, you are dead! You know I'm friends with several of the officers at work, and they would take my side!" he roared. He looked down at the red splotches of blood on his crisp, white shirt and gray tie. "Ugh. Look what you did to my shirt. Now I have to go change." He stomped away.

His words rang in her head like a church bell. They were the last words Dean said to her before he drove off to work, probably with a smile on his face, as if he had won some great victory.

Dean was a bounty hunter now, but he had been a police officer for a short time. He didn't make his one-year probationary period as an officer, but he made a lot of friends while he was on the force by going out and drinking with them after work. Because he didn't follow department policy on arrests and was overly violent, he was terminated early on. So, he became a bounty hunter instead, so he could be his own boss. However, he swore his friends would do anything to help him, even lie for him.

He held that over her head every day.

Dean would find reasons to start a fight in almost everything. The most random, insignificant situations enraged him.

She had nowhere else to go. This was her house, and now that she'd stupidly let him move in a few months ago, she couldn't get him to leave. She'd tried to leave him before, and she had the scars to prove it.

She hated the thought of leaving this house behind after she'd inherited it from her friend Shirley, who had been like a grandmother to her, but now she was seeing no other way out of this toxic, dangerous relationship.

Dean's threats crept under her skin, haunting her very existence.

Outside was below freezing, but she couldn't stand to be in the house a moment longer. As soon as she heard Dean's car leave the driveway, she went outside.

Freya's tears froze on her face before they even fell to the ground as her ears started to sting, then turned numb like the rest of her body. Her brain was too busy conjuring up a way out of this living hell to notice anything else. Her senses were shut down, her aching heart drowning out everything else, yearning for the days when she did not have to worry about staying alive.

For the first time, she clearly understood. Yes, her life was in danger. She had always wondered why nothing she did seemed to please Dean in any way. For so long, she'd thought it was her own fault. She'd thought she wasn't good enough, caring enough, or attentive enough to him. She'd thought she wasn't fast enough at anticipating what he wanted and providing it, soothing enough to divert his anger once aroused, strong enough to fight, quick enough to escape, or smart enough to end any argument before it got out of control.

Freya sat down on the front steps and lowered her head in her hands, defeated. Now she saw it for the first time. It wasn't her. It was him; no matter how hard he tried to convince her, it was all her fault. Dean was a monster dressed in a man's skin that seemed to have been sent straight from hell to terrorize her very existence.

Snow crunched under somebody's feet. A shiver sped down her spine. Had he come back to finish the job? She didn't even dare lift her head to see.

She felt a gentle touch on her shoulder. Her immediate reaction was to jolt backward—an automatic reaction. She had no idea if and when Dean was going to hit her, so her brain was under constant stress and fear.

A kind voice pierced through the cold. "Don't be scared, child. I just saw you crying all alone here in the snow, and I came to see if you were all right."

She slowly lifted her head. It was Victor, her kind, elderly neighbor.

"I'm fine. Don't worry about me," she said while trying to wipe her frozen tears off her face.

Victor was the embodiment of the typical middle-class elderly man. Always careful with his house, his car—even if it was older than Freya—and his property. During the summer, his lawn would look impeccable, and he would trim the hedges near the sidewalk. Freya had noticed that his brown dog was his only companion.

"You don't look fine to me at all," Victor replied, pushing his wire-rimmed glasses up on his nose. "You are crying all by yourself out here in the cold, and you aren't wearing a jacket. You know, I've heard the shouting and things breaking. I was the one who called the police before."

Freya looked down, remembering the times the police had come to Freya's house, asking if anything was wrong, and Dean had always had some explanation to make them go away. She was not about to contradict him to the police. Before they left, she would always insist she was fine.

"I know he's hurting you," Victor pressed.

Tears stung Freya's eyes. There was no getting around it—he knew. She didn't know what to say to him. Why deny it? She didn't want to lie, but she didn't want to put him in danger either. Who knew what Dean would do to him if he found out that Victor knew the truth?

"I'm sorry. I'm really sorry," she murmured, trying to walk away, but her feet were too frozen for her to be able to make a single move. "I should not get you involved in this. I am fine, trust me. I had just come out to get some fresh air."

"And cry out here in the freezing cold?" Victor insisted. "And you have bruises on your face and neck. It's obvious something is wrong here. I can help you get away from him, you know, if you don't want to go to the police. I can help you with anything you need. Do you need a car to get away from him? Money for gas or a plane ticket?"

Freya turned her head away from Victor, trying to avoid his eyes. But he was not there to judge her, rather to offer a hand to a person in need.

She did not know what she felt or how to react anymore. In her head, there was a storm smashing and crashing everything in its path, and it was fueled with fear and despair. All she knew was that if this man helped her, he was as good as dead, and she couldn't have his death be her fault.

"I'm fine," she insisted as she finally managed to get up. She was planning on going inside, but something in her heart told her she should wait for another minute and hear what this old man had to say.

There she went again, following her same old patterns of hiding her injuries when it only protected Dean, not her.

"You can say whatever you like to me right now, but I am old enough to know that you're most likely being abused," Victor replied with a kind voice. "I've seen it before with other couples. I was happily married for fifty-three years, and I know what being married truly means. I know that fights are inevitable, but they shouldn't happen like this. What is happening to you, my dear, is just wrong."

Chapter Two

"Please, don't assume I have spied on you, because I haven't. I could hear the noises, the fighting, and all those screams. Our houses are not so far away from each other, you know. I called the police before. What I have witnessed today is too much. I would never forgive myself if I saw a woman suffer the way you suffer and did nothing about it besides calling the police a few times," Victor said.

Again, Freya's eyes were filled with tears, the last ones she had left. She was engulfed by a feeling of sadness and regret and could not believe at the same time that such chivalry still existed in the world.

She turned away from the front door and towards Victor, covering her face with her hands.

Victor looked at her with compassion. "I know you are scared, child. You still have many long and beautiful years ahead of you. You just need to dare and take that opportunity while you are still breathing."

Victor's words rang through Freya's head. They sounded just right, exactly the thing that she needed to hear and, more importantly, do. She looked at the old man for a moment; he was indeed the embodiment of kindness with his warm brown eyes and wrinkled eyelids. Then, without a warning, she plunged into his arms. A cascade of feelings pulled her up and down like a rollercoaster.

"What am I going to do? What am I going to do?" Freya muttered in the old man's shoulder. "He used to be a cop. His friends are police officers. They will find me if I run. And this is my house, not his. I can't make him leave. If I call the police, he says his friends will take his side."

Victor patted her slowly on the back and listened to her weary breathing. Now that she was so close to him, she noticed him seeing all the bruises and all the marks on her neck and face. It looked like a terrible war had been waged on her skin, and now he was witnessing the aftermath.

After a few more moments, she pulled back and tried to wipe her tears. She could hardly breathe—the frigid air felt like acid burning her throat.

Through the pristine snowflakes that started to fall out of nowhere, Victor looked at the sky and smiled.

"It looks like this is a sign!" he said with a kind voice; his arms were wide open trying to catch a snowflake.

"What do you mean?" Freya asked in a confused voice. Snowflakes were getting caught in her hair, and those falling on her skin were melting right away. Her skin was still warm, and her heart was still beating, meaning that she still had enough energy to make a change.

Victor looked at her again. "They say that every time it snows, somewhere an angel is born."

This funny remark made Freya smile for a moment. "I've never heard that before."

"Maybe it's not true, but this pile of wood and glass you are calling a home is the biggest lie of all."

The words sank deep in Freya's heart as if they had been cast in the lead. She looked at her house, three stories tall with a Victorian feel. It looked almost perfect, and it used to be filled with good memories, but on the inside, it was a horrific prison now.

Freya just stood there on the porch watching how the snowflakes were falling peacefully on the old layer of snow.

"It's never too late, you know," Victor said.

Victor's encouraging words gave Freya goosebumps all over her body, and this time, they were not caused by the freezing cold outside. She started picturing herself free—running and going wherever she wanted without fear of being beaten, or worse, killed by Dean during one of his manic episodes. Her aching heart started pushing blood through her body faster and faster, and suddenly a flicker of hope sparked in her soul.

Freya had nothing anymore. Shirley had left her a large inheritance and this house. Dean had taken it all from her within mere months.

Her feet were still cold and wet, but at least she had heard some words of wisdom from someone who clearly understood life better than she did. She looked at Victor.

"I don't have anywhere to go," Freya muttered. "I have no family. We have a joint bank account, and he's taken everything from me. I have nothing anymore. He will use his police connections to find me."

Victor took off his gloves. "So? Is that an excuse?"

Freya looked up at him.

"You see, when I married my beautiful wife all those years ago, I had nothing, just like you. No money. Nothing. Just the sky above my head. We still managed to build a happy life. With these two hands," Victor added as Freya noticed his wrinkled and battered hands. "When the love of my life passed away—God bless her soul—I had nothing once again, but I got through it. I was devastated, but I kept going. You will get through this. You have resources you are not aware of, and all you need to do is take that first step. After that, you will certainly figure out a way. I can help you."

Freya took in Victor's every word and quickly realized the truth in them. Yet, she could not muster the courage to make that first step. Her freedom felt so far away from her.

In the back of her head, there was this constant fear lurking: Dean would try to kill her, regardless of where she was going to run. He had promised her countless times that he would not rest until he killed her if she ever ran away from him.

She looked at her feet in her slippers. They had gone numb, just like her overall existence. She could not feel joy anymore. Freya could barely remember the last time she genuinely laughed. She lived in constant fear, terrified of what her fiancé would do to her next. Her heart and soul and her own pride and decency were broken. Her bones were still intact so far because he'd been careful not to leave visible injuries before today. But now she had bruises on her arms, neck, and face that Victor had quickly picked up on. Now that Dean had crossed that line, how long would it be before she ended up in a hospital?

Her ribs ached, but she wouldn't go to a hospital, even if they were broken. She wasn't sure if there was anything that could be done about them, anyway. They would have to just heal on their own. If she went to a hospital, Dean would use his connections to access medical records.

"Where should I go? I have no one," Freya muttered.

"Anywhere. It doesn't matter as long as you can find your happiness. I am willing to help you. Where is that violent beast you're calling your man right now?" Victor asked.

"Dean is at work right now," Freya said. "Why?"

"Now is the perfect moment," Victor replied with a strong voice.

Freya hesitated when she heard those words. "Now? Perfect for what?"

"To run, to go away. To be free, to live and love again. Not all people get a second chance at life, you know. I don't have many days to live on the face of this earth; I am fully aware of that. But you have quite a lot of years ahead of you," Victor added. "Take my car and some money I've put aside, and go before it's too late. As for the car, I'll sign the title over to you, but I'll leave the date off. Don't put it in your name just yet."

"I can't take your money or your car," Freya said, shaking her head. "What if I get pulled over? What if Dean realizes you let me use your car?"

"Try not to get pulled over, of course." He gave a small smile. "How would Dean know I gave it to you? I've always kept it in the garage."

"He's a smart guy. He's a bounty hunter. What if I buy it from you? Then I could sell it and get a different one once I reach somewhere safe."

"But then you'd have to register your car under your new address. I don't know much about these things, but wouldn't Dean be more likely to notice that?"

"I suppose so."

"Just take the car, and I will pay for the insurance and registration for you under my name, but I'll put you as the driver on my insurance."

"You would do that?" Freya put her hand on her heart, astounded by this man's kindness.

Victor waved a hand and huffed. "I don't need two cars. It was my wife's car, but I could never bring myself to drive it again. Please, she would want you to have it."

"I don't know what to say. You barely know me, yet you are being so kind to me." Tears stung her eyes.

"Listen. My wife and I had one daughter, and she was going to inherit everything once we both passed, but my daughter died a few years ago," Victor said, his eyes brimming with tears. "Her boyfriend was also abusive, and he killed her before killing himself. We had no idea he was hurting her until it was too late because she hadn't spoken to us in years. I just wish I could go back and change things so it never happened."

"I am so sorry. That is terrible," Freya said.

"Anyway, she didn't have any children, and I have no one left to give the money to, and you remind me of her. I want to give it to you, and I want you to have the car."

Freya's heart tripped. She put a hand on her chest. "Me? Are you sure? I don't even have my own bank account. He took over mine."

"So, open a new one. It's pretty easy, you know. Just take the money out of the joint account and close that account right away, then open a new one in your name only with whatever money you have left, keeping a generous amount in cash. I'll transfer some more money to you because I want to help. For now, I'll get you some cash so you can leave right away. Use cash, not credit, or he can track your purchase locations."

Could she really believe him? What if he was trying to con her somehow?

As she looked into this man's eyes, surrounded by crinkled smile lines from a life well-lived, she knew deep in her heart she could trust him.

"Please. I've lost everyone. Let me do this for you," he pleaded. "It will make Dean angry, but if you leave, he will take all the money you have left. Hopefully, one day you can get the house back. Right now, all that matters is your safety. If you stay any longer, I'm afraid he'll kill you. Please, do this for me, if not for yourself. Every day I live with worry that he will kill you, and I know he is hurting you severely. It pains me to think that you live in the same house as him. I want you to be safe."

Freya burst into tears, hugging him again. Victor's words seemed so surreal that her brain was close to incapable of processing them. She blinked her teary eyes a few times, pulled away, then looked at Victor, who was still waiting for an answer.

"Come on, child, what are you waiting for?" he asked.

"Thank you. Thank you so much!" she cried, feeling as though her heart would burst from fear, excitement, and gratitude.

"Go pack your things." He shooed her away.

"I only need a few minutes." Freya turned without wasting another moment and ran into the house. Maybe she could go to Canada. She had some relatives in Canada she'd never met. They could have raised her if they'd chosen to, but instead, they'd chosen not to and she'd gone into foster care. She'd never told Dean about them because it was a painful topic for her to talk about. He had no idea she had any connection to Canada.

Hopefully, Dean wouldn't look for her there.

Chapter Three

She hurried upstairs to the bedroom and started shuffling through her clothes. She didn't have that many things, but even so, she could not take everything, only a few things. The less she took, the longer it would take Dean to realize she was really gone, especially if she left her favorites. She grabbed one bag, stuffing it with clothing from the back of her closet that she hadn't worn in a long time.

Dean had thrown out most of her belongings when he moved in, replacing them with his own and claiming there wasn't space to store them, so there wasn't much she could take with her. She grabbed the small amount of cash she'd been hiding under the rug that she'd saved up doing odd jobs for neighbors that Dean hadn't known about.

As she approached the doorway, Freya rested her hand on the door frame. She'd lived here for a few years with Shirley, and she smiled at the happy memories they'd shared. After Freya's drug addict mother hadn't been able to take care of her and didn't even want her, she'd been placed in the foster system. She'd never known what it was like to have a real family. Shirley was the closest thing she'd ever come to one—she had been something like a mother or grandmother to Freya, she guessed. Freya had never met her grandmother.

"I'll miss this place," Freya whispered as she took one last look at the house. Now, when she looked around, the recent memories Dean had created in her mind overtook the good ones she'd shared here with Shirley.

If it was ever safe for her to return, could she ever live here on her own again? Selling this place was a painful thought, causing her to feel as though she were betraying Shirley. No, for now, she wouldn't sell it.

For now, she had to go. She'd think about that later.

Freya emerged from her house with the single bag stuffed with clothes in her hand. The engine in Victor's car was running, already blowing a thick trail of whitish smoke in the back.

"Here, take it," he said, handing Freya the keys to his car. There was a key chain with a photo of his wife on it. When Freya wanted to return it to Victor, he refused.

"Take it with you," he added, smiling. "I will be reunited with my love in heaven soon; I can feel it. I don't need that anymore. I will meet her again soon in person."

Freya had never felt that sort of bond in her life before. No man had ever made her feel that way. She felt a bit envious of Victor, but not in a bad way. Right there, she prayed she would find someone someday that would truly make her feel safe, whole, because there was an emptiness in her chest she could not shake.

Victor pressed an envelope into Freya's hand, filled thick with cash. Written on it was a phone number. She opened it, revealing several large bills. Her eyes went wide.

"That's my number on the envelope. When you get your bank account set up, call me and I'll send you a check or do a fund transfer from my bank." The look on Victor's face was so serene and calm. "The tank is full. When my wife went through chemo, she collected several wigs. I put a bag of them on the passenger seat with some of her glasses and hats. I figured you could use them to disguise yourself. I know what your fiancé does for work, so stay away from cities and try to avoid security cameras. Whatever you do, stay out of trouble."

Freya took Victor's hands. "Thank you so much. I have no idea how to repay you."

"God bless you, child. I hope you can find somewhere safe and put this all behind you. That is all the repayment I want."

Freya looked at the old man and could not find her words to thank him. She knew she might never see him again. Victor's kindness would certainly mark her existence for all the days she had left.

"I just want you to be happy. I want you to take the money, and I don't want you to repay one cent of it. Just promise me you will spend it or save it wisely."

Freya nodded. "I promise I will be wise with it."

"And remember this: there are things in life that could never be bought even if you had all the gold and money in the world, like spending every moment you can with your family until they are gone," Victor replied with tears in his eyes.

Freya's own eyes filled with tears. "This is one of the kindest things anyone has ever done for me. I have to repay you somehow."

"No, I don't want you to. I'm old and don't have much time left. I don't need the money, and I want one of the last things I do to be helping someone else."

Freya gave Victor a final hug. The old man's hands were cold as ice.

"Thank you so much, Victor," Freya murmured. "You've saved my life."

"I am more than convinced that you will find a man one day who will know how to treat you properly. You are a beautiful young woman inside and out who deserves to be happy. Now get going while you have a head start. Who knows when he will be home?"

"He still has several hours until he gets off from work," Freya replied, but then she remembered all those instances when Dean had come home irregularly just to see what she was doing. Victor was right—she needed to go. "Thank you, Victor. You may have just saved my life." She threw her arms around him.

He patted her on the back. "You're welcome, dear. I just want you to be safe and have a happy life. You deserve so much more."

"I will call you soon," she said, pulling away, giving him one last grateful glance.

"Yes, thank you. I want to know when you are safe, but be careful. Use a public phone. Go, now. Hurry." He made a shooing motion with his hands, a small smile on his face.

She opened the door of the car to get in. The car was already warm inside. Her hands and feet started warming up. Outside, it was still snowing, a layer of a few inches of fresh powder already covering the ground.

She grabbed the bag on the passenger seat and unzipped it to reveal the wigs and other accessories. Freya put on a blonde wig, a scarf, and some plastic glasses, then looked in the mirror. She looked different enough, especially in this blinding weather.

Freya drove away, the image of Victor in her rearview mirror fading quickly as the snow continued to fall.

As she drove, Freya had a slight smile on her face, even though she hadn't been driving more than a few minutes. She was actually starting to feel the taste of freedom with every inch she traveled as she drove farther from what she could no longer call home. Dean's attack that morning had seen to that.

She just focused on keeping the car on the road and drove on without looking back. As she continued to drive, she became more relaxed and began thinking of how her life was going to start over. Maybe she could be a teacher again. She had a degree for teaching, thanks to Shirley putting her through college. Unfortunately, Dean had not allowed her to work because he was afraid that she would meet someone else and leave him.

With the money Victor had given her and her own savings, she had enough to buy a plane ticket to France, but would he be able to track that? She honestly had no idea. She'd always wanted to go to Europe. Hawaii would be nice too.

Her phone dinged, and her heart froze. Freya strongly suspected that Dean had been tracking her with it. With his training, he had the know-how to do it.

The phone beeped again, signaling a text message. She didn't have any numbers saved in her phone, except for Victor's. Dean had thrown away her old phone and bought a new one so she couldn't talk to anyone else. Her right foot automatically pushed the brake pedal to the floor, and the car drifted slightly.

Her body shook, and she could not feel her feet anymore despite the warmth inside the car. She was terrified to grab that phone and check the message and knew already it would only be threats of the worst kind.

After a few deep breaths, she grabbed her phone and looked to see the message.

I told you I would kill you if you left.

You thought I was joking?
Just waiting to get my hands on you.
I am coming for you, and I will kill you.

Dean was determined to haunt her existence until her last breath. He would go to the ends of the earth in order to do so.

In the past, she had even pondered about killing herself at times when she felt as though she could not take it anymore. Maybe she should just end it all now. If Dean did find her, he would kill her anyway, and it would be horrific. She could drive off a cliff in this weather, and if the fall and resulting impact didn't kill her outright, she would bleed out or succumb to hypothermia relatively quickly. She'd heard hypothermia lulled its victims to sleep, so in the end, they felt quite warm and cozy before going comfortably numb. Comfortably numb sounded appealing right now.

She was just so tired of the pain, of the fear, of the constant need to be on the alert.

But then she remembered her vow. *I will do whatever it takes to make sure he can't hurt me again.*

What was she thinking? Why give up now? Her life had meaning. Every life had meaning. She had come this far. She would survive.

"No, I am not going to let myself be terrorized again. It is either freedom or death!" she roared, focusing on the road ahead.

Now Dean was trying to call her, and she stiffened. She did not want to hear his voice or see his face ever again in her life.

Freya saw a bus stopped up ahead, then pulled her car over. Perfect. The light-up sign on the top of the bus showed that it was heading south, the opposite direction of where she was headed.

She hurried toward it, shielding her face with little success from the biting wind, then handed the driver money for a ticket. Freya wandered to the back of the bus, then nonchalantly sat down. Turning the phone on silent, but keeping it on, she shoved it under the seat while looking around to make sure no one was looking. Then she went back to the front of the bus.

"I just forgot my bag in my car. I'll be right back," she told the driver.

"I don't have all day, miss. I got a schedule to keep," the rotund man said, but she was already halfway out the door.

Freya stepped back out into the cold, and when she reached her car again, she cranked up the heat. She drove away, watching the bus also drive away in her rearview mirror, going the opposite direction. Now Dean would track her going south. It might not take him long until he figured it out, but it should be enough to buy her just enough time to get a head start.

She got on the highway, going north toward Unity, Maine.

***

Victor was right.

Only a half-hour after Freya fled the house, Dean came back out of nowhere to check on Freya.

Victor peeked through his curtains as the abuser pulled his car into the driveway in a rush. As the bully walked to the door, his face was bitter and tense.

Dean looked towards the old man's house as if suspecting something. Victor quickly dropped the curtain and backed away from the window. Had Dean seen him?

The last thing Victor needed now was to get into a fight with a raging bull like Dean. In his younger days, he had stood up to men like that regardless of the consequences. But his strength was long gone. What would a narcissist like that do to an elderly man?

Fortunately, Dean turned his gaze away from Victor's house. With one swift movement, he opened the front door and strutted inside the same way a lion would prowl his domain: triumphant and certain.

"Freya... Freya!" Dean ground his teeth as if they were hers, trying to break them into a million pieces.

Usually, Freya would come rushing to greet him whenever she heard Dean's voice. It did not matter if she was in the kitchen, upstairs, or in the basement. She would hurry to meet him at the door as if her own life was on the line. Because it was.

Why wasn't she answering? Where was she? Anger frothed up inside him and instantly overflowed. He slammed the door behind him so hard the wood screeched in pain.

"Where is that woman?" he mumbled to himself as he started to search the house.

He started in the kitchen. All the pots and pans were in their usual place. The room looked neat and clean; the blood spatters from her earlier lapse in judgment invisible to the naked eye. Freya worked herself day and night in order to keep the whole house clean and tidy; that had been one of Dean's express requirements. He had taught her —with the back of his hand—to keep the entire house spotless.

He walked upstairs into the bedroom. When Dean opened the door, the room was immaculate, as usual. Dean opened the closet and pushed the clothes in the front aside to see several empty hangars at the back of the wardrobe. Those weren't empty before.

He looked under the bed and pulled out a box, opening it to see several of Freya's important papers missing, including her passport and birth certificate.

He sat on the bed, holding the box. Had she just gone away for a few days to cool off? If she had, why did she take her passport? Maybe she'd come sniveling back when she realized how useless she is without him. If that were the case, she would have taken her favorite clothes and left the papers.

His face turned red with anger, his fists tight at his sides.

She was gone. She'd left him. Did she really think she could get away from him? She'd tried this before—he'd found her, and she had the scars to prove it.

He tore the bedroom apart, smashing the ceramic castle she'd painted as a child and the knickknacks Shirley had given to her. He punched the bathroom mirror, the jagged edges of the glass slicing into his knuckles.

"She'll pay for that," he muttered angrily and slammed the wall with his fist. "She'll regret this for the rest of her days."

He would find her...and he would make her pay. Then he remembered he could track her. Until now, he hadn't had to use it except for that time she'd tried to leave him. He turned on his phone, checking to see where Freya's location was. She had no idea, but he could track her phone and find out where she was at any time.

He sneered when he saw the screen light up, seeing that she was driving down the highway, going south.

All he had to do was follow the signal, but he had to hurry to catch up with her.

First, he had some questions for the old man who lived across the street.

He walked over to the man's house and pounded on the front door. "Victor? I know you're home. I have some questions for you."

"Go away or I'll call the police!" the old man shouted from inside.

"Did you help Freya leave? I know you called the police, claiming I was abusing her."

"Who?"

Dean's blood boiled with frustration. "My fiancée, Freya. Don't play dumb. I know you made those domestic violence calls," Dean growled. "I wasn't arrested, as you can see."

"Doesn't mean you're innocent," Victor retorted through the door.

Dean pounded his fist into the door. "Where is she, old man?"

"Who?"

"My fiancée!" Dean growled.

"I don't think she's your fiancée anymore. Think whatever you want, but I'm on the phone with the police right now. Hello? Yes, this is Victor Johnston. I'm calling to report my neighbor, who is yelling at me and pounding on my door, harassing me," Dean heard the man say.

"Fine, I'm leaving," Dean said, backing away. "If you helped her, you'll regret it, old man."

Dean turned and stormed off to his car. It wouldn't take long to catch up to Freya if he hurried.

She wouldn't get far.

Chapter Four

Maria paced the floor of her in-laws' house as she waited for her husband to return. "Robert should be back by now. He's been gone for an hour. Where is he?"

Aaron stood by the window, staring out into the storm. "Perhaps the horse wandered farther away than we realized. Maybe Robert just can't see anything in the storm and can't find his way home."

"We need to start a search party," Adam said, getting up off the couch with a blanket wrapped around him.

"You're sick, Adam. You need to stay put," Hannah said, wagging her finger. "You should be in bed."

"I can't sleep or just sit here while my brother could be in trouble. I need to go look for him now. I say we find people who can help us search," Adam said, already putting on his boots and jacket. "I should have gone with him, so I have to do this. I'll go knock on the neighbors' doors."

"Adam," Hannah protested. "You're sick. Sending you out there won't do any good."

"I should have gone with him," Adam argued. "He probably just got turned around in the storm. I'll be right back." With that, he put on his boots and coat and walked out the door.

"I'll go with you," Aaron said.

"Me too." Maria rushed to join him, pulling on her boots and jacket. Her insides were wrought with anxiety and worry for her husband. What if something had happened to him?

"Well, then, I'm coming too," Hannah said, and a moment later, they were knocking on the neighbors' doors, and within minutes, several people had joined them outside and were hitching up their buggies.

As Adam and Aaron broke them up into groups and sent them in different directions, Maria wrapped her arms around herself.

"I'm so worried about him," she murmured, and Hannah leaned in closer.

"God will protect him, Maria."

Maria's parents, Mary and Gideon, came rushing out of their house and hurried over to Maria.

"We heard what happened. We are praying for Robert's safety," Mary said.

"I will go with them to search." Maria's father kissed her on the forehead. "Don't worry, darling. I'm sure he's fine. It hasn't been that long. Maybe he got stuck or lost in the storm."

She nodded as Gideon joined the other men and rode away in a buggy down the lane, the way Robert had gone. But what if he had turned around and gone in a completely different direction?

Several of the women came up to her, telling her that the Lord would keep Robert safe and that they were praying. She was grateful, and she wanted to believe them, but doubt crept into her heart.

What if You choose not to protect him, Lord? What if he's hurt, or...

No, she wouldn't think that. Not now. She couldn't.

"I'm going with them to search," Maria said, charging forward to one of the buggies that was about to leave.

"No, Maria," Mary said, grabbing her arm. "You're pregnant. Robert would not want you going out into a blizzard and freezing."

"She's right," Hannah said. "They will go search. We should go to the house and wait there in case he comes home. It's not safe for you to go out there. Think of the baby."

Maria heaved a sigh. "You're right, I suppose. Let's go."

She had to get out of here.

As the storm subsided, Freya sped down the winding country road through the Amish community, wiping tears from her eyes as fast as the windshield wipers swatted away the snowflakes on her windshield. What if her car was damaged? Panic struck her. Would a dent on the front of her car be enough evidence to have her arrested?

Freya pulled over on the side of the road, got out of the car, and walked around to the front. She let out a sigh of relief when she realized there was only a small dent, something she could easily have repaired as soon as she was somewhere safe. She had been going slow when she had hit the man, and he had probably died from hitting his head on the road rather than from the actual impact of her car.

Still, the dent brought back all the memories of the man, lifeless and cold on the snow-covered pavement. She scrambled to get back in the car and started driving again.

"What have I done?" she cried, letting out a sob.

She'd left that man lying in the road, dead. What kind of sick, horrible person was she? Guilt tore at her, and she was certain it would never fade.

As she approached a street sign directing her to the highway, she stopped at the stop sign and paused, her blinker flashing.

Should she get out of this town before anyone figured out what she'd done?

Or should she stay and at least make sure the family found out what had happened, maybe return his hat to them?

The black hat on the passenger seat seemed to be glaring at her. She sighed and picked it up, turning it over in her hands. Then she noticed something on the inside of the hat—the initials *R. L.* were stitched into the fabric with white thread. Who was that? How could she find out who this man was?

Guilt and fear warred within her—one half of her wanting to go back, and the other half wanting to run for her life. But guilt and her conscience would not let her make that turn toward the highway.

"Ugh!" she roared, turning the car around and heading back toward Unity. Who would she even talk to about this? How would she find the man's family?

As she drove down the long country road, she passed a police officer and instantly stiffened, looking straight ahead, heart hammering in her chest. Good thing she was still wearing her wig and glasses. Her heart raced even faster as she looked in the rearview mirror. When the police car's brake lights lit up, her heart launched into her throat. Was he coming for her?

The police car continued down the road and disappeared into the distance. Freya let out a sigh of relief.

"What am I doing?" she asked herself. She shook her head, her wig loosening just a bit. This was preposterous. What could she do now besides confess to them what she'd done?

The fear set in. Freya gripped the steering wheel with pale knuckles, arguing with herself in her mind. If she stayed here, they might realize it was her and have her arrested.

Then Dean would find her. What if he was out looking for her?

No, she had to get out of this town. At least for several months until things settled down. If she stayed in town, people might find it suspicious that she showed up at the same time that the man was killed.

Freya's heart ached as she drove toward the highway, heading north. She promised herself she'd return to this place one day.

Whether she liked it or not, she was tethered to this place now, and it would never let her go. For now, she had to go to Canada—and even if her relatives still didn't want her in their lives, hopefully, she'd be safe there.

Maria and the other women made hot coffee for the men who were out searching. Wrought with worry, she busied herself with making the coffee and praying, except for when people came up to her to encourage her.

"It will be okay," Leah, her friend, said. "Don't worry."

She was so sick of people saying that. How could she not worry? Her husband was lost in a blizzard, and no one knew where he was.

A few moments later, the door opened, and Maria whirled around at the sound. Sid Hoffman, an Amish man who lived down the road, walked through the door. Snow swirled in behind him as he closed it. He took off his hat, stepping closer to her.

Her entire body filled with dread, and she felt light, as if she might evaporate right then and there. What had happened to Robert? Why did Sid look so devastated?

Suddenly, Mary, Aaron, and Hannah were beside her. "Sid?" Hannah asked. "What's wrong?"

Sid finally met their eyes, focusing on Maria, Aaron, and Hannah. "I'm sorry. I... I witnessed Robert's death and came here as fast as I could. He's...gone. I'm so sorry." He wrung his hat in his hands.

"What? That can't be!" Maria cried out, grabbing her mother-in-law for support as her knees buckled beneath her.

"He hasn't been gone that long. We thought maybe he just got lost in the snow," Aaron added.

"I'm very sorry. He was killed in a car accident," Sid said somberly. "I saw it from a distance. I'm so sorry to be the one to have to tell you."

"No!" Maria screamed, not caring about the people around her who were staring with concern. She felt as though no one else was in the room as devastation gripped her, bringing her to her knees. Even though Sid tried to explain how the accident had happened, Maria couldn't hear a word he said.

"No! Not Robert, no! No, Lord!" she cried out over and over again, weeping on the floor, barely aware of her mother and mother-in-law crying beside her and holding her. Time seemed irrelevant as she slipped into a void of tears.

Adam stepped inside the house, shook the snow from his jacket, and realized that everyone in the room was staring at him. Though they didn't have cell phones, word still traveled fast in the Amish community of Unity, Maine, even in snowy weather. He'd only been out looking for his brother for less than an hour, and several of the neighbors had already gathered to show their support.

He stopped moving, feeling the weight of every eye in the kitchen and living room upon him. He slowly removed his black-rimmed hat. "What?" he blurted. "Was ist letz?" he asked in Pennsylvania Dutch. "What is wrong? Did anyone find Robert yet?"

Many looked away from him, staring at the floor and shifting their weight uncomfortably.

"He doesn't know yet," he heard one woman whisper to another.

"Well, we just found out," another whispered back. The long white ribbons on their prayer kapps swayed as they shook their heads in pity.

A suppressed sob turned Adam's head. His mother, Hannah, wept quietly in the corner. Adam had only seen his mother cry a few times in his entire life. And Maria, his sister-in-law, was also sobbing.

Adam's heart constricted, squeezed by a fist of dread. His stomach sank, filled with a sick feeling that had nothing to do with the flu he'd had last night and was still recovering from.

No. No. It couldn't be, could it?

"What is going on?" Adam asked again, louder, moving toward them, pushing through the crowd that had gathered. He pulled his mother into his arms. His voice was soft. "Mamm, why are you crying? Someone has to tell me what happened. What happened to Robert? Where is he? Is he hurt?"

Adam's father, Aaron Lapp, rested a work-roughened hand on his son's shoulder. "Son, I'm so sorry. Robert has been killed. Sid just arrived and told us a few minutes ago after bringing his body here. We were about to send someone to go find you."

Adam sucked air into his lungs, but he couldn't get enough oxygen. His veins ignited with panic, despair, and disbelief. The room spun, and he took a step back for balance.

His older brother and best friend was…dead?

"No. Maybe he was just injured," he stammered. "He can't be dead."

"He's dead, Adam. I'm sorry." His father's eyes pooled with tears, something Adam had rarely ever seen in his life.

"How?" Adam croaked out. He should have gone with Robert to look for the horse instead of letting him go out into that blizzard alone. How could he have let him go alone? Guilt wracked his chest.

"Sid Hoffman found him in the road near his house. It was an accident."

Adam's head swam. "Robert said his horse was probably in the lane. He said he'd just go look on the lane and then come right back. Why did he go all the way out to the road?" he demanded, not caring how everyone was watching.

"You know how he loved that horse, Adam. We don't know what happened. It doesn't matter how he died. He is with the Lord now."

"Someone killed him? An *Englisher* hit him with their vehicle?" Adam all but shouted. Several people jumped at the sudden noise, then looked away out of respect. "How did this happen? Why?"

"Son," Aaron said in a low, soothing voice. "You know it is not the Amish way to ask these sorts of questions. Your brother has passed on. That is all that we need to know. Do not ask questions like you always do."

"That is not all I need to know!" Adam pulled away, ignoring the stares. "I want to know who killed my brother. They can't get away with this." He turned to face Sid. For a moment, the room spun as dizziness swept over him, a symptom of his flu. "Sid? What did you see?"

Sid Hoffman stepped forward, his balding head bent in sympathy. His long beard bobbed as he spoke, and he wrung his black hat in his hands. "I'm sorry it took me a while to get here. I loaded him into the buggy by myself."

"What happened, Sid?" Adam persisted, his voice almost a whisper. "What did you see? Did you see who did it?"

"Adam," Adam's father protested.

"Adam should know the truth, Aaron." Sid furrowed his brows, and Adam's father stiffened. Sid turned to Adam. "I heard something and looked outside to see if I could help."

Adam nodded, silently urging him to go on.

"I saw a silver car with a young blonde woman driving. It looked like she tried to avoid the horse and hit him instead, but there were signs she'd tried to revive him. She tried to use her scarf to stop the bleeding. Maybe she tried CPR. You could tell by the imprints in the snow that she'd knelt beside him," Sid explained somberly. "By the time I made my way outside, she had already driven away."

Adam shivered and turned away, closing his eyes. Just hearing Sid's words, he could imagine the scene as if he was standing right there. Oh, how he wished he'd been there to witness it, to see who had killed his brother. Anger scorched his veins. How could she have just driven away and left his brother there in the road?

"Perhaps she left to get help. By the time I got to him, he was gone. I'm sorry." Sid bowed his head apologetically as if it had been his fault.

The room was deathly silent except for the soft sobs coming from his mother.

"Thank you for telling me, Sid," Adam choked out.

Sid nodded and stepped back.

Indignation burned a fire in Adam's belly at the injustice of it all. His brother had been such a good man. He turned and headed for the door.

"Where are you going?" Aaron called to his son.

"I have to find out who did this to Robert, and why she left him there in the road, alone to die. I'm going to find her and make her pay for what she did." Maybe if he got justice for his brother's death, it would help relieve the guilt he felt for not helping Robert find his horse.

Adam's mother gasped, then let out another round of heart-wrenching sobs. Maria, Robert's pregnant widow, cried onto her mother-in-law's shoulder. Some of the other women gathered around to try to comfort them.

"Adam," his father said sternly, "that is not the Amish way! We must forgive and move on. Don't go trying to figure out what happened like you always do."

"That's exactly what I'm going to do. You know, I told Robert a long time ago that I wanted to be a police officer one day and help other people get justice."

His mother gasped. "Adam, no. Please. You haven't even recovered from the flu yet."

"Adam! Please don't leave. Don't make any rash decisions right now," his father pleaded.

Adam pivoted on his heel and flung open the door, stepping back out into the clawing, swirling snow.

Sid followed him out. "Adam, I'm sorry you had to find out like that."

"Thank you for telling me."

"Adam, wait."

Adam turned to see the older man coming toward him, his hat in his hand. "His body is still in my buggy. If you're leaving, you might not get the chance to say goodbye." Sid gestured to his buggy parked in the driveway. "I'm going back inside the house. Take all the time you need."

Sid turned and walked back inside, then Adam turned and walked toward the buggy. With every step he took, his feet seemed to sink lower and lower into the snow.

He stepped up into the front seat of the buggy and closed his eyes. Was he sure he really wanted to see this? He'd never seen a dead body before, and this was his brother.

"If I'm going to be a police officer, I better get used to it," he muttered under his breath, then he opened his eyes and turned his head.

Robert's body was lying in the back of the buggy, dried blood marring his face and neck. His eyes were closed, and though his body had been bruised and bloodied, he looked so peaceful. A white scarf stained with blood was beside him.

"Robert, no!" The strangled cry escaped Adam's lips as he climbed into the back of the buggy, reaching out to touch his brother's face. "You always looked out for me. How could this happen?"

Adam wept, holding his brother's cold hand. Anguish and agony ripped through him, and his chest ached. Several minutes later, he wiped his eyes. "I will find the person who did this, Robert. You were the only person who believed in me, who believed I could become a police officer. I'm going to do this for you, brother. I love you."

Adam heard the sound of voices coming out of the house, and he gently set Robert's hand down on his chest, then climbed out of the buggy.

He had packing to do.

Chapter Five

Dean sped down the highway, going south, trying to catch up with Freya. He glanced at his phone, seeing that he was gaining distance on her and catching up to her. A few hours later, she stopped moving. Perhaps she had stopped at a rest stop or gas station.

He pulled into a rest stop parking lot where truckers often stopped to sleep or use the bathroom. A few buses were in the parking lot along with several cars. According to the GPS signal, she was here.

He got out of the car and followed her signal, which led him to a bus. That made sense. He thought maybe she had borrowed a car from a friend, maybe the meddling neighbor, but perhaps she had taken the bus instead. He stepped inside the bus, where the driver was playing a game on his phone.

"I'm just looking for someone," Dean said, and the driver barely looked up. Dean walked down the aisle of the bus, scanning the seats. Mostly everyone had gotten off the bus to get food or use the restrooms, but a few people remained.

A young woman with her sweatshirt hood partially hiding her face stared out the window. Red hair poked out from her hood, cascading down her shoulder. Was that her?

He surged forward, grabbing the woman's shoulder roughly. "Freya?" he rasped.

She was a teenage girl—definitely not Freya. "Back off, man!" she shouted.

"We got a problem, buddy?" the driver called from the front seat.

"Sorry. I thought you were someone else. Did you see a phone on the floor or on a seat here?" He raised his hands defensively, dialing Freya's number. "I'm calling it."

"We found one here, man," a teenage boy said, holding up a phone, which was now ringing. "Is this it?"

"That's my fiancée's phone," Dean said, then turned to the girl. "I thought you were her. Sorry." He took the phone from the boy. "Thanks."

Dean whirled around and stomped off the bus, anger pounding within him as he got back in his car and slammed the door.

"She tricked me!" he roared, slapping the steering wheel and hurling the phone on the seat beside him. She'd put her phone on the bus on purpose and had probably gone in a completely different direction.

Now he had no idea where she'd gone. He would look into it, but he was sure that the bus made dozens of stops. It could have happened at any of those. It could take months to sift through the video footage, if he could even get access to it. He wasn't a police officer anymore, but maybe one of his friends could get it.

He longed to wrap his hands around Freya's neck and shake answers out of her. Why had she left him? Did she really think she could get away from him?

How would he find her now?

※※※※※ ※※※※※

Adam turned from Robert's body in the buggy and shuddered as he walked back toward his house, his mind wandering back to the time when he and Robert were kids. Adam was about eight years old and had convinced Robert to sled down the hill onto the frozen pond.

"Come on!" Adam had taunted as snowflakes fell from the sky. "Or are you a scaredy-cat?"

"I am not," Robert retorted, dragging his sled behind him. "If you're so brave, you go first."

"Fine." Adam climbed to the top of the hill, sat on his sled, and went flying down the hill. He hollered as the sled bumped down the incline and skidded over the ice. Finally, the sled slowed to a stop. "Wow! That was fun! Your turn."

Adam stood on the ice and watched as his brother sat on his sled, pushed off, and sailed down the hill. Suddenly, the sled hit something under the snow, maybe a stump, right before landing on the ice. The sled flipped over, causing Robert to land hard on the ice.

Robert screamed out in pain.

"Robert!" Adam cried, his smile quickly dropping as he rushed toward his brother, his feet sliding all over the ice. Adam finally reached him and knelt beside him. "What hurts?"

"My ankle!" Robert sobbed, holding his limp leg. "It hurts! Get *Maam* or *Daed*."

They're going to be so upset with me when they find out this was my idea, Adam thought, but he couldn't dwell on that now. Robert might have a broken leg or ankle.

Adam turned and hurried off the ice, running up the hill with snow kicking up behind him. He ran all the way to his house and burst through the door. *Maam* was standing in the kitchen, kneading dough.

"*Maam*! Robert fell on the ice and hurt his leg. I think it's broken," Adam said, out of breath.

"Oh, no!" Adam's mother cried, her hand on her chest.

Daed came into the kitchen. "Take me to him. We may need to take him to the hospital."

Adam and his father raced down the hill to see Robert, who was still lying on the ice.

"Robert?" *Daed* said, rushing to him. "Can you move your leg or foot?"

When Robert tried to move his foot, he cried out in pain. "No. I can't move it."

"It could be broken, then, but I don't know for sure," *Daed* said. "Let's get you to the hospital. Thank the Lord it isn't too far away."

Daed scooped up Robert in his arms and carried him home, then placed him carefully into the buggy. After Robert was settled, *Daed* looked at both of the boys.

"Whose idea was it to sled down the hill onto the pond? I've told you before that hill is too steep for sledding," *Daed* said.

"It was—" Adam began to confess.

"It was my idea," Robert blurted. "I talked Adam into it. I'm sorry."

Daed grumbled and gave them each a stern look. "Well, I hope a broken bone is enough to teach you to never do it again."

Both boys nodded adamantly.

As *Daed* got into the buggy, Adam climbed in for a moment to talk to Robert.

"You didn't have to do that," Adam whispered. "Thanks."

"You should do something that scares you now and then," Robert said with a mischievous smile. "Even if you get hurt sometimes."

As Adam watched the buggy drive away, guilt ripped at him. It should have been him with the broken bone, not his brother, who'd taken the blame.

Robert had always looked out for Adam. Now, Adam had to do this for his brother—find the woman who killed him.

As he flung open the door to the home he'd grown up in, he was brought back to the present with a jolt. He'd been planning on buying a piece of land down the road and building a small house for himself that he could add onto if he got married and had children, but now he knew that would never happen. Not here, anyway. He couldn't stay here an hour longer.

Adam loved his family, but the rage and burning desire to find the person who killed Robert was the only thing that mattered to him right now.

"Adam?" his mother called, surrounded by neighbors in the kitchen.

Silently, Adam walked up the stairs.

"Thank you all for coming and showing your support, but we need some family time right now," Adam heard his father say downstairs, followed by the shuffle of many feet as people filed out of the house.

Reaching his room, he pulled a bag from his closet and started throwing clothes into it, his plain white, brown, gray, and black shirts and dark pants. They would have to do until he could buy some *Englisher* clothes.

Adams' mind swam with questions. How would he even go about applying to the police academy? What about getting his GED? How long would his training be? Would he find a place to live? Hot tears blurred his vision as he threw things into his bag.

Suddenly, footsteps pounded up the stairs. "Adam!" his father roared. "Let's talk about this."

"You don't mean it, do you? You're just angry and upset. Don't do anything rash," his mother, Hannah, called out as she also came up the stairs, followed by Maria. "I remember you saying before that you wanted to become a police officer, but I thought it was a phase you would grow out of. You were just talking about that piece of land yesterday. I thought maybe that meant you were ready to get baptized and maybe find a nice girl—"

"Clearly, I'm not going to get baptized into the church after this," Adam said, thrusting a pair of pants into his bag. "I just can't agree with the rules about not pursuing justice. Why can't we report this to the police? I'll never understand."

"Vengeance is the Lord's," his father said, shaking his fist passionately. "Leave it to God."

"I think God put us on this earth to help each other, and that includes putting criminals in jail," Adam insisted. "It helps keep everyone safer. It helps keep the peace."

"It's not the Amish way," Maria said, her hand partially covering her mouth as she watched Adam packing in a frenzy. "Would Robert want this?"

"I know it's not the Amish way, Maria," Adam said, taking a deep breath as he tried to keep his voice steady. He stopped packing so he could look each of them in the eye. "I don't know if Robert would want me to do this, to find the woman who killed him. But I know he would want me to do what I know in my heart is right, even if it's against the Amish way." He threw a pair of boots, his Bible, and a few books into the bag, then hefted it onto his shoulder. "I'm sorry, but if I don't do this, I'll never have peace in my heart. I have to at least try."

"Please, Adam." Hannah rushed forward and grabbed his upper arms. "I've already lost one of my sons. I can't lose you, too. You're the only child I have left." She sniffed and wiped her eyes.

"Maria and *Daed* will take care of you," Adam reassured her. "You'll all take care of each other."

"If you leave, you're not welcome back here until you repent and promise to stay, even though you're not shunned," Aaron said, staring him in the eye. "This is my house and those are my rules."

Hannah let out a gasp, covering her mouth. "He can't even visit?"

Aaron shook his head.

"I know, *Daed*. At least I won't be shunned. It's a good thing I wasn't baptized. I just knew in my heart it wasn't the right choice for me."

"You're really going to leave us?" Hannah said, her eyes filling with tears again as she still held onto him.

"Did you know about this?" Aaron asked his wife.

Hannah hesitated. "He told me he was thinking about it when Robert and Maria announced the pregnancy."

"What? No one told me. Not even you, Hannah?" Aaron demanded.

"I asked her not to tell you because I knew you would get upset. I wasn't sure yet, anyway, but now I know. I'm sorry, *Mamm* and *Daed*. I have to go. I have to do this."

"Will you come back?" Hannah asked, her grip tightening around his arm.

"I don't know."

His mother threw her arms around him, hugging him tightly. "I love you."

"I love you too," he said, his voice cracking with emotion. He pulled away and looked at his father, who was still eyeing him sternly. Adam stuck out his hand for his father to shake, but his father just crossed his arms.

"You're breaking your mother's heart, son."

"I'm sorry. I'm sorry I can't just forgive and move on like you all. But I have to do this. For Robert."

Adam gave Maria a quick hug, gave his father one last look, then pushed past him to walk out the bedroom door. He kept going down the hall and marched out the door into the frigid cold, then headed to the phone shanty where he'd call the local driver.

Adam didn't know where he would even ask Bob to take him—maybe the bus station. He didn't know where he was going, but Adam would find this young woman.

And she would pay for what she did to his brother.

Chapter Six

One year later

Freya's mind reeled as she approached Unity, Maine, once again. After hiding from Dean in Canada successfully for a year, she'd finally mustered up the courage to return to this place. Hopefully, by now the investigation, if any, had gone cold, and no one would suspect her of anything. She'd even had the dent in her car fixed. She wanted to buy the car from Victor so she could sell it and buy a different one, but Victor had told her that might raise flags because she would have to register her new car with her new address, and Dean might see that. So, she kept using Victor's car, and he paid the insurance and registration for her.

The next thing to do was to find a place to stay for a while.

As Freya continued down the back road, she approached a sign: *Millers' Bed and Breakfast.*

From the buggy in the driveway, she guessed that this was an Amish house. After grabbing her bag and letting out a deep breath, she knocked on the door.

An Amish woman who looked to be in her mid-sixties answered the door. "Hello, how may I help you?"

"Hello, I'm looking for a place to stay. Could I rent a room on a week-by-week basis?" Freya asked, having no idea how long she'd be in town.

"Of course. Come on in." The woman opened the door wider. "I'm Mae Miller."

"I'm Freya. Nice to meet you. It smells so good in here," Freya said, stepping inside to be welcomed by the scent of cinnamon rolls and pastries.

"This is also where we bake for local stores and the market," Mae explained as Freya noticed the large kitchen in the simple home. "My two daughters and I. We bake very early in the morning, but we won't disturb you. Follow me, and I'll show you to your room."

Freya followed the woman upstairs, the wooden steps creaking under their feet. Two teenage girls came out of one of the bedrooms.

"This is Freya, and she will be staying in one of the rooms," Mae said. "These are my daughters Laura and Lydia." She gestured to the younger one, then the older one.

"Nice to meet you," they both said.

"Are you from out of town?" Laura asked.

"Yes," Freya said, not sure how much information about herself she should reveal, so she left it at that. After an awkward silence, Mae opened one of the bedroom doors.

"Here you are," Mae said.

The full-size bed was covered with an intricate handmade quilt, and the furniture looked handmade and perfectly crafted. There was a battery-operated standup light on the nightstand.

"We do have indoor toilets and showers," Mae said. "I will get you some soap and towels. There is a bathroom down the hall."

Relieved, Freya smiled. So, she wouldn't have to use an outhouse after all.

"Breakfast will be ready for you between six and seven if you'd like to eat with us. Do you need anything else?" Mae asked.

"No, thank you. Actually, this is a long shot, but do you know whose hat this is?" Freya pulled the black hat out of her bag and showed it to Mae.

Mae touched the inside, noticing the initials stitched in white thread. "Hmm. *R. L.* Let me think of which last names around here begin with L..." She pondered for a moment, looking up at the ceiling. "It could be Lantz, maybe Lambright, or Lapp. Each of the families has several children, and many of them are adults now. You might have to ask around. I don't remember all their names. My memory isn't what it used to be." Mae chuckled, handing the hat back. "Can I do anything else for you?"

"No, thank you. That helps a lot. I appreciate it."

"I will let you get settled in then," Mae said with a nod. "Please let me know if you need anything." She turned and walked down the hall.

Freya gently closed the door and put her bag on the bed. She knew there was no phone here, and even if there was, she wouldn't be able to call Victor to let him know she was safe. Dean had boasted about computer forensics and forensic accounting, and how he could track down anyone anywhere by using his police connections. Dean once told her that fugitives often go somewhere familiar or contact someone they know, and that's how they get caught.

But Freya didn't have anywhere else to go or anyone else she could contact. Because of moving so often from family to family growing up, she had no real friends, and her relatives hadn't wanted her as a child, so she'd lost contact with them.

However, she'd looked them up, and they did live in Canada, as she'd suspected. She even got as far as standing on the sidewalk across the street from their home, and she could see the family eating dinner at the table, but she hadn't been able to muster up the courage to go knock on the door and introduce herself. After all, they hadn't wanted her in their home as a child—why would they want to meet her now? If they had raised her, perhaps they would have saved her from so much heartache during her years in foster care. But if they didn't even want her, perhaps they weren't the nice people she'd imagined them to be.

In Canada, even though she'd gone there to find those relatives, she'd found a job and a small apartment where she'd lived on her own.

Mae's kind eyes and friendly face reminded Freya of Shirley. Freya's mind wandered back to the day she had moved into Shirley's house.

"Home sweet home," Shirley had said as they walked through the front door of her home.

Freya had gasped and turned around slowly in a complete circle, taking it all in. It was an old Victorian-style house with old-fashioned wallpaper, chandeliers, and hutches filled with fine china.

"I raised my three children here, but none of them visit me anymore, so it's just me now," Shirley said, ushering Freya into the kitchen. "I'm so glad to have someone to share it with. You can pick any of the bedrooms you'd like, except mine, of course." She winked as they sat down at the kitchen table.

"Oh, thank you, Shirley. This means the world to me," Freya said, still stunned that this woman had invited her to live with her after only just meeting for the first time at a diner. "I'm still shocked you invited me to stay here with you. I'm very grateful."

Shirley waved a hand. "I have good instincts about people. As soon as we met, I could tell you have a heart of gold."

Freya smiled, deeply honored.

"I'm lonely here, my dear. Trust me. I'm getting the better end of the deal. I could use some company around here, and you'll be helping me tremendously. I'm old and I can't do things as easily as I used to, and I never was much of a cook."

"I love to cook," Freya said.

Shirley waved her hand. "See? I knew we'd make a great pair."

Freya knew deep down inside that this would work out wonderfully. Then she paused, remembering something Shirley had said. "When you said your children don't visit you anymore, why is that?" Freya shook her head, realizing she was prying. "I'm sorry. That's none of my business."

"No, it's all right, dear. They don't visit me anymore because their father drove them away from me, convincing them I was a terrible person, that it was my fault we got divorced, but it was his own fault. He was an abusive, mean drunk." Shirley leaned forward. "When I married him, he was such a sweet liar. Promise me, Freya, that you won't fall for a man like that, a man who puts on an act until you're stuck with him." She shook a finger for emphasis.

"I promise," Freya said, blinking.

Even with all of Shirley's warnings, Freya still fell for Dean's smooth-talking deception, and she hated herself for it sometimes.

Shirley leaned back in her chair. "They're so slick, they have you thinking they're the nicest man, then boom, they have you convinced." She shook her head. "I was brave enough to leave the jerk after he hurt the children and me too many times, but when the kids were older and were able to see him, he convinced them everything was my fault. He was the most manipulative man I've ever met. He's dead now, but they still won't talk to me, and I don't have many relatives, so I'm all alone in this big world." She looked up at Freya and grinned. "But now I have you."

Freya's heart went out to the lonely woman. She patted Shirley's thin, frail hand. "Yes, you have me. And as long as you'll have me, I'm not going anywhere."

"Well, that's good to hear, darling. Now, come on. I'll show you the bedrooms, and you can pick out which one you want."

Shirley died only a few short years later, leaving Freya all alone. Now that she was finally away from Dean, all she had was herself to rely on.

No, a small voice told her. *You have Me. I will never leave you.*

"Are you really there, God? Because right now, I feel so alone," she whispered.

Deep in her heart, she already knew the answer. When her neighbor had brought her to church, the pastor had spoken about how God is always with us and has a plan for us.

On the nightstand, there was a Bible. Freya went over to it and picked it up, then sat on the bed, opening the pages.

She wanted to learn more. And right now, she hoped it would comfort her soul.

***

The next morning, Freya awoke to the smell of cinnamon rolls. She rolled over and checked her watch. It was only six, and it smelled as though they'd been baking downstairs for hours.

She hurried to the bathroom to see a regular shower along with a toilet and sink. She didn't know much about the Amish, but before coming here, she had wondered if they used outhouses or even if they used toilet paper. Now that she thought about it, she felt silly.

"What a relief," she muttered to herself as she turned on the hot water. She let it melt away her stress and anxiety, even for a few moments.

After getting dressed, she went downstairs to see several trays of baked goods on the table and countertop.

"Wow! You baked all of this already this morning?" Freya exclaimed.

All three of the women looked up at her.

"We sure did," Laura piped up. "We start at five-thirty."

Freya shook her head in amazement. "It smells so good."

"I hope you slept well," Laura said.

"I slept better than I have in months," Freya said. "Maybe years."

"Oh, good. You're just in time for breakfast," Mae said, pouring a pan of scrambled eggs into a dish. "Let's sit at the table."

"Thank you," Freya said. She couldn't remember the last time someone had made her breakfast.

"Good morning," Ed said as he came through the front door.

"Good morning," Freya said as they all moved to the dining room. They sat at a large, handmade wooden table that could seat at least eight people. Along with the dish of scrambled eggs, there was a plate of cinnamon rolls, sausage, bacon, and fruit.

"Freya, we say a silent prayer before we eat, if you'd like to join us," Ed said, folding his hands.

"Oh, absolutely," Freya said, and they all bowed their heads and closed their eyes for about thirty seconds.

Thank you, God, for bringing me here, Freya prayed. *Please help me find the family of the man I killed, and please give me the strength to tell them what happened.*

When she heard the sound of spoons and forks scraping plates, Freya looked up to see the family dishing out the food.

"This is the loveliest breakfast I've ever seen," Freya murmured. Did they always eat like this? In foster homes growing up, she was lucky if she got some cold cereal for breakfast.

"These ladies are the best cooks in town," Ed said, grinning.

"Oh, Ed," Mae said bashfully, waving her hand.

"It's true," he said, patting his round belly. "And they're the best bakers."

"Are you staying in town long?" Laura asked.

"I'm...not sure yet," Freya murmured, scooping some eggs onto her plate.

"Where did you say you were from?" Ed said.

"I'm from Boston," Freya said, figuring she might as well tell them where she was from. "Much different from here."

"Boston?" Laura sighed, tilting her head to the side with a dreamy look in her eye. "Oh, I'd just love to go there someday. What's it like?"

Lydia rolled her eyes.

"Well, it's very crowded and dirty, and there's so much traffic." Freya inwardly cringed, remembering how Dean had stopped letting her go out alone. "Honestly, it's so much nicer here. You're very blessed to live in a place like this."

"Thanks, and you're right, but I do hope to travel one day," Laura mused. "Maybe I will on my *Rumspringa*. That's a time when we're allowed to leave and explore the world to decide whether we want to be baptized into the church."

"Not me," Lydia said. "I like it right here."

"Boring," Laura muttered under her breath, and Lydia shot an annoyed look at her. Laura looked at Freya and giggled, and Freya smiled, enjoying the banter between the two sisters, who couldn't be more opposite.

After breakfast, Freya got in her car and drove down the road to a store she'd seen earlier, the Unity Community Store. She walked in, immediately enveloped by the calming environment. No music played; only conversations could be heard.

"How may I help you?" a young Amish woman asked, walking up to her.

"I was wondering if anyone knows whose hat this is," Freya said, handing it to her. "I found it." It wasn't exactly a lie, but the guilt ate at her, anyway. "I heard it could belong to someone with the last name Lantz, Lambright, or Lapp. Do you know if any of them have a first name that begins with R?"

The young woman tapped her chin, thinking.

"Ella Ruth, take your break when you're done," an older man said from behind the counter.

"I will, *Daed*," the woman, Ella Ruth, said. She turned back to Freya. "It could be Roland Lambright's, or it could belong to Ralph Lantz. But they're children, and this is a man's hat." She paused, looking at the floor. "Or it could have belonged to Robert Lapp. I can't think of anyone else."

Freya's blood ran cold. *Belonged. It could have belonged to him.* "That sounds right."

"Where did you find it?" Ella Ruth asked. "He was killed a year ago."

"Uh..." Freya stammered, her heart racing. "I found it by the road." She wanted to give herself a facepalm for not thinking of something better. She should have lied.

"How is that possible?" Ella Ruth handed it back to her, a bewildered look on her face. "After all this time? One year? How did it not blow away?"

"It stuck under a branch." She wanted to wince for the terrible lie. "I heard he was killed by a car."

"*Ja.* It's a shame, a terrible tragedy. It's so sad." Ella Ruth shook her head slowly. "He left behind his wife, who was pregnant at the time. The baby is about a year old now. We knew Robert well."

"Do you know where the Lapps live?" Freya asked.

Ella Ruth turned. "Just go down the lane until you see the big gray house. That's their house." She pointed out the window, and Freya could see the house in the distance.

Freya's heart seemed to flip and sink all at the same time. "Do you by any chance know where he is buried? I'd like to pay my respects."

"The little cemetery is on that hill, behind the trees." Ella Ruth pointed out the window again, then eyed Freya quizzically. "Did you know him?"

Freya looked at the floor. "No. I just...feel a connection to his family. I want to bring some flowers to his grave and return the hat to his family."

"That is very nice of you."

Hardly, Freya thought. *It's the least I could do.* "Thank you so much."

"Is there anything I can help you find while you're here? We have the best donuts in town made by the Millers' Bakery." She gestured to the counter where Freya saw dozens of cinnamon and chocolate donuts displayed.

Her stomach churned. Normally, she would have jumped at the chance to have a homemade donut. And since they were made by the Millers, she was sure they were divine. But the thought of food right now made her sick.

"Sorry, no, but thank you. Maybe another time. Thanks so much for your help." She hurried out the door.

Freya gulped in the chilling fresh air, welcoming the cold entering her lungs. She knew where the family lived. What now? Should she knock on the door and offer them the hat?

No. They would suspect something. Perhaps she could leave the hat at the grave and hope that a family member would find it.

"What do I do?" she muttered, walking back to her car. She got inside, wanting to bang her head against the steering wheel.

God, please tell me what to do, she prayed, yet she already knew the answer.

But that would be too hard. There was no way she could possibly do it.

Would she have to just learn to live with this guilt that continued to eat away at her?

"No," she said to herself. "I have to do this."

Chapter Seven

Freya drove down the lane until she reached the Lapps' house. She parked across the lane and rested her head on the steering wheel.

What do I do? Just go knock on the door? she thought. Before she could talk herself out of it, she grabbed the hat, got out of the car, and started walking toward the house.

The snow seeped into her boots, but she didn't care. She approached the house and heard laughing and talking coming from the inside. Though she was still in the driveway, she looked through the window to see an elderly woman holding a little boy, laughing with him. A younger woman came and took the boy from her, also laughing. She was smiling, but it was a sad smile that didn't reach her eyes.

Was that his mother? And was the younger woman maybe his sister? Or, what if she was his widow? The young woman at the store did say that Robert had left behind his wife and little boy.

Freya's stomach churned, threatening to lose the eggs and cinnamon roll she'd had for breakfast with the Millers.

No, she couldn't do this. Before they could see her, she whirled around and hurried back to her car as fast as she could without slipping on the ice.

A few days later, Freya was in town getting groceries when she saw the same two women and the little boy she'd seen at the Lapps' house.

She ducked behind the aisle of bread, watching them. The baby suddenly cried out.

"Shhh, Carter," his mother said, patting his back as she held him. "It's okay."

Carter. The baby's name was Carter. Freya's heart lurched when the boy turned, and she saw his face more clearly. Though Freya had only seen Robert's face for a few moments in the blizzard, his face would forever be burned into her memory. Carter looked so much like him.

"Oh, Maria, let me hold him for you while you shop," the older woman said.

"Are you sure?" Maria asked. So, she was Robert's widow.

"That's what grandmothers are for," the older woman said with a chuckle, taking the child.

So this was Robert's mother, widow, and son, according to what the young woman had told her at the Unity Community Store.

It's all my fault that this baby doesn't have a father, she thought. Heart breaking, her eyes filled with tears, and she turned her cart around. Freya retreated back into the bread aisle, almost bumping into someone. She muttered an apology, distracted as she pushed her cart.

Should she go talk to them? What on earth would she say, especially in the grocery store?

No, this wasn't the time or place. Freya grabbed a loaf of bread, tossed it in her cart, and followed them from a distance. She had to admit she was a bit surprised to see them in a grocery store—she had just assumed they made all their own food from scratch. As they put boxes of cereal, graham crackers, and toilet paper in their cart, Freya became even more intrigued.

"I can't believe it will be one year since Robert passed away," Maria said. "Let's do another dinner in honor of him."

"Of course," the older woman said. "I just wish Adam could be there. It doesn't seem complete without him."

Who is Adam? Freya wondered.

"I know you miss him." Maria put a hand on her mother-in-law's arm.

"So much. I just wish I could reach him somehow. He never wrote or called to let me know where he is. If I knew his address, I would write to him."

"Even without Aaron knowing?" Maria whispered.

"My husband can be so stubborn sometimes. I know he loves Adam, but I think it's wrong how he won't speak to him. If I had the chance to call or write to Adam without him knowing, I would do it. It would be the right thing to do. The thing is, I don't know how to reach him." The woman spoke in a quiet voice but hiked her chin confidently. "I have heard of mothers who still write to their shunned children."

"At least Adam wasn't shunned," Maria reflected.

Freya was listening so intently to their conversation that she almost rammed her cart into someone else's. Muttering an apology, she steered her cart away. Carter, who looked over his grandmother's shoulder, locked eyes with Freya and smiled.

Her heart melted at the baby's grin, and she waved to him. Maria looked at him and turned around to see who he was looking at, but Freya ducked her head and quickly turned to steer her shopping cart down another aisle, heading for the flower section.

She walked towards the flower section to buy some roses. She couldn't put it off any longer—it was time to visit Robert's grave.

Freya carried a bouquet of red roses through the small Amish community's cemetery. Now they felt like a cheap, measly excuse of a peace offering in her hands. She chose red ones because they'd reminded her of the way Robert's blood had looked on the snowy road. She shivered at the thought, but for some reason, she felt compelled to buy that particular color.

Her boots crunched the snow with each step she took—the only sound to be heard in this bleak graveyard besides some snow falling off nearby tree branches.

Freya had been too ashamed and afraid to come before today, but she couldn't live with the guilt haunting her anymore, even though she risked her ex finding her if she was arrested or questioned. Now that she had seen Robert's mother, widow, and son, she could no longer stay away.

She stood before the tombstone and wiped away a tear, her heart aching in her chest. "I saw your family today. I am so sorry," she whispered before hearing footsteps behind her. She whirled around to see a tall, incredibly good-looking man approaching, dressed in jeans with a nice shirt and tie under his partially unzipped jacket. His brown hair was cut in a short military-style cut, and his warm brown eyes searched hers.

"Hi. Did you know my brother? Never seen you around here before. I'm Adam Lapp," he said, extending a hand for her to shake. "I left the community a year ago to become a police officer, so I haven't been here in a while."

He was a cop? She didn't expect to see anyone here, so she hadn't worn her blonde wig or glasses. Her instinct was to turn and run, but she found herself reaching for his hand and shaking it.

"I guess you could say I knew him. I'm Freya."

"What a lovely name," he said with a dashing smile, but her heart sank as his gaze settled on the headstone. "He was a wonderful man. Too young and newly married. He left behind his wife Maria, who was pregnant at the time with their son Carter."

Freya's heart caught in her throat.

"I still miss him every day," he said. "He was the only one who supported my dream of leaving the Amish to pursue a career in law enforcement." He looked at the grave and sighed. "His horse had gotten loose that night, and he took the buggy out to look for it in a snowstorm. It was a hit and run. Maybe a drunk driver. We still don't know. But you probably knew that."

Freya had already been wracked with enough guilt, but this new information nearly crushed her. She wrapped her arms around herself and lowered her head. Swallowing bile, she tried not to cringe or tremble at the memories.

If she told Adam the truth, would he arrest her on the spot or hear her out? Could he realize it had been an accident and that she'd been running for her life?

"Are you okay?" Adam asked.

Freya wiped away another tear, unable to speak.

"How about if we go for coffee or cocoa around the corner and we can talk?" He smiled at her again, and this time she let his charm wash over her. "I'd love to hear about how you met my brother."

Freya nodded eagerly. "I'd like to learn more about Robert. And honestly, I have something to tell you about him, and I hope you will forgive me."

If that is even possible.

"Well, whatever it is, everyone should get a second chance, Freya. That's what God's grace is all about."

Did he really believe that? Her spirit lifting a little, she allowed a slow smile to brighten her face as she set the red roses on the snow in front of the tombstone.

She definitely didn't think she deserved a second chance, but at least Robert's family would know the truth. All she could do was pray for the best. Freya wiped away another tear and shivered.

"Come on. Let's go." Adam's voice was gentle. "You're obviously very upset. And cold."

Was she that obvious? "Now? Don't you want to pay your respects?"

"I will come back and do it later. I'd like to be alone when I do. Come on. A cup of coffee or hot cocoa will warm you right up. Besides, Robert wouldn't want us freezing out here." Adam softly touched her elbow and led her away from the grave. Freya could hardly feel his light touch on her arm through her jacket.

"I have my own car. I could meet you there," Freya said.

"Sure. I'm parked over here," Adam said as they reached the cars.

With each step she took, her heart felt as though it was dropping lower and lower to the ground. What would he say? Would he blow up in her face? Call the cops right then and there?

If Adam did call the police, she knew her ex-fiancé, Dean, would find her. Freya had no doubt that he had asked his police friends to tell him if they heard anything about her.

"It's just around the corner. You can follow me," Adam said, getting into his car. He drove away first, and she followed him to the coffee shop. When they arrived, she got out of the car.

"Here it is," Adam announced as they approached the coffee shop which was on a street lined with quaint shops. She had been so absorbed in her own thoughts while being here that she'd barely noticed it before. As they stepped into the coffee shop, a small bell rang on the door. Inside, one brick wall was covered with local framed art and photography, while another wall was lined entirely with shelves displaying books for sale. Wooden tables and chairs were scattered beneath a chalkboard menu.

"Have a seat." Adam pulled a chair out for her. "What would you like? Tea? Coffee? Hot cocoa?"

"I'll have a hot cocoa, please. Thank you," Freya said, flustered by his chivalry. Dean had never pulled out a chair for her except during the very beginning of their relationship.

"You're welcome. And this is my treat."

"You don't have to do that."

"Please. I insist. I'll be right back." Adam flashed her a smile and headed toward the counter to order. She unzipped her jacket and took it off, letting her long red hair drape over the back of the chair. Even after Freya removed her mittens, her hands kept on sweating, despite the snow outside. She rested her head in her palms and took a deep breath.

She had been so careful ever since she had left Boston. And so far, Dean had been unable to find her. Freya had turned coworkers down when they had invited her to hang out, not wanting to get too close to anyone. She had been paying for everything in cash, using her fake name. Would all her hard work be for nothing? Was she wasting it all just to tell this man the truth about his brother's death?

I have to do this.

Freya shook her head. She couldn't live with this secret one more day. If Dean came for her and killed her, so be it. Because if she continued to harbor this secret any longer, it would eat her alive. She had to tell Adam what happened to Robert.

Chapter Eight

Adam returned to the table, grinning as he set down two hot cocoas and two croissants. "These are the best. I thought you might like one, but if you don't want it, it's okay."

"These look great. Thank you," Freya said, but her stomach churned at the thought of food. Not wanting to be rude, she took the croissant anyway.

"It's beautiful here, isn't it?" Adam said, gesturing to the scenery out the window. From where they sat, all you could see were the shops lining the street, but she knew he was referring to the vast farm fields, long stretches of road, and the woods in the distance.

"It is. I see why you came back. So, you work in law enforcement?" she asked.

"Yes, I'm a police officer at the Covert Police Detectives Unit in Augusta."

"What was it like going from being Amish to working as a police officer?" She leaned forward, genuinely intrigued.

"Honestly, at first, it was a bit of a culture shock to move out and live on my own, but I really love my work, so I adapted quickly. Before I got into CPDU, I had to get my GED. The Amish only go to school until eighth grade. I left home and applied to train to work as a police officer, but I had to put on my application that my high school equivalency, or my GED, was pending."

"But you were still able to get in?" Freya asked.

"Yes, it all worked out. Fortunately, I passed about a month after I left home. I updated my resume, and they put a rush on my application because I couldn't start until I passed my GED, so that was a blessing. After that, I had to pass CPDU's written tests, interviews, background checks, a polygraph, application screening, and things like that." Adam let out a long breath. "Sorry. That was a lot of information."

"Wow. That sounds complicated, but I think it's really interesting. You're obviously passionate about your work." Freya wrapped her hands around her warm cup of cocoa. "I didn't realize you had to do all of that to get into police training."

"It's quite the process, but it was worth it. The timing worked out because I was one of the last applicants to get my paperwork filed before the interviewing process started. I've only been an officer for a very short time."

"Do you like it so far?"

"I really love it. Many of the guys at work make fun of me for growing up Amish, but now I've quickly realized they are just joking around. I took it personally at first, but not anymore."

"Well, your family must be so proud of you." Freya uncovered her hot cocoa and blew on the brown liquid.

"No, they aren't. Not at all. At least, I don't think they are. They haven't spoken to me since I left."

Freya drew her eyebrows together. "Why?" she couldn't help but blurt out. She took a sip of her drink.

"When an Amish person leaves their community, they are shunned if they've been baptized into the church. I haven't been baptized, so I wasn't technically shunned, but my father told me I wasn't welcome back unless I repented and promised to stay. I know my mother would talk to me, but I haven't told her how to contact me. Besides, I'm sure my father told her not to speak to me, so I don't want to put her in a difficult position."

"I'm so sorry, Adam. I don't even know what to say," Freya said, her eyes filled with concern. Freya didn't even have parents, but if she did, she could only imagine how painful it would be if they wouldn't speak to her.

Adam shrugged. "It is what it is. The Amish don't report crimes to the police or pursue justice. Don't get me wrong, I loved growing up here, and the Amish are wonderful people, but that is one thing I do not agree with. I value justice, and now I make sure other people get justice."

Freya nodded, taking a sip of her hot cocoa, her thoughts racing. She studied the scratched table. Should she tell him now? Or would it just make everything worse?

"Once my brother died and my family refused to report it to the police, I knew I had to leave. I think the police should have investigated his death and tried to find who killed him, but the community wanted to forgive and move on. Whoever hit Robert just left him on the road and drove away." A tear glistened in his eye, and he slowly shook his head. "I couldn't just stay here and pretend like I agreed with what was happening. Out of respect for my family and community, I never reported the crime, but I hoped to find the woman on my own. I left so I could find that person, arrest them, and make them pay for what they did to my brother. What kind of heartless woman just leaves a man lying dead in the snow?"

Freya set down her cup and lowered her head, feeling the blood drain from her face.

It was her. She was that heartless woman. The hot cocoa she had swallowed threatened to come back up her throat. She swallowed again, hoping to keep it down, but her stomach just churned even more. Her heart pounded as she looked up at Adam.

"I really need to tell you something," she choked out.

"What?" Concern covered his face, and he reached out and touched her hand. "Freya, you look very pale. Are you okay?"

"Just listen. This is hard for me to say. I've been thinking about how I would say this for so long, but I still don't know how to word it, so I'm just going to say it. Adam, I was there the night your brother was killed."

Her heart ached when he leaned forward, looking as though he was trying not to leap out of his chair. His eyes widened, and he squeezed her hand. "Did you see anything? Sid, a family friend, was there but couldn't see very much through the snow. He saw a young blonde woman drive away in a silver car. Did you see her?"

Freya closed her eyes, trying to shut out the memories, but they still came rushing back—the way her head hit the back of her seat as the airbag exploded, the way the melting snow had mixed with the blood on the road surrounding Robert's limp frame.

So much blood...

"I saw everything." She couldn't bear to look at Adam, so she just kept her eyes closed and lowered her head. She heard his chair creak as he shifted anxiously in his seat.

"Please, Freya. Tell me. I want to know. No matter how bad it is."

"Well, it was snowing really hard. I was driving down that road. It was so hard to see, and it was icy. I had just left Boston because my ex-fiancé was abusive. I'd tried to get away from him before, but he found me. He told me if he found me, he'd kill me. I was on my way to Canada. He has a bunch of friends who are cops, so I've been staying under the radar. That night, I was driving..." She stopped mid-sentence as a sob escaped her lips. Freya wrapped her arms around herself, feeling her cheeks warm as a couple in a nearby booth looked her way.

"Let's go outside." Adam helped her up, and she put on her jacket. He put his arm around her and guided her out the door as another sob shook her chest.

They stepped onto the snow-covered sidewalk and walked back toward the cemetery.

Adam patted her shoulder, trying to comfort her, but it was no use. Freya didn't feel any of the weight lift from her heart.

"So, who did you see, Freya? Did you see the blonde woman in the silver car? Don't be afraid to tell me. I just want to know the truth."

She couldn't keep it in any longer. Freya threw her hands up. "It was me, Adam. I'm the one who hit Robert!" she cried in a strangled voice.

She looked to Adam for a response, but he just stared at her, his eyes full of fire. Would he hurt her? At this point, she didn't care—it would hurt more to keep the truth caged inside her than a blow to the face would.

"It was an accident. I wasn't drinking or anything, I swear. I don't even drink," she went on as the words tumbled out of her. "The roads were so icy, and the snow was coming down so hard. He was standing in the road. I didn't see him in time. I tried to steer the car, but it careened out of control." She sank to the ground, barely noticing the cold of the snow as it wet the knees of her jeans. Tears streamed down her cheeks. "I was running from my ex, and I was afraid he'd find me and kill me. I was wearing a blonde wig. It was me. I'm so sorry, Adam. I'm so sorry. Arrest me if you want to." She held out her hands toward him, expecting him to cuff her right then and there.

Freya looked up after a few moments to see Adam standing there, just staring down at her. She tried to read his face, but she couldn't tell if he was angry or sad or just shocked. Maybe it was all three. Finally, after several moments, he spoke.

"Why are you telling me this now? Why come forward after all this time?" His voice shook with emotion, and tears ran down his red cheeks.

"I told you, my ex has connections with the police. I was afraid if it was reported that his friends would find out and tell him. And then, if I was arrested, he would know where I was. That's why I left Robert there in the road. I was afraid that Dean, my ex, would come after me if I reported it. So, I just left your brother there, dead. I was so scared. I tried, but there was nothing I could do for him. I have regretted it ever since."

"So, if I go report this or arrest you, your ex will find you and kill you?" Adam asked. Freya couldn't tell if he believed her or not.

"If that happens, so be it. I can't live with this secret any longer. I'd rather die or go to prison. Your family deserves to know the truth. I will accept whatever you decide to do, but I do hope you forgive me somehow. If you don't, I understand."

Adam continued to stand there with clenched fists, silent. Freya finally found the strength to stand. When she did, she looked into Adam's eyes and saw only sorrow and confusion.

"I left the Amish to find the person who killed my brother and make them pay for what they did," Adam said in an even tone, taking slow breaths, clearly trying to keep himself calm. "Thank you for telling me the truth, Freya. But I'm sorry. All this time, I've imagined arresting the person who killed my brother, but I..." He blinked as a snowflake caught in his eyelashes. "I can't bring myself to arrest you. Clearly, you were running for your life and you regret it, if you're telling the truth. But...I can't forgive you for this. It won't bring Robert back. What you did is unforgivable." He whirled around and stomped away.

As Freya watched Adam's retreating back, she felt something die within her, as if she hadn't been broken enough already. What had she been expecting, for him to sigh in relief and hug her, then take her out to dinner? She knew this would happen, that he'd reject her, possibly even hate her, yet it still hurt.

Well, she'd done what she'd set out to do. Now it was time for her to leave this town again.

Chapter Nine

As Adam stalked off to his car, the snow crunched under his feet.

It was Freya. How had he not seen it? Sure, she was obviously a natural redhead with those freckles and green eyes, but how could he have not seen her as a possible suspect who'd worn a blonde wig?

She's beautiful and charming, he admitted to himself. *She got you to let your guard down.*

Normally, he could read people. Even though he'd only been a police officer for a short amount of time, he could normally tell if someone was sincere or not. He could tell Freya was sincere. That's why he hadn't suspected her.

He got what he thought he wanted, hadn't he? Adam finally knew who killed his brother. He could see how tormented she was by guilt, and maybe part of him felt glad that she was anguished. It wouldn't have been fair for her to have stolen his brother's life and not suffer because of it.

But if her guilt and anguish were punishment enough, why didn't he feel better? Why, instead of being consumed with revenge, was he afraid for her safety? Why did he believe her when she said she was afraid for her life? Her ex could still be looking for her.

Why, in the midst of all of Adam's anger and indignation, did he feel compelled to find out if she was telling the truth about her ex? Dean, was it? She hadn't given a last name.

And why on earth, most of all, had he not wanted to arrest her? He'd been wanting to arrest his brother's killer all this time, and when the moment came, he didn't do it. When he'd seen the pain and fear in her eyes, he knew it just wouldn't have been right.

If she was telling the truth, then Adam could hunt down that man down instead—the person who was really responsible for Robert's death—and bring him to justice instead. If Freya hadn't been running for her life, she never would have been driving in that blizzard, and she wouldn't have killed Robert.

Yes, now it was clear to Adam—Freya's violent ex, Dean, was the one responsible for Robert's death.

Now he just needed to do some digging and find out who this vile scumbag was and if Freya's accusations about him were true. Deep in his heart, he knew she was telling the truth. He just had to prove it, for both their sakes.

As Adam got in his car and drove back to the cemetery, his mind wandered back to when Robert and Maria first announced that they were expecting a baby.

"We are so happy for you!" his mother had cried, pulling Maria into her arms.

"What a blessing," Aaron had said, clapping Robert on the back.

"This is wonderful news," Adam said, and though he truly was happy for them, a pang of jealousy pinched his heart. When would he find a wife to love and build a family with? Would he ever find someone to love?

"Don't worry, little brother, it will be your turn soon enough," Robert murmured into his ear, as if reading his mind.

Adam waved away his comment. "This is your day. Don't worry about me."

"I see that look on your face. I know you want a family of your own, too. I just pray it will be soon."

As Hannah and Maria began talking excitedly about baby names, even pulling Aaron into their conversation, Robert and Adam slowly made their way toward the porch.

"Honestly," Adam said quietly. "I don't have any interest in any of the women here."

"Still? What about Leah? Or Ella Ruth? They're both nice and very pretty. Or what about—"

"I know, they are. It's not that though. Any Amish man would be blessed to court them. It's just that...I feel most of the time like I don't belong here."

"You mean...you want to leave? Become an Englisher?" Robert whispered as they leaned against the porch railing.

Adam nodded, then looked at the carefully crafted deck. "I've been thinking about it. Please, don't tell anyone. *Mamm* and *Daed* would be so upset."

"You know I won't," Robert assured him. "But why? You still want to become a police officer?"

Adam nodded again. This wasn't the first time they'd discussed Adam's dreams.

"And now you're seriously considering it? I thought that was just a daydream of yours," Robert added.

"*Ja*, I am seriously considering it. I know it would crush *Maam* and *Daed*. It would kill me to have them disappointed in me, and I know it would break *Maam's* heart." Even the mere thought sent guilt ricocheting through him.

"If she knows you're doing what you believe you've been called to do, then she will accept it and be happy for you secretly," Robert said. "I know it."

"There are just so many things I don't agree with," Adam blurted. "I think we should be allowed to go to high school and college if we want to. And what is so wrong with electricity? I know plenty of Englishers who have close relationships with the Lord. What about Jeremiah Bromwell down the road? He is one of the godliest men I've ever met, and he's an *Englisher*."

"True—" Robert began.

"And I know they want me to get baptized, but how can I when I know I'll be shunned if I leave after? I don't agree with shunning at all. If a brother or sister is turning away from Christ, we should reach out to them, not ignore them. Why shun someone for leaving? Leaving isn't even wrong," Adam continued, his face heating with frustration. "I just want freedom. I feel trapped."

Robert sighed. "I know this life is hard, and it's hard to understand. I've found peace and happiness. I hope you do too one day, my brother, no matter where that is. You know I will always support you, right?" Robert put a hand on Adam's shoulder.

Adam nodded. "Thanks. Truly, I'm so happy for you and Maria. You must be so excited."

Robert leaned forward. "Secretly, I'm hoping for a son. I'd just love to have a son I can go fishing with and show him how to sled like we used to."

Adam laughed out loud. "I'm not sure that's such a good idea. It was dangerous the way we did it."

Robert smiled. "True. I'll be happy with a boy or girl, though."

"Of course, you will."

"I just hope I can be half the father *Daed* was to us. He was always so patient and attentive. I never realized until now how blessed we are to have a father like him."

Guilt tore at Adam again at the thought of leaving the community. "You'll be a great father, Robert. I know it."

But Robert never got to be a father or even know if he had a son or a daughter. Adam knew in his heart that Robert would have been the best father.

The brothers walked back inside the house, opening the door to see their mother standing there, hands on her hips.

"I couldn't help but overhear your conversation. I was coming outside to get you and I heard you say..." Hannah lowered her voice to a whisper. "You are thinking of leaving, Adam? To become a police officer?" Her lower lip trembled. "Why would you want to do such a thing?"

Robert and Adam exchanged worried glances.

"*Mamm*," Adam said, reaching out for her. "I know you and *Daed* want me to get baptized into the church, but it's probably obvious I don't fit in here. I need to do something more with my life."

"What is wrong with our simple way of life?" she demanded.

"Nothing. It's just not for me."

Hannah huffed, looking at Robert.

"I support him either way, *Mamm*," Robert said, hands raised defensively.

"Your father would be so disappointed if he knew about this," Hannah said.

"I know. Let's not tell him. This is Robert and Maria's day. I don't want to spoil their good news. Please, let's just enjoy the rest of the day," Adam pleaded. "Please, don't tell *Daed*."

"I'm begging you, Adam, please get this idea out of your head. You belong here. No one wants you to leave," his mother said.

Adam sighed. "I've been thinking about this for a long time, to be honest."

A tear slid from his mother's eye, causing his heart to ache. "I couldn't bear to lose you."

"You wouldn't be losing me. If I don't get baptized, I won't be shunned. I could still visit you."

Hannah turned away slowly. "You're right. Let's not talk about this now. Let's enjoy Robert and Maria's announcement." She returned to the kitchen, and they spent the rest of the day fellowshipping.

That seemed like such a long time ago. Adam shook his head, bringing himself back to the present as he drove back to the cemetery and got out of his car. He had been so focused on his memories that he barely remembered the short drive here. He walked to his brother's tombstone and sighed.

"Oh, Robert. I finally know the truth," Adam said, his words catching in his throat as it constricted. "I know who killed you." The words came out in a rasp. "It was a woman named Freya. I always pictured the woman who killed you to be a heartless person, maybe an alcoholic who had been drinking and driving. But she's not what I imagined at all. She's lovely and sweet and beautiful, Robert. She told me everything and even told me to arrest her, but I... I couldn't. I think she's in danger." Adam continued talking to his brother, telling him the entire situation. "I have to help her, right? I have to find out who her ex is. Is that what you'd want me to do?"

He stared at the simple tombstone as if waiting for it to speak to him, but he didn't need to hear anything. In his heart, he knew it was what his brother would want him to do.

"I have to go find her and ask her what his last name is. She only said his name was Dean. I have to find out more. Ugh," he groaned, scrubbing a hand over his face. "I was horrible to her. You would be ashamed of how I acted when she told me."

He stared at the tombstone again. Nothing.

"If I find this Dean person, he would be the one to pay for your death, not Freya. I forgot Freya is a victim in this, too. She was running for her life. That scumbag tried to kill her."

Guilt began to gnaw at his heart, soon devouring it ravenously. "Robert, I have to find this Dean. I can still get justice for your death if I find him and prove him guilty of domestic violence and battery."

Maybe this was why God had him leave the Amish—to get justice for his brother's killer in this way, a way he'd never expected.

Adam turned and drove back to the coffee shop. He burst through the door, his eyes darting around.

"Can I help you, sir?" the barista asked.

"I'm looking for the woman with the red hair, the one I was sitting with earlier. Have you seen her?" he asked.

"She left with you and didn't return," the barista said.

"Thanks." Adam dashed back out the door and stood outside, still trying to catch his breath. Was she staying in town? She hadn't said anything about it.

"Adam," Mae Miller said, approaching him on the street. "It's great to see you. How are you doing?" She paused, squinting at him. "Are you okay? You look worried about something."

"I'm looking for Freya," Adam said. "She was just here. Have you met her yet?"

"Of course," Mae said. "She's staying with us at the bed and breakfast."

"She is?" Adam breathed a sigh of relief. "Oh, good. I have to go talk to her."

Adam drove to the Millers' and knocked on the door. Ed Miller opened the door.

"Hello, Adam," Ed said, smiling warmly. "I heard you were back in town for…you know…Robert's anniversary," he stammered. "It's nice to see you."

"It's nice to see you too, Ed," Adam said. "Is Freya here?"

"She was here, but she just left," Ed said, his eyebrows knitting together. "Is something wrong? You look troubled."

"Do you know where she went? Is she coming back?" Adam asked in a rush.

"No. I mean, she checked out. I don't know where she went," Ed said. "I'm sorry. I asked her, but she didn't answer. She left in a big hurry. Is everything alright?"

Adam sighed. "I said some things I need to apologize for. She was honest with me about something, and I reacted terribly. I also have some questions for her. I'm worried about her. Did she say anything about a man named Dean who was bothering her?"

Ed shook his head. "We shared several meals with her, but she wasn't much of a talker. She didn't say much about herself when we asked where she was from and where she was going. We just figured she was a private person, but she did finally mention over breakfast that she was from Boston."

"Do you think she's coming back?"

Ed shook his head. "I asked her, but she said she didn't know. I'm sorry. She's a hard one to figure out. I wish I could help you more."

"Do you think she told more to Mae or Laura or Lydia?"

Ed tilted his head. "Maybe. You could ask them. You know how women talk." He chuckled.

Freya was so unlike most women; he doubted she'd told them much more than she'd told Ed. "I'll call them down." He turned to the stairs and hollered up, "Laura! Lydia! Come down for a minute."

A moment later, footsteps sounded on the stairs, and the two young women appeared.

"Hi, Adam," Laura said cheerfully. "It's great to see you. How do you like working as a police officer? It must be so exciting."

"That's one word for it," Adam said, and normally he would have chuckled at Laura's enthusiasm and never-ending questions, but he knew if he didn't cut her off then, she'd just keep asking them. "Did Freya say anything to either of you about where she was going?"

Lydia shook her head. "No."

"I kept on asking her, but she just said she didn't know," Laura said, sighing. "And I asked her many times."

"Did she ever mention a Dean? Did she say a last name? Or do you know Freya's last name?"

Lydia shook her head.

"No, sorry. She was a quiet one. I asked her all about her life, but she barely said anything about it. She did talk about a Shirley, a nice elderly lady who took her in and left her a house when she died. That was so nice of her because they hadn't known each other that long. She said Shirley had children, but they hadn't spoken to her in years, so she left the house to Freya."

"Hmm. That's interesting," Adam said. "Did she give a last name for Shirley?"

Laura shook her head. "No. Sorry."

"Did she say anything else? Anything might help."

"What's going on? Is she in some kind of trouble?" Lydia asked.

"I'm worried about her, and I need to apologize to her. I really need to find her and talk to her."

Laura shrugged. "I talked to her a lot, but she didn't say much other than that. She did mention she was from Boston. I'm sorry, Adam. I wish I could help more."

She had said she was leaving Boston the night she'd killed Robert. Maybe he could check the obituaries in Boston for a Shirley, and maybe he could find an address from there and check for any recent reports of domestic violence.

"Actually, you've been very helpful, Laura," Adam said. "Thank you. Do you think your mother knows anything besides the information you just gave me?"

"Probably not," Lydia said. "But you could ask her."

"I saw Mae near the coffee shop," Adam said. "If I hurry, maybe I can find her to ask if she knows anything more."

"She said she was going to the Unity Community Store on the way home," Ed said. "You might find her there."

"Thank you all. This was helpful."

"Of course," Ed said.

"Glad to help," Laura piped in.

Adam left to find Mae at the Unity Community Store, but she hadn't known anything else besides what Laura, Ed, and Lydia had told him, not even Freya's last name.

Adam turned away, defeated. He'd pushed Freya away with his words; he knew it. Would he ever see her again?

If he couldn't find Freya, how could he protect her from the mysterious Dean?

At least he hoped that if he didn't end up finding her, maybe he would see her again at the cemetery next year.

Chapter Ten

It didn't take a lot of sleuthing for Adam to find out where the mysterious Freya had lived and what her last name was.

He did an online search for obituaries in Boston for a Shirley and found a few that fit the time frame. Then he looked up those names with the county recorder to see if they owned property. He could see that one of the properties was transferred to a Freya Wilson from a woman named Shirley Connors.

So, she was Freya Wilson. With that, he found the address of the house. It was a Victorian-style house in a neighborhood in Boston. He'd found her house, but was she even there, or was she still on the run?

Adam wondered if there were any police responses to that address concerning domestic violence or any other matters and if any of them contained Dean's name and surname. He decided to walk a fine line and call Boston Police Department and tell them he was from the Covert Police Detective Unit and investigating a criminal matter that traced back to that address. He then requested a CAD, or Computer Aided Dispatch Report, for the past three years. Fortunately, they granted his request, and he could see that calls had been made reporting shouting and suspicions of domestic violence involving a Dean Hamilton.

Yet, every time an officer had gone to investigate, it was unsubstantiated and nothing had ever been investigated beyond that —all dismissed for some reason or another, such as Dean saying Freya had fallen down the stairs, walked into a door, etc. and that Freya had confirmed it even when the officer had questioned them separately. Well, a scared woman might not tell the truth and deal with the consequences, or the police really were corrupt.

It has been known to happen, Adam thought. Freya had said that her ex had connections with the police, so maybe his buddies had pulled some strings for him or dissuaded Freya from making a complaint somehow.

Adam dialed a number on his phone, and his coworker Charles picked up. "Hey, Charles, it's Adam. Can you look up the name Dean Hamilton, a bounty hunter from Boston?"

"Sure, I can do that. Why?"

"He's after a woman I know... A woman I need to keep safe. When I come in, I'll do some digging of my own. Don't tell anyone I asked, okay? He can't find out about this... Neither can the woman I care about."

He thanked him and ended the call. At least Dean couldn't sell the house without Freya's consent since she owned it. It appeared that someone paid the property taxes last year, and they were current.

The 911 calls had been made by a Victor Johnston, who apparently lived right across the street, so Adam figured he'd make the drive down to Boston and see if Victor would give him any more information. He could also check to see if Dean was home and maybe question him too.

First, he had to talk to Officer Jackson in Boston. She was the officer who had investigated the last call that Victor Johnston had made. Fortunately, she agreed to meet him, and he drove to the Boston Police Department to see her.

"You responded to the Wilson residence a year ago, according to this report. What did you think? Do you remember this call? Did it seem to you like a domestic violence situation? The other officers seemed to think it wasn't," Adam asked her in a conference room while visiting the Boston Police Department to follow up on Freya's story.

Officer Jackson nodded. "Oh, I remember that one. The woman kept on insisting she had fallen down the stairs, and that's how she'd gotten the black eye. But Dean Hamilton was standing right there, just out of earshot, so she might have been intimidated."

"Dean Hamilton. What was your impression of him?" Adam asked.

"I think he was abusing her. Probably still is. What else could she have said? I pulled her aside and away from his view and asked her again if he was abusing her, but she kept on saying no, that he wasn't. She didn't want to press charges and wouldn't look me in the eye. She seemed scared to me. Her face still haunts me. I wish she would have just let me arrest that guy." She shook her head slowly, then sipped her coffee.

"So, your hands were tied," Adam added.

"Right. She didn't want to report the abuse, and we didn't have an eyewitness, so we didn't have enough probable cause to bring him in and keep him. It's one of the worst parts of the job, when your gut is telling you something isn't right, but you can't do anything about it."

"Do you happen to know if Dean Hamilton is close friends with some of the other officers?"

"He absolutely is." Officer Jackson gave him a knowing look, raising her eyebrows, but not elaborating. "You know, he used to be a police officer, but he didn't make his probationary period and was fired for being too violent."

"Interesting." Adam's eyebrows knitted together.

"I hope you get to the bottom of this, but I am surprised you are here in Boston. A little out of your jurisdiction, isn't it?"

"Yes, but I am working to connect Dean Hamilton to crimes and domestic violence incidents in my jurisdiction in Maine. I think there is a connection, and it would be helpful to show he is a repeat offender. I'm going to speak to the neighbor who made the calls reporting the domestic violence," Adam said.

"I talked to him, but he said he didn't see anything—just heard shouting and screaming. The other officers said they could have just had an argument." Officer Jackson shook her head slowly, staring into her coffee. "We both know it wasn't just that."

"It's worth a try."

"Good luck."

When Adam arrived on Freya's street in Boston, he pulled into the driveway, looking at the house that Shirley had given her. This was the house she'd shared with Dean, now filled with terrible memories. Adam got out of the car and knocked on the door. There was no car in the driveway, so he assumed Dean wasn't home. When no one answered the door, Adam drove across the street to Victor's house.

He knocked on the door, and an elderly man answered but wouldn't open the door more than a few inches.

Adam held up his badge. "Mr. Johnston, I'm Officer Lapp from CPDU. I saw that you made some calls to report domestic violence at the house across the street. I was wondering if I could ask you some questions," Adam said.

"I don't know anything," Victor said, looking Adam up and down.

"I'm very concerned about Freya Wilson's safety. Can you give me any information on Dean Hamilton? It might help me build a case against him. I noticed he wasn't home. Do you know where he is?"

"He's been gone for days," Victor said.

Maybe he was looking for Freya.

"Look," the older man said, his eyes darting back and forth. "I already told you people I don't know anything."

Why was he being so guarded? *Maybe Victor thinks I'm one of Dean's buddies,* Adam thought. "So, you've been questioned before by police officers?"

"Yeah, and they didn't do anything to help Freya. I'm guessing you won't either." Victor frowned.

"I want to help Freya Wilson. Like I said, I'm trying to gather more evidence to build a case against Dean Hamilton so we can arrest him for domestic violence. That's why I drove all the way here from Augusta, to see if Dean was home so I could question him and to see you. I was hoping you'd tell me something that you didn't tell the other officers. Did you ever see Dean Hamilton hurt Freya Wilson? Anything at all could help."

Victor furrowed his brow as he stared Adam down. "No, I never saw anything. He's slick and smart. I heard shouting, and I heard her screaming. I heard what sounded like him throwing her across the room and her landing into the wall. That's all I know. Sorry." He started to shut the door.

"Thank you, Victor," Adam said, handing Victor a business card. "If you think of anything else, give me a call."

"Sure." Victor shut the door.

Well, he hadn't learned anything new, but Adam hoped maybe Victor would change his mind and give him a call once he realized he wasn't one of Dean's friends.

Chapter Eleven

Dean's phone buzzed as he drove, and he grabbed it off the passenger seat and answered it. It was Officer Curtis Brookes, one of Dean's old friends from the Boston Police Department.

"Dean. Some officer at Covert Police Detectives Unit up in Augusta, Maine, is investigating you."

"All the calls that the neighbor made were dismissed," Dean countered. "Why is CPDU investigating it now?"

"He's looking into your history with Freya all on his own," Curtis explained.

"On his own?" Dean's eyes narrowed as he focused on the highway ahead. He was on a job, looking for a man who had failed to show up at court. "Why Augusta? Maybe that's where Freya is."

"He found the house, Dean. He knows where you live."

"What? How?"

"It's not that hard. Probably just some simple online searches."

Dean slammed the steering wheel. "Who is this idiot? Doesn't he know who he's messing with?"

"A friend of mine at Boston PD overheard him talking to Officer Jackson, the officer who almost convinced Freya to press charges against you. Do you think he has something on you?"

"He has nothing on me," Dean snarled. "If he had enough evidence to bring me in, they would have. He doesn't even work in Boston! He doesn't have jurisdiction here, and I've done nothing in Maine. So why, after all this time, is he looking into things here all on his own?"

Curtis fell silent on the other end of the line.

"Because he's in love with her, you dimwit," Dean snapped. "She must be somewhere near Augusta, and he's trying to protect her. So, what's his name?"

"Adam Lapp."

"Lapp? That's a weird last name."

"Apparently, he used to be Amish."

"Amish?" Dean laughed out loud. "Are you kidding me? An Amish cop? That's ridiculous."

"Well, I just heard that Lapp's brother was killed by a hit-and-run driver, then he left the Amish to find whoever did it. That's what my buddy said, anyway. Lapp has been searching for his brother's killer on his own for a year now."

"Did he ever find them?"

"No, not that I know of."

"So he's not as bright as he thinks he is. That's good." Dean tapped on the steering wheel with one tattooed finger. "Do you know where he lives and where he's from?"

"I'm not really sure. He probably lives in Augusta now. Isn't the closest Amish community in Pennsylvania? He may have come from there."

"I have no idea," Dean muttered. "I'll look into it. I might not be able to track down where he lived, though. Can you ask your friend for this guy's address history?"

"Sure. I'll ask him, but he might not know. It's not like I can just look him up in the phone book. You know that's confidential."

"Can you follow him home from work one day then? Or look in his personnel records?"

"That's illegal, Dean."

"Oh, come on. You owe me, man. How many times did I cover for you when we worked together?" Dean asked, laying on the guilt.

"Fine. I'll do my best."

One side of Dean's mouth turned up in a wicked grin as his vision focused on the road ahead. "If I find Adam Lapp, that's where I'll find Freya."

Then I'll kill her, he thought. *And she'll never run away from me again.*

On a quaint street lined with shops, Freya stepped up to a payphone to make her regular call to Victor. She called him every few weeks to check in and see how he was doing and to let him know she was still safe. She didn't know how calls were traced, but just in case, they always kept their calls less than one minute long.

"Oh, Freya," Victor said, breathing heavily into the phone. "I was hoping you'd call. A police officer was here asking about you and Dean, about what happened. I think he's one of Dean's goons trying to see how much I know. He gave me his business card, but I lost it and I forgot his name. I'm sorry. You better watch your back."

"Really?" Freya gripped the phone tighter, her heart pounding. "Was his name Adam Lapp?"

Victor groaned in frustration. "Ugh, I'm sorry. I can't remember. I'll keep looking for it, but I think I threw it out. My memory isn't what it used to be, dear."

"Do you think Dean knows where I am? I should move again just to be safe."

"Yes, I think you should," Victor said. "I'm sorry. I know last time you called, you said you had a job as a waitress, and you made some friends."

Freya sighed. "I knew it seemed too good to be true, but I have to do what I have to do."

"I'm sorry, angel. I just pretended like I didn't know anything. I remember his card said he worked in Maine, too, which seemed odd to me. Why would he be asking about a local domestic violence incident?"

"He was from out of state? From Maine?" Freya's skin went cold. "I wonder if someone is investigating the accident. That must be it."

Could it really be Adam? she wondered. *Why would he go all the way to Boston to talk to Victor about Dean's abuse? Is he worried about me?*

She shook her head, chiding herself. Adam wasn't worried about her—he was probably trying to make a case against her.

"Do you think someone reported it?" Victor asked. "I thought the Amish don't report crimes."

"Well, that's what I thought too. Maybe someone did."

"Please be careful, dear," Victor said. "Thanks for calling."

Freya sighed. "Thank you for letting me know. Well, I better go. I have to start packing."

It was time to move again.

Chapter Twelve

Two years after the accident

Freya dusted the snow off the top of Robert's tombstone and set her bouquet of red roses on the ground just like she had the year before. She had vowed to herself that she would come back here on the anniversary of his death every year.

She had waited for the day that the police would come knocking on her door every day since she had told Adam the truth, but they had never come. Since she had not left Adam her number or any other contact information, he had never called her. She even worked under a fake name. Sure, Adam hadn't arrested her on the spot as she imagined he would, but she thought maybe after some time he'd come to his senses and track her down.

As time passed, she realized the truth.

Adam had not reported her, and Dean still had no idea where she was, as far as she knew.

But the nagging question remained: Had Adam ever forgiven her? She'd heard that the Amish always forgive no matter what, but Adam was no longer Amish. She didn't blame him if he hated her guts.

Freya lifted her head when she heard footsteps. She looked around the snow-covered cemetery, then turned.

Adam Lapp walked toward her, stopping when he saw her. "Freya. I've been searching for you."

She sighed. So, he wanted to arrest her after all. "So, now you're going to take me to jail?"

"No," Adam said, coming closer. "I was worried about you. Did Dean ever find you?"

"No. I was hiding from him, moving often. You went to Boston and talked to my neighbor, didn't you? You talked to Victor, asking about me?" she demanded. "He thought you were one of Dean's friends, you know. You scared him."

"No, I didn't," he lied. "That wasn't me. Boston is out of my jurisdiction. However, I spoke with Officer Jackson on the phone, who responded to the last call your neighbor made. She's still worried about you. She suspected Dean was abusing you, but you insisted he wasn't."

"Of course, I did. I was afraid he'd kill me if I said anything."

"Every time domestic violence was reported, one of his officer buddies just swept it under the rug. I confirmed this, and I do believe you," he said.

"Yeah, he would just tell them I fell down the stairs or walked into a door." She wrapped her arms around herself, looking away. "He was never arrested."

"I'm so sorry, Freya."

She looked up at him, her eyes wide. Did he mean he was sorry for how Dean had hurt her, or for what he'd said last year?

"I'm sorry for how I reacted when you told me the truth," Adam said. "I went back to the coffee shop to find you. I wanted to apologize and ask you for more information about Dean so I could help you and protect you; and I looked for you at the Millers', but you were gone. They didn't know where you went. They said you didn't tell them."

"I didn't tell them much of anything." She stared at him, stunned.

"Why did you leave, Freya?"

"I thought you hated me. I didn't see the point of staying."

"I was shocked," Adam said, coming closer. "I'm sorry I reacted like that. I feel terrible about it."

"I killed your brother, Adam. You had every right to react the way you did. If you hate me, go ahead and say it. I don't blame you. I understand. What I did was horrible. Though, I do appreciate you not arresting me, because Dean would find me and probably kill me. So, thank you for that."

"I don't hate you." He shook his head. "I've had a whole year to think about this. I've asked myself what I would have done in your situation, and honestly, I don't know. But I do know that you telling me the truth took a lot of courage. And I admire that."

Freya's eyes widened and shock spiraled through her. He didn't hate her? "What about your family? What do they think?"

"Well, I never told them, since they don't report crimes or pursue justice. I thought it best to leave well enough alone. But you could tell them. I could take you to them."

Freya took a step back, dread seeping into every pore of her body. It had been hard enough telling only Adam about what she had done, but an entire family? She couldn't possibly do that.

"Okay, obviously that makes you uncomfortable, and I don't blame you. But my family will be understanding and forgiving. And I think they would want to hear the truth from you. I tried to reach you, but you're a hard person to find."

"I'm sorry. But I hope you understand why."

"Yes. I know. Because of your ex." Adam reached out and took her hand. "Listen, Freya. I'm not like my family. I usually can't let things go and just move on. But I want you to know that I played your words over and over in my head for months. I prayed and prayed about it, and it took me a long time to get to where I am now, but I want you to know that I do forgive you. We all make mistakes. And as I said last year, we should all get a second chance."

Freya smiled as new tears coursed down her cheeks, the first tears of joy she had cried in such a long time. "You forgive me? Really?"

"Yes. It wasn't easy, but yes."

Freya threw her arms around Adam and sobbed into his shoulder. For several minutes, he held her there until her tears finally slowed. When she pulled away, she saw that he had been crying too.

"Come on. Let's go to my family's house." He held out his hand.

"I... I don't know if I can face them," Freya said, taking another step back.

"Don't you think some of the guilt might subside if you tell them the truth and they forgive you? Don't you feel better after telling me, especially now?"

"Well, yes," Freya said hesitantly.

"I'll be with you every step of the way. Come on."

"Promise?" She took his hand.

"I promise."

As they made their way to his parents' house, guilt gnawed at Adam for lying to Freya about talking to Victor. He knew that if he told her that he'd been investigating Dean, trying to make a case against him, that she would panic and possibly leave again. He didn't want to lose her again, not after finally finding her. He wanted to protect her, and how could he do that if she ran again?

Adam had even told her that he spoke to Officer Jackson on the phone and not in person—another lie. He didn't want her to know he'd gone to Boston at all.

Adam knew that if he told her the truth, he would completely lose her trust for good. He was closer to gathering enough evidence to arrest Dean, and he couldn't blow it now.

He had to focus on helping Freya face her fear and confess to his family. Only God knew what she was feeling right now, but he imagined she must be terrified.

Deep in the Amish community of Unity, Maine, there was no traffic or zooming of cars on the lanes, especially in winter. Nothing to keep you from your thoughts. No distractions.

Freya would have given anything for distractions from her own thoughts. Guilt and anxiety knotted in her stomach as she thought about what she was going to say to the family.

Adam Lapp had been leading her in silence, aside from the occasional warning to watch out when she stepped on a patch of ice, so all she had to think about was how her stomach felt like it was gnawing itself from the inside as they crunched through the snow.

She couldn't even imagine being in Robert's parents' shoes. All this time, they had no idea who had killed their son or why. How would they react when they met his killer? Freya's mind immediately played the worst-case scenarios, as if she were watching a movie.

No, Freya. You're not going to get cleaved in the back by a vengeful Amish man with an ax.

The silver lining of this nightmare was taking comfort that the Amish didn't report crimes. Or at least, that's what Adam had told her. Was it really true? Would they really not report her for killing their son?

Guilt boiled in the forefront of her mind as she looked to Adam. His family hadn't spoken to him since he'd left the Amish two years earlier because of the rift she had caused in his family—and yet he was bringing her to them. If they refused to speak to their own son just for leaving, how would they react to her, the complete stranger who had run over their other son with her car?

Perhaps they just hadn't known how to reach him after he left. They didn't have phones, did they?

Would his family speak to him now if he visited?

A rock tumbled down the path she walked along with Adam, clicking and clacking until it fell into the snow off to the side of the lane, distracting her only for a moment.

Adam's voice broke through her thoughts. "We're here."

A knot of anxiety formed in Freya's heart as she looked up to see a small cluster of homes that seemed to be right out of a postcard. She would've enjoyed the view a lot more if it didn't mean an arduous undertaking was about to happen. It truly was a quaint and beautiful little town—part of her was surprised they weren't all white with black shutters like in the occasional Amish movie she'd seen. Instead, they were different colors—one was tan with green trim, another maroon with a tin chimney, and a third was indeed white.

Some of the houses had neatly stacked tarp-covered firewood. Bales of hay were being hauled out of a large storage shed by two men and tossed into pens with animals. Another man used hay tongs to put tightly packed sheets of hay in the feeding troughs of the stabled horses. Freya's breath hitched in her chest, and her stomach ached as though she'd been punched in the gut.

Horses.

She was behind the wheel of that car again, her wig feeling odd and itchy on her head as the memory filled her mind. The car smelled stale and rumbled oddly as she drove, and a vibration in the steering wheel caused her fingers to go numb. The snow fell down so heavily, it was a wonder she could see the road at all. She should have slowed down more before she turned the corner.

She should have pulled over because of the snow as soon as she thought about it. Why hadn't she just *pulled over*? If she had, Robert would still be alive. She'd just wanted to keep moving, to get as far away from Dean as possible.

The horse came into view, standing out starkly in the headlights. It looked so surreal, as though it almost couldn't have been real. Her numb hands jerked the steering wheel to try to avoid it.

Her foot pounded the brake pedal with a desperation she'd never known, then in her mind, she could see his face clearly as she sped toward him. That night, she hadn't recognized the shape of a man because it had happened so fast, let alone make out his face distinctly. Her memories warped, and now she could see his face in her mind's eye clearly—she could see Robert's terrified face, his wide eyes, mouth open in a scream, holding his hands up in defense. Other times, she could see him shouting angrily at her, shaking his fist; sometimes he was crying.

Then the memories of the impact came—she hit him, and he didn't move or react to her. He simply crumpled under the speed of her vehicle.

She barely remembered getting out of her car. The neighing of Robert's horse had echoed in her ears as she looked down at the swelling pool of crimson at her feet. Her hand had fumbled for the rumpled hat as she staggered back into her car with a sob.

Back in the present, a sob broke her out of the trance she was in, the snow stinging coldly against her knees when she dropped to the ground and retched. She hardly registered an arm over her shoulder and a rather startled Adam was kneeling down, keeping her hair away from her face. A wave of nausea came over her as her heart pounded in her ears, and her vision darkened. She closed her eyes, waiting for the dizziness to subside. Despite the cold, her hands grew clammy. Freya knew the symptoms of a panic attack all too well.

The men who had been hard at work looked over at them.

"It's Adam. I don't know who is with him," one of the men said to the other, who turned toward one of the houses.

What if they assumed she was drunk?

Adam's concerned words began to finally register in her ears. "Freya? Freya, are you okay? Are you sick?"

Poor guy. Freya imagined he was probably thinking he had dragged a woman with the flu all the way out here.

"No, I'm not sick in the usual sense. It's a panic attack. I get them when I get flashbacks sometimes."

"Oh. I'm so sorry."

"I was already having panic attacks before all of this because of Dean. They're part of my life now." She reached a hand out to scoop up some untouched snow on the ground to put into her mouth. After it melted, she swished it around her mouth to get the taste out, then she spat it out. "I saw one of the horses, and it reminded me of... I'm sorry, I need a minute."

Crunches in the snow told her someone was walking toward them, and her eyes lifted. A man who looked similar to Adam, but older and with a long beard, approached them.

"I saw you from the window," the man said. "Are you alright, ma'am?"

Freya looked to Adam and back to the man. Was this Adam's father? Was he really not going to say anything more to his son whom he hadn't seen in so long?

"I'm fine," Freya said, gulping. "I just had a panic attack."

"Panic attack?" the man asked.

Adam spoke up. "Hello, *Daed*. This is Freya Wilson. She needs to speak with the family. May we come in a moment?"

"Adam, I told you when you left that you are no longer welcome here until you repent and decide to stay Amish. Is that why you're here?" Aaron said in a cold voice.

"Well, no, but—" Adam stammered.

"Then you are not welcome inside the house, Adam. I'm sorry." Aaron gave a decisive nod.

How could this man treat his own son this way? What would he say to her, especially if she was without Adam in that house?

"No, Adam, I need you to go with me," Freya whispered to him, glancing up at him. "I can't do this without you."

Aaron furrowed his brow, studying her, then glanced at Adam.

"I know. Let me see what I can do," Adam reassured her in a soft voice, then turned to his father.

"I know you won't speak to me and you don't want to let me inside, but Freya needs to talk to you about something really important. She has something to tell you that I know you will want to hear. It's going to be hard for her, so she needs my support. I need to go in with her. You don't have to say a word to me. Just let us go inside together," Adam pleaded.

Aaron Lapp's eyes widened. "Very well, Adam. You may come in." He looked at Freya curiously. "Hello, Freya. I'm Aaron Lapp. When you're ready to come inside, you are welcome to. Adam will know where to take you." Adam's father only gave Adam a final nod before he turned to walk back inside.

No hug, no asking how he was, no welcome home. Nothing.

Now she saw what Adam meant by his father not wanting to speak to him, and it was all because of her. No matter how she looked at it, the problems here came down to one person—herself.

The next half an hour was a bit of a blur for her, swimming in and out of waves of nausea before she was finally well enough to follow Adam to the house.

Chapter Thirteen

Adam pushed open the door, guided Freya inside, and helped her onto a bench in the entryway. "Feel free to take your coat off. It might help you feel better." Adam's gentle voice put her at ease, at least a little. He took off his shoes, and she followed suit.

He was right. Pulling off her coat made it easier to breathe. Adam hung both of their coats by the door, then led Freya into the kitchen.

A woman in a long dress and prayer *kapp* turned and stared at Adam, then blinked. "Adam?"

"Hello, *Mamm*," Adam murmured.

"My son!" the woman cried, then ran toward Adam and threw her arms around him. "Oh, I missed you so much. How have you been? Where have you been living?" She released him and held him at arm's length.

Adam glanced at his father, who also stood in the kitchen, watching them, but made no move to stop them from talking.

"I've been living in Augusta working as a police officer. I didn't call or write telling you my address because…" Adam glanced at his father again, then at his mother. "I'm sorry. Should I have?"

"All that matters is you're here now. Are you staying?" She looked up at him, her round eyes full of hope.

"I'm sorry, no. I'm here because my friend Freya has something very important to tell you."

"Oh," Adam's mother said, her smile and her arms dropping simultaneously. "I thought…" She glanced at her husband, then back at Adam, and now Freya understood. She had thought that because Aaron had let Adam back into the house that he must have come home for good. Freya couldn't even imagine Adam's mother's heartbreaking disappointment.

"We will let Freya say what she needs to say, Hannah," Aaron said coldly. "Adam isn't staying."

Adam's mother wiped a tear from her eye and gave a weak smile. "Well, I'm glad to see you, Adam. So, this is Freya?"

Freya nodded. "Nice to meet you. I'm Freya Wilson."

"Aaron told me you were feeling sick. I'm Hannah Lapp, Adam's mother." Hannah darted back to the table and handed Adam and Freya each a steaming beverage. The beverages smelled a little spicy, similar to some of the plants Freya had smelled at the farmers' market.

"Thank you." Freya wrapped her hands around the mug, looking into the amber-hued fluid before she took a small sip, sweet with honey and sharp with ginger. Her stomach settled as the warmth of the tea began to trickle down her throat.

The home was simple but cozy. Battery-operated lanterns flickered dimly in the room, providing much of the light. The chairs were hand-carved and surprisingly comfortable, even without cushions to soften them. The smell of wood ash filled her nose. Hannah pushed another log into the wood-burning stove. The heat warmed the entire room, and Freya wondered if it warmed the upstairs, too.

Bundles of herbs and flowers were hanging to dry, and baskets lined with cloth and partially covered with a towel held what looked like potatoes or onions.

Freya built up the courage to break the silence after a few more sips from her mug, her hands shaking a little. "This really helped settle my stomach, thank you. Your home is very lovely, Mrs. Lapp." Her voice wavered past the golf ball-sized lump in her throat.

"I certainly try my best to keep it that way. Thank you." A grin stretched across the woman's face as she rubbed her hands dry with a small towel she kept in a loop on her apron. She looked like the kind of mother you'd see in a storybook for children, with her gray hair pulled back into a bun, covered by her prayer *kapp*, and crow's feet that crinkled and grew deeper when her smile raised her cheeks.

"Sometimes you'd be amazed to find a clear table or counter in here, especially during canning season."

Look at how happy she is, Freya's mind nagged at her. Hadn't she caused enough pain to this family? The pit in her stomach deepened as she thought about having to tell this woman, to her face, at her own table, that she was the one who had killed her son. That this was her fault.

A woman and toddler walked in. "Freya, this is our daughter-in-law, Maria Lapp, and her son Carter. They live here with us. Maria, this is Freya Wilson."

"Nice to meet you, Maria," Freya said. Maria looked to be around her age now that she was up close, though worn down. Clearly, she had experienced a great deal of stress. Seeing the woman and little boy again—Robert's son—undid all the good the tea had done for settling Freya's insides. The blood drained from her face as she focused on her mug, and her shaky hands turned clammy.

"*Spiele,*" the little boy said to his mother, and Freya wondered what he had said.

"Yes, Carter, you can play," Maria said.

Freya watched as Maria set the adorable pudgy-cheeked little boy down on the floor to play with some wooden blocks. Maria looked up at Freya. "He mostly speaks Pennsylvania Dutch," she explained. "Children here don't learn English until school age, normally."

Freya nodded, wiping her sweaty hands on her pants, unable to respond. She had taken this child's father away from him, and the realization that she was responsible for the tragedy settled on her like a shroud.

Adam was the first to break the silence as he looked at his father. "You don't need to talk to me. You don't need to say anything to me. Freya is the one who needs to speak to you." He looked among his family members and swallowed hard before continuing. "I came here with Freya because she needs to speak to all of you, and because I wanted to support her." His gaze then moved from his family to her.

"Please, have a seat," Aaron said, and everyone sat at the table, except Adam. He stepped closer to her, bent down, and whispered in her ear, "I know it's hard, but you're already here. You can do this." He then took a seat near her at the table.

But could she really do this? Her hands idly traced the indents in the wooden table, thumbs pressing into the perfect rounded edge while she took a deep breath. She could back out, couldn't she? That would be quite the waste, she knew, to come all this way just to crumble and never tell them what she did to their family. That kind of knowledge eats at a person like poison, and his parents not knowing was even worse.

She couldn't live with herself if she left without telling them.

God, please give me the strength to get through this, she prayed.

After a deep breath, she began to speak past what felt like a wad of iron wool in her throat. "It's about something I did that affected all of you." Her voice was far quieter than she'd intended it to be, so she cleared her throat and spoke louder. "I've been too scared to do this until now."

They watched her intently. She wanted to be anywhere but here.

"I was running from someone who wanted to hurt me. Someone who wanted to kill me. I wasn't thinking clearly. I hadn't slept, eaten, or stopped driving for hours. It was so dark, and it was snowing so hard."

Aaron walked over from his seat and stood close to Hannah, placing a hand on his wife's shoulder with a solemn look on his face as if he knew what Freya was about to say. Hannah's eyes filled with tears.

"I couldn't see far down the road, and I swerved to avoid hitting a horse—" Tears stung Freya's eyes as her hands clutched at her stomach. "And he was just...there. I couldn't stop on the ice. I didn't know what to do. I got out of the car and tried to revive him, but it was too late. I took his hat. I panicked, got in my car, and drove away. I'm so sorry. Oh, I'm so sorry for what I've done." Her voice cracked, and her head lowered in shame. "If it's any consolation, he died instantly. He didn't suffer." She couldn't even bring herself to look at them, to see their reactions. She opened her purse and pulled out the black hat, then solemnly set it on the table. "This was his. I took it at the scene of the accident. I saw the initials inside, and I was going to try to find you, his family, to tell you what happened..." She hesitated. "I see now that I shouldn't have taken it. I'm sorry. I'm so sorry."

The silence was suffocating. All she could hear was the hammering of her heart in her chest and a tense inhale from Adam. The quiet was shattered by the sharp wailing sob that escaped Maria and the rustling sound of fabric. Maria leaped forward, picking the hat up from the table and clutching it to her chest. The sight was so heartbreaking, Freya couldn't watch.

Freya squeezed her eyes shut and heard the poor widow run upstairs, her mother-in-law following swiftly after her.

A wave of nausea washed over her once again.

"It was her!" Maria cried, flinging herself onto her bed. "She is the one who killed Robert!"

"At least she told us," Hannah said, touching Maria's back gently. "That took courage."

"I don't care!" Maria snapped. "What she did is horrible and unforgivable."

"We must forgive her, my dear. It was an accident, after all," Hannah said soothingly.

"How?" Maria lifted her tear-stained face. "How could you possibly forgive her?"

"We must, Maria. God calls us to. It's the right thing to do."

Maria shook her head, sat up, and crossed her arms. "I never will. I can't."

Hannah sighed. "Maria, you have to. You will be able to in time."

"No. That woman"—she pointed toward the door—"killed your son. You're going to forgive her, just like that? What about *Daed*? Will he?"

"Yes, we both will." Hannah nodded slowly. "This is what will help us move on. We finally have closure, Maria. We finally know what really happened, and she's sorry. Doesn't that help you feel any better?"

"No." Maria shook her head adamantly. "It makes me angry, her waltzing in here, thinking she can just apologize and everything will be fine."

She wasn't like her in-laws. How could they just accept this woman's apology?

Maria vowed to herself that she would never forgive Freya Wilson—not now, not ever.

Chapter Fourteen

Aaron still stood near where his wife had sat, his hand clenched tightly around one of the chairs.

"We should give them a minute," Adam muttered quickly to Freya, grabbing her hand and pulling her outside into the cold winter air.

Instead of relief, she just felt...numb. She thought maybe she'd cry, but no tears came. She looked toward the house, worried about Maria.

They ended up near the barn. Freya found herself feeling rather grateful that the horses were out of sight inside the barn, and Adam had taken her far enough away from the house that she could tune out the distressed crying of the woman inside.

"Adam, I'm sorry. I should have taken it slower. I should have said it more gently. But the words spilled out of me. There had to have been a better way." Freya turned to look at him.

He shook his head and offered a consoling pat on her shoulder. "There's no graceful or immediately well-received way to bring up something like this. Sometimes you have to rip off the bandage. And it was good that you didn't keep them in suspense once you began. It can hurt, and it's hard to pull it off sometimes, but in order for the wound to heal, it has to be done. This is what's best for everyone."

"How can you be so sure this is better for them?" Freya rubbed her temples to alleviate the pain in her head. She leaned against a sturdy wooden fence post.

"Because the truth will set you free. It will set them all free. Nothing is worse than not knowing, and at least now they know. And it's better for you, too. You don't have to carry this burden around in you like poison."

She reeled a little at his words, since she hadn't given much thought to how confessing would make her feel. All she had thought about was the family's reactions.

The sound of stomping hooves inside the barn was enough to draw her attention away from the conversation, the visible flinch causing Adam to look concerned. "Freya, are you afraid of horses?"

"I think so." Her right hand flew to her chest. Her heart hammered heavily through her ribs as she took a step away from the stables. "I don't recall ever being scared of them before. Never saw them much growing up, except for during things like parades. Now they just remind me of the accident." Her stomach churned at just the thought of being near a horse.

"That's Robin. He was Robert's horse. My parents and Maria take care of him now."

"That's the horse Robert was looking for that night?" Freya asked in a shaky voice.

Adam nodded. "Robert loved that horse. That's why he went out to look for him in that blizzard. I should have gone with him in the blizzard that night to search, but I had the flu. I still feel so guilty. I wonder if I had gone with him…

"None of this is your fault, Adam. It's mine," Freya insisted.

"No, Freya, it wasn't your fault. I see that now."

Freya sighed, shrugging. "Still, if it's anyone's fault, it's mine. Definitely not yours."

"It's not anyone's fault. Sometimes terrible things just happen. These horses are usually very calm, especially if you're calm around them." Adam walked into the barn. He noticed she wasn't following, so he added, "You don't have to come in."

Freya moved to stand by the door of the barn, peering in while Adam coaxed Robin over to him. "See, he's a big sweetheart."

Freya took a step closer, then another step closer, and she surprised herself by walking over to stand next to Adam. The horse leaned its head away, huffing, a little bit reluctant to come near her. Perhaps her own fear made the animal uncomfortable.

Or did he remember her from that night?

"I'm sorry, Robin," she murmured. "Maybe you do remember me."

"Horses are very smart. If he saw you that night, he might remember you," Adam said in a low voice.

"No wonder he doesn't want to be near me." Dejected, she began to turn away, then the horse was within arm's reach of her, standing calmly and looking down at her with big brown eyes.

"See?" Adam patted the horse's neck. He gestured to it to encourage her to reach out and touch him. "He's very wise. He knows you have a good heart."

Freya smiled and reached her hand out reluctantly, slowly gliding it over the brown hair of the massive horse, causing him to huff and stamp one of his hooves into the dirt. "His hair is kind of wiry. I expected it to be softer."

"This part, on the nose, is very soft." Adam took Freya's hand and guided it down the horse's nose. Her heart, which had been heavy with anguish, fluttered for a brief moment, but soon the moment was gone once her heart began hurting again.

Freya turned away. Distractions couldn't last forever, even if Freya wanted them to.

Adam stared at Freya as she turned, confusion muddling his thoughts. Had he overstepped by taking her hand like that? He couldn't deny the way his heart had tripped over itself at her touch, but clearly she hadn't felt the same way, now that she wouldn't even look at him.

"I'm sorry, Freya, if I made you uncomfortable," Adam said.

"No, no, it's not that. It's just that..." Freya slowly turned to face him. "I'm really worried about Maria. Will they let us back in? I'd like to see how they're doing. Ugh, I feel awful." She collapsed on a bale of hay.

"You told them the truth. It's expected for them to be upset. Let's give them some time. Maybe they'll ask us to come back in."

As they sat in comfortable silence, Adam's mind wandered back to the night when his brother was killed.

Maria and Robert had come over for dinner, but when it started snowing, they'd decided to stay the night. After dinner, Adam suddenly felt sick and went to bed after losing his dinner. When he heard a commotion in the kitchen, he wandered into the kitchen, wrapped in a blanket.

"Robin is loose," Robert said, coming inside. As the door opened, snowflakes swirled in and landed on the hardwood floor. "I have to go find him."

"Please, Robert, don't go out into this storm," Maria said, her hand resting on her round belly.

"I can't just leave him out there," Robert said. "He's probably just down the lane."

"Adam, what are you doing out of bed?" Hannah demanded, waving a dish towel in the air.

"Let me go with you, Robert," Adam said, stumbling forward. "It's dangerous out there. You need help."

"No, no, Adam." Robert lifted his hand, making a shooing motion. "You go back to bed. I don't want Maria getting sick."

Maria took several steps back. "You look so pale, Adam. Go back to bed."

"I'll go with you, Robert," Aaron said, walking toward the door.

"No, *Daed*. It's freezing out there. I don't want you out there with your asthma. You could get bronchitis," Robert said. "Please. It'll be fine. I'm sure he's not far. I'll just go down the lane; I'm sure he's nearby."

"It looks dangerous out there," Aaron said. "Can it wait until it stops snowing?"

"I know you love your horse, Robert, but your safety is more important. Please, don't do this. You can barely see anything out there!" Maria cried.

"Robin needs me. I'll be right back, I promise." He stepped forward, kissed Maria on the cheek, and grabbed a battery-operated lantern. He walked back out the door, leaving a flurry of snowflakes puffing behind him as the door closed.

"There was no talking him out of it," Hannah said, hands on her hips. "Maria, you tried. He'll be back soon. He knows this lane like the back of his hand." She turned to Adam. "You, Adam, get back to bed before you get all of us sick!"

A wave of nausea overcame Adam, and he hurried down the hall to the bathroom. He remembered praying, *Please, Lord, keep Robert safe in the storm. Please forgive me for not going with him.*

Would Freya feel a little better knowing that Adam also felt responsible for Robert's death? He opened his mouth to tell Freya when suddenly the house's front door opened, snapping Adam back to the present.

Adam looked out the barn window to see Aaron standing in the doorway of the house. Aaron looked somber but calm, and Freya couldn't hear Maria crying anymore, which was another good indication that things may have simmered down.

"You may come back inside now, if you'd like!" Aaron called before retreating into the house.

They went inside and took off their shoes, and Freya followed Adam into the kitchen. Everyone was gathered at the table, with Hannah's hand on Maria's shoulder. The widow looked twice as worn down as when Freya had first seen her. Her son sat in her lap, leaning against his mother, and both of them were still red in the face from crying.

Hannah was the first to break the silence. "Please, take a seat. There are some things that need to be said." Her tone was gentle and marked with sadness.

Freya certainly couldn't blame her. She moved over to one of the chairs across from them and slowly lowered herself down into it.

Aaron began, leaning forward a little in his chair. "You coming here to tell us this was brave. It's later than I would have liked to know but brave all the same. But we want to know some things."

"Whatever questions you have, I'll try my best to answer." Freya's hands clutched her knees.

Maria rubbed her son's back slowly as she held him. "And we appreciate you coming here. You said you were running from someone. Why?"

"My ex-fiancé. He was very controlling. I'd tried to leave him before, but he said if I ever tried again, he'd kill me. I couldn't talk to the police, either. He's a bounty hunter, but he used to be a police officer, and he has too many close friends in the police force."

Hannah winced in response. "Did he hurt you?"

"Yes. The morning I left, he attacked me so violently that I was afraid he'd kill me. That's why I left. He hasn't found me yet, but he could still find me."

"But why didn't you report the accident? Couldn't you have gotten help?" Maria asked.

Maria's emotional voice caused pangs of guilt to bubble up in Freya, reminding her that the emotion had a permanent home within her. "If I had reported it, the police would have known about me. Like I said, he has police officer friends who would have heard about it. He would have found out where I was. He would have found me and killed me. I know it. I'm still not safe from him."

"Do you think there is a chance that Robert suffered?" Maria looked straight ahead with a blank look on her face as she held her son, her voice flat. "Or do you know for sure he died instantly?"

"I think he was gone the moment the car hit him. He was gone by the time I got out to check his pulse. I tried CPR, but it was too late. I got back in my car and left. I wasn't even thinking right when it all happened, I just wanted to hide."

The family briefly exchanged looks. Whatever messages their expressions carried were lost on Freya, but they seemed to be in agreement by the time Aaron spoke. "I'll begin by saying that we're not angry at you. It sounds like you are in a very difficult situation, one that made it hard to think clearly or react in a way that would be considered reasonable and sound. Robert was out looking for his horse in the blizzard. It must have been very hard to see and very slippery."

Freya nodded slowly to him, her gaze moving to Hannah when the woman cleared her throat.

"And I think everyone can certainly understand why your first instinct would be to run," Hannah said. "But a person's first reaction to a problem isn't who they are. It's what they do next."

Freya must have looked a little surprised to hear such words, since Hannah let out a chuckle. "What you did next was you felt remorse, and now you've tried to make amends. No coward would be sitting here talking to us, telling us the truth."

Freya almost let out a nervous laugh. She sure felt like a coward.

"Now we know that it wasn't someone who didn't care about his life in the slightest. I was so convinced that the person who killed

Robert was nothing like you, but I'm glad I was wrong," Hannah added.

This made Freya's eyes widen with shock as she leaned back in her seat. "What do you mean by that? I don't understand."

"You felt guilty, you valued his life, and you knew that something terrible happened. I was convinced that whoever did it would never have cared enough to find out his name, let alone sit at his family's table and confess. I don't know if you came here looking for forgiveness, but—"

"I wasn't," Freya interjected. "I wasn't expecting that. I just wanted to give you answers. I've wanted to tell you ever since it happened. I plan to go to his grave every year on the anniversary of his death and leave flowers."

"That was you?" Maria whispered, tears in her eyes as she held her son closer.

Freya nodded. "I met Adam there last year; that's when I told him what happened. He encouraged me to come to you with the truth. That's how this all began."

Aaron interjected, "Coming here shows that you feel remorse. Not because you just want it off of your mind. You knew it affected people besides yourself."

From the corner of her eye, Freya could see Adam was in shock, too. Freya looked at the family, her mouth opening and closing several times before she found the words she wanted to say. "I have to admit, I didn't expect this reaction. I expected..." her voice trailed off.

"Anger? Yelling?" Hannah said.

"I didn't expect this type of reaction at all," Freya admitted, nodding.

Aaron shook his head. "I imagine Adam told you a bit, but we won't call the police." He ran his worn hand over the table, feeling the grain. He must have made that table. "We'd call an ambulance if someone got hurt so they could get help, but we don't report crimes. Robert was already gone when his body was found, so we didn't. Vengeance is the Lord's."

Freya gawked, frozen with confusion. "I don't understand. What does this mean in terms of us? This whole situation?"

Hannah reached over the table, giving Freya's hands a gentle squeeze. "We can't hold this against you. It was an accident, and you never intended to hurt anyone, and you told us the truth. That's enough for us to forgive you. We'd also like to invite you to come here again if you'd like. You might want to get to know us. We also want to get to know you, and our community would be open to you."

Part of Freya was delighted at this sort of invitation, her heart warmed by the kindness being offered. This part of her was so touched, in fact, that tears streamed down her cheeks. She covered her mouth with her hand. "You're not shunning me?"

Aaron shook his head. "No, you're not Amish. It doesn't work that way."

"But what about Adam? He said you haven't spoken to him since he left the Amish to find justice for Robert's death. Why can't he be allowed back too?"

Aaron held up a hand, sighing heavily before he spoke. "It's not that simple. He wasn't baptized before he left, so he wasn't shunned, but I told him he wasn't allowed back here unless he repented. We don't believe in seeking justice, and he couldn't live with that. That is his choice. Please don't mistake this for animosity or malice toward him, and…" He paused, looked at his son, and took a deep breath to mull over his next words. "And I hope he knows we love him and don't hold anything against him. We could never hold anything against him. We just want him to come home. While we love him, we don't support his choices." He looked at Freya while wrapping his arm around Hannah's shoulders to console the teary-eyed woman.

How can you do this to your son? Freya wanted to blurt out, but she just stared at the floor. She glanced over at Adam. He watched his father, his mouth in a straight line. How must he be feeling?

Maria spoke up, her voice flat again. "I know it's hard for you to understand, but this is what Aaron thinks is best."

Freya still didn't understand, though. Why would they accept her, a stranger who killed their son, but not speak to their son just because he left?

"I'm sorry. This doesn't seem right to me. He left the community to try to do what he thought was right. There has to be some way to rectify this, isn't there?" She surprised herself, trying to plead Adam's case while his family shook their heads somberly. But she'd already mended some fences. Might as well try to fix all of them.

"Well, we are thankful to know what caused Robert's death," Hannah said, her voice cracking with emotion. "And Adam no longer has a need to seek justice. Now that we have that closure, maybe Adam will reconsider rejoining the Amish. We would welcome him and be overjoyed to have him back."

"He feels guilty about Robert's death," Freya blurted, then hesitated. "I don't know if he told you, but you should know. He regrets not going out with Robert that night to search for Robin."

Adam stared at the floor. Was he angry with her?

"Adam was sick. It was no one's fault," Aaron said somberly.

The few minutes of quiet, remorseful silence were cut off by Adam himself, who spoke from the doorway. "We should get going. I don't want to walk back down the lane in the dark." He spoke matter-of-factly, only getting a simple nod of acknowledgment from his family. "I'll try to send a letter some time. Maybe I'll leave a message on the community phone. I'm sure you'll all see Freya around." He paused, putting his hand on the doorknob. "I love you all. I'll be outside when you're ready, Freya." He exited the house, leaving Freya alone in the kitchen with the family.

Hannah spoke up, looking at Freya. "I do appreciate your kindness. Thank you for coming here to tell us what happened. Terrible things happen, and it doesn't always have to make sense. Please, do get home safely."

"Thank you for everything. You will never know what your kindness means to me."

Hannah gave Freya a hug, and Maria did too, to Freya's surprise. However, while Hannah's hug was warm and inviting, Maria's hug was stiff and awkward. When Maria released Freya, she gave her an artificial smile, then Aaron shook her hand. Well, Freya couldn't blame Maria at all for her cold farewell. She completely understood why Maria hadn't truly forgiven her. She was going through the motions with her in-laws, but it was clear from her body language that she had not truly forgiven Freya. And why should she?

Chapter Fifteen

A lump grew in Freya's throat as she walked out of the house. Tears stung her eyes again.

Adam smiled at her. "I appreciate what you said about my parents not speaking to me, Freya. Even if it doesn't change anything, it's nice to know you tried to help, anyway."

"I'm sorry about blurting out that you felt guilty for not going with Robert," Freya said. "That wasn't my place."

"No, I'm glad you said it. I never told my parents, and they should know. They're listening to you more than me right now."

Freya nodded while they walked back down the lane. "I still don't understand. It doesn't make any sense to me. This should have helped fix things."

"It did help fix things. I got to see them again; you got to apologize. They have the consolation of knowing what happened. Freya, they're a totally different culture even though they live right here amongst the rest of the world. It may take you a long, long time to begin to understand what things are like for them, and you might never understand. I grew up here, and I still don't even understand."

Freya looked down at her shoes as they trudged through the snow. Only now did she begin to appreciate the scenery they'd traveled through, now that she didn't have the weight of a confession bearing down on her. The sights, the sounds, and smells of clean Amish living surrounded her in all their beauty and simplicity.

Freya had spent most of her life in Boston. As she walked around the city, she had often smelled the whispers of baking bread and busy kitchens preparing for the day ahead. The aromas weren't quite enough to mask the chemically-harsh smells that came from a jungle of asphalt and litter, where exhaust from cars was so deeply permeated into the concrete and brickwork that even an industrial power washer couldn't chase the stink out.

Here, she smelled the scent of burning wood, and she remembered catching a stray whiff of it when she had visited the cemetery. This is what she occupied her mind with to keep her thoughts from what had just happened at the house.

The path the wagons and buggies took snaked down the dirt lane, entombed in snow and ice. Where the horses often clomped along, the remnants of large hoof prints marked the path.

She listened to the crunch of the snow under their feet, and she felt the way the snow seemed to shudder under her weight as it packed down with every step. Barren tree branches rustled in the cold winter breeze, reaching desperately for the sky. If she strained her ears, she could even hear a little trickling from a stream nearby. This was the kind of place she wouldn't mind walking to clear her head—it definitely cleared her lungs.

As snippets of the conversation came back to her and she kept going over it in her mind, she worried. Had she stepped out of line and said something inappropriate?

Adam gave her a reassuring smile before he pointed toward the bushes beside them. The branches were weighed down by snow. "When the weather is warmer, wild raspberries grow here. My mother picks them and cans them and makes all sorts of delicious food with them. Ever had wild raspberries?"

Freya found herself quite thankful for something to fill the silence that didn't weigh heavily on her mind—there were already hundreds of other troublesome thoughts tumbling and clattering around in there.

Taking a moment to compose herself while she moved to look at those branches curiously, she offered him a shake of her head. "Not wild ones, no. I've only had ones from the grocery store." Another fringe benefit of going into hiding in a place as rural as this was being able to try things grown locally.

"Oh, there's nothing like raspberries from your backyard. One of the things I will always admire about the Amish is how resourceful they are, how they grow their own food. If all the grocery stores shut down, they would still survive. Although, they do often go to the grocery store, contrary to what some people might believe." Adam stopped and pointed. "When that dug-out pond over there freezes over, my family uses it for ice to keep the food cold in an insulated room under the house. Many of the families do it. I prefer my fridge now, thank you very much."

"I can't even imagine having to harvest my own ice just to store food." She watched him nod as they began moving along the road again, the snow crunching under their feet. "I'm from the city. I don't even know how to garden. If the grocery stores shut down, I don't know what I'd do."

The snow on the ground had caught a thin layer of ice, a crystalline crust that was crushing under the weight of their feet, making a crunching noise with every step they took. There was something special about winter in the Amish community, something holy that the rest of the world had lost a long time ago. Freya felt drawn to it in a sort of mysterious way she could not understand completely. She had not been born Amish and barely knew anything about this way of life until she met Adam, and yet she felt a longing in her chest. What exactly she was longing for, she wasn't sure.

Adam turned to her and smiled. "I'm glad you faced your fear."

"I need to thank you for taking the time to talk to me in the café last year. For thinking about what I said, and for being willing to give me a second chance." Freya stepped up to him, looking upwards as she continued. "You brought me all the way out here to see your family, coming back here even with how all of it would affect you. And you still did it; you still helped me have this chance. There aren't enough words to thank you for this."

Adam couldn't help but smile a bit, holding out a hand towards her. "Well, you can thank me by talking to me more often and staying in touch. After all of this, and with my family inviting you back, I was hoping maybe you could be a go-between for my family and me. If I go with you, maybe they'd let me go back to visit."

"Absolutely," Freya said, hope rising within her. "That would be wonderful. I'd love to see your parents speaking with you again."

Adam scratched his ear uncomfortably, a blush creeping up his neck. "Well, yes, it would. Not only that, I'd like to get to know you more. I could tell you all about Robert. What do you say?"

Freya sighed inside, smiling. That sounded amazing. She paused before placing her hand in his, squeezing it and giving it a firm shake. "It's a deal, then. How about we start with that cup of hot chocolate we never got around to finishing? My treat this time."

"I think I'd rather like that. When it comes to hot chocolate, I'm a child at heart. I love it," he said, smiling.

Something about that image made her laugh. She laughed for the first time in what felt like years. When she tried to remember the last time she had laughed, she realized it could well have been years.

Maybe that cup of hot chocolate would be her first taste of what healing tasted like, especially now that she would share it with her new friend.

After the short ride in Adam's car to the café, they walked into the same place where she and Adam had that first cup of hot cocoa together after they met in the cemetery. The café looked different to Freya, though maybe she was one that had changed. Although she couldn't pinpoint anything specific, the booths looked friendlier and more inviting than when she had entered the last time. Perhaps it was a shift in her own perspective. It was a lot warmer and inviting now that she didn't have something weighing so heavily on her mind.

"Want to sit in the same booth as last time?" Adam asked her.

Freya glanced over at the table where she'd made her confession to Adam last year and hesitated. "Let's try somewhere else. Maybe we can make some happier memories."

Adam chuckled. "Good point."

Chapter Sixteen

After they got their hot chocolates and sat down in a different booth, Freya smiled at the view outside the coffee shop. "Last time I felt almost claustrophobic, knowing what I had to tell you. Now I can enjoy the scenery. It looks like a picture-perfect Christmas card." She gestured to the little town square lit up with Christmas lights. "It's lovely here."

"It sure is. I loved growing up here. You know, there's something I feel like I need to confess to you. The night Robert died, I should have gone with him to look for his horse, but I didn't. I was feeling sick. I had the flu." Adam groaned just thinking about it. "I had been vomiting all day. But I should have gone with him." He lowered his head. "I've always felt like if I had been there, I could have stopped the accident. I should have just convinced him not to go at all, but he loved that horse. He wouldn't let anyone talk him out of going, not even his wife."

"You were sick," Freya said, briefly touching his hand. Was it just her, or had his heart fluttered the same way hers had when their hands touched? She pulled her hand back. "None of this is your fault. Who could blame you for that?"

"I knew he wasn't going to let anyone talk him out of it, so I should have just toughened up and gone with him." Adam shook his head. "I could have been watching for headlights. Something."

"There's nothing you could have done, Adam, trust me. The snow was coming down so hard I could barely see three feet in front of me.

Please. This is my fault, not yours. Don't blame yourself." She gave a tiny smile. "It sounds like your brother was very stubborn."

"He was the most stubborn person I ever knew," Adam said, one corner of his mouth pulling up in a crooked smile. He chuckled. "He got into a lot of trouble by being dared to do things and not backing down. He liked to prove he could do anything. One time our friend dared him to go knock on the door of the old mansion on the hill. It used to be a creepy-looking place. Anyway, he did it, but he was so scared he wet his pants running home. We were all cackling with laughter the entire time."

Freya laughed out loud. "Sounds like you had a lot of fun together."

"We sure did. My parents always wanted more children, but my mother had some complications and only had the two of us. We had a wonderful childhood. She spoiled us with homemade cookies and pies." Adam smiled. "She's a saint, that woman, especially for loving my serious father. I mean, he acts all serious, but truly, he is a very loving person once you get to know him."

"I'm sorry he won't say much to you," Freya said, sipping her cocoa. "If I had parents and they didn't speak to me, I'd be heartbroken."

"He's doing what he thinks is right," Adam said, shrugging, then he smiled at her. "Maybe you'll make him see the light, and he'll change his mind."

Freya stared into her mug. "I hope I can do something right around here."

"You already got me into their house. That's major progress. Now," Adam said, leaning forward with his elbows on the table as he sat across from her. "Please, tell me about yourself. I want to get to know you."

Freya opened up about herself a little, at least about some of her quirks growing up, like how she used to mispronounce certain words. Adam seemed so easy to talk to, now that guilt didn't constantly wedge itself between them. Granted, they were not talking about particularly heavy subjects. No, it was mostly the vegetables they hated eating when they were children and how they used to pass the time and play.

Their childhoods had been completely opposite. Even their chores seemed to be entirely different. She'd never had to milk a cow or help turn a fallen tree into a hundred firewood logs. She never had to shovel manure or load hay into a barn.

Adam chuckled. "It's funny. My gut reaction is still to say, 'Really? You've never done any of that?' whenever someone trades stories with me about growing up. So many things still seem alien to me. The guys at work make fun of me for being Amish."

"Really? That must be annoying."

"I don't mind. I know they're just joking around." He shrugged. "I took it personally at first, but they have become like brothers to me, and now I know they didn't mean anything by it."

She was about to ask if he liked his job just to make conversation, but then she remembered why he'd become a police officer in the first place—to find the person who killed his brother.

Adam continued, "When I first left my community, I was like a tourist attraction to people when they found out I used to be Amish. They always wanted to ask me weird questions. It used to feel like that growing up, when we'd head out to town to sell stuff at the market or buy things we needed at the store. People always assume that we don't shop in stores because they think we make everything we need." He held up a hand, tallying things off on his fingers. "But we buy cereal, crackers, containers, normal stuff like that."

Freya remembered thinking the same thing when she first saw Hannah and Maria in the grocery store.

He continued, "They think all Amish don't use mirrors, buttons, bicycles, or solar panels when in reality, each community has different rules..." His voice trailed off, and he sighed. "Sorry. I could go on and on."

"No, I think it's interesting. That seems so different compared to what most people think when they hear Amish. I hope that didn't come out sounding rude or anything."

"No, no, I understand. I've found that most people tend to get the wrong idea. When you think Amish, some people think of things like buggies, children being kept out of school, and people stuck in the past refusing to learn. People think they're naïve, backwards, and there are many stereotypes about them." He frowned as he said those words, shaking his head. "I wish people would take the time to learn more about the Amish before judging them and realizing that there are different rules and customs for each community."

He was a good man. A really good man, Freya realized. He had the patience of a saint to bring her all the way out here, to face down his own challenges at home with a stoic sense of grace and poise that Freya could admire and hoped to find in herself one day. Maybe she had come a little closer to it today, staring down one of her inner demons and coming out of it as a victor. But she didn't do it alone, and for that she was grateful.

There was one question she had to ask. "Do you think you'd ever return to being Amish again?"

"No. There are too many things I don't agree with. I love my family and the community, and I agree with most of their ways. I'm still a Christian. But I think justice should be pursued. I think kids should go to high school and college if they want to. I think people should be allowed to play instruments and wear what they want. There were too many rules for me. I wanted to do more with my life than stay in that small community forever and be a farmer or a carpenter."

"They don't even allow high school or instruments?" Freya asked.

"Nope."

"Well, I'm glad you found your way. Even if they don't say it, I hope your family is proud of you."

He shrugged. "Probably not, but I accept that. I'm just glad you got to say what you needed to say to my family." Adam sighed, looking out the window. "I used to get into all kinds of mischief around here. Remember that pond I showed you earlier? Robert and I used to go sliding on it."

"Sliding? Not skating? Sounds a little dangerous."

"Yes, sliding, as in sledding down the hill and onto the ice. It was dangerous. Robert fell wrong on the ice one day and *snap!* His leg was broken."

"Ouch. That must have been scary for a couple of kids."

"Terrifying, especially since it wasn't the man-made pond in the village itself, so help was further away. I had to leave him there alone while I went to get my dad, and he was so brave. He told me everything would be okay. I hated leaving him there alone on the ice, but I went to get my father, and he took Robert to the hospital. Afterward, my parents were so upset with us. Even though sliding down the hill and onto the ice was my idea, Robert took the blame so I wouldn't get punished." Adam chuckled at the memory. "He did that more times than I can count."

"Sounds like he was a wonderful person," Freya murmured, a stab of guilt slashing through her heart.

"He was." Adam paused, looking at his hands on the table. "I hope this isn't too bold of me, but I wanted to ask you something."

Freya noticed a shift in his tone to a more serious one as she looked over to him. "Go ahead. I can't promise I'll answer it, but I won't be upset if you ask me something I don't feel comfortable answering."

He offered a small nod, turning a little in his seat to look at her. "Will you tell me more about your ex, Freya?"

Being asked that point-blank left her reeling, the blood draining from her face as her hands clutched at her knees.

He reached over to touch her arm gently. "You don't have to tell me about him, but I want to be able to help if I can."

She swallowed and looked down with a shaky sigh. "I've been keeping most people at arm's length because I'm scared about him finding me. I'm scared that the more people I tell increases his chances of finding me. What if he comes around looking for me, asking people if they know me?"

"You can trust me with your secret. If you tell the church not to answer any questions from a strange man, they won't."

Freya gave him a small, grateful smile.

"I don't feel safe sharing that information with anyone yet. But..." She ran a hand over her face. "I need someone to talk to sometimes, I think. I guess right now, a friend I can talk to would be a help."

"Freya, I want to help you. I want to protect you. How can I do that if you won't give me the information I need?" Adam asked.

"I have trust issues. I'm sorry, especially after all you've done for me. I hope you understand. Also, I don't want to put you or your family in danger. I hope you understand."

Adam nodded. "Of course. I won't pry further. It does sound like it must be rather hard for you."

She took a deep breath to calm herself.

"Let me know if there is anything I can do for you. Anything at all," he said.

Freya spoke softly, looking at Adam across the table. "I appreciate that." She felt indebted to him so much, especially after he'd taken her to see his family.

"I wish I'd never met him." The words spilled from her mouth, and now that she'd started, she couldn't stop. "Dean. I met him after my friend's funeral. It's a long story."

"I like long stories. If you want, you can tell me. You want someone you can talk to, right?"

Freya nodded. "Well, then. In that case, I'll start at the beginning. I don't really have any family. I was raised in foster care until I got out at age eighteen. After that, I was on my own."

Freya's mind went back to the day she'd met Shirley. "Foster care was more often bad than good. Sure, I had a few nice families, but most of them weren't great. Some were terrible. After I got out, I was so alone. Then I met Shirley at a diner I was working at. We connected right away. The diner was empty except for her, so I sat down and we talked for a long time. We had a lot in common."

"What happened to your parents, if you don't mind me asking?" Adam asked.

"I don't know who my father was, and my mother was a drug addict. The state took me away from her when I was a toddler. I don't really remember her, but she couldn't take care of me," Freya said.

"I'm so sorry," Adam said, briefly touching her hand.

She flinched, a reflex she'd developed throughout her life. "It's okay. Like I said, I don't remember. Anyway, Shirley invited me to go stay with her. At the time, I was homeless. I didn't trust anyone, but I just knew I could trust her. So, I went home with her. Her house is beautiful, three stories tall, Victorian style. She needed someone to cook and clean and run errands for her, so she hired me, and I quit my job at the diner. When she asked me to stay for good, I was happy to."

Freya's eyes filled with tears at the warm memories of her dear friend. "We became best friends. She was also raised in foster care, but she'd been adopted by a couple with no other children. When they died, they left the house to her. She'd been married and had had three children of her own, and her husband had been abusive. Before he died, he turned the children against her, so they'd grown up to resent her and moved far away. She was all alone. It was terrible. But that's why we connected so well."

Adam nodded thoughtfully, motioning for her to go on.

"One day, I found her sitting in her chair by the window, dead. I was devastated. After that, I found out that she'd left everything she had to me, which was a fortune, including the house. I had no idea she was wealthy. Her children were so angry. She'd tried for years to reconcile with them, but they'd rejected her."

"Wow. You must have been shocked," Adam put in.

"Yes. I mean, I just didn't think she'd leave anything to me instead of her own children. Anyway, after her funeral, I went to a coffee shop just to think. Some guy started hitting on me, and I asked him to leave me alone. He got aggressive, and that's when I met Dean. He got the guy to walk away and leave me alone. I thanked him and invited him to sit with me." Freya shook her head, shutting her eyes tightly. "It was the biggest mistake of my life. He seemed so nice. I had no idea he had a split personality."

"Abusers can master the art of seeming like a kind and caring person in public," Adam told her. "It's not your fault."

"To say he is a master is an understatement. Before I knew it, I was telling him about Shirley and how she'd left me her house and her entire inheritance. He wanted my money. He charmed me into one date after another until he convinced me to let him move in. He said he just needed a place to stay for a week or two until he found a place of his own, so I let him stay. That was the second biggest mistake of my life. One thing led to another, and then I was adding him onto my bank account. He said he just needed to borrow money to pay for his father's medical bills, that he'd pay it back. He used the money for gambling."

"I'm guessing he never had any intention of paying it back," Adam surmised.

Freya clenched her fists, wanting to slam her head against the table. "How could I have been so stupid?"

Adam grabbed her hand again. This time, she didn't flinch or pull away. "Freya, he manipulated you. You were lonely and grieving, and he took advantage of that."

"He sure did. Then he started abusing me. He'd apologize, then do something nice for me or buy me a gift with my own money. He started staying out late, especially on the weekends. Soon enough he drained most of my bank account. When I suspected he was gambling, I asked him where all the money was going, and he attacked me. My neighbor called the police a few times, but he always talked his way out of it, and I was too afraid and lied to protect him in order to avoid a future, more severe beating. I think it was his police buddies who let him off the hook as the responding officers were suggesting to me that everything was okay now and putting words in my mouth that nothing wrong happened, assuring me I did not want to press charges. I wanted him to leave my house, but he wouldn't go, and those police officers left, telling me that was a civil matter and not a police matter. Dean just intermittently threatened me, keeping me off balance. I regretted everything so much, especially letting him move in with me when we got engaged instead of insisting on waiting until after we got married. Although he would have just kept up the façade longer, and if I had married him, I don't know if I could have gotten away from him. Now I see how wrong and immoral the entire situation was, living with him like that. I'd give anything to change it."

"We all make mistakes," Adam said. "He sounds like a monster. I'm just sorry he targeted you like that. I wish I could make him pay."

"A woman down the street invited me to church, so I went with her while he was out one Sunday. Her church was so friendly, and I wanted to go back. But when I got home, Dean was there, and he attacked me again, telling me I was forbidden to leave the house without him. He told me if I ever left him, he'd use his connections to find me."

Freya looked out the window, remembering how he'd thrown her into the wall. The house that had once only been filled with fond memories of the time she'd shared with Shirley had become tainted and marred by the memories of Dean's abuse. "I was too afraid to even call the police because of what he'd said."

Adam let out a slow breath as if to calm himself. "I'm sorry. My blood is boiling. I can't imagine anyone treating a woman that way."

"I'm sure with your line of work, you see it more than you'd like."

"It never gets any easier," Adam told her.

Chapter Seventeen

At first, Adam had only brought Freya to the coffee shop to get more information from her about her abusive ex.

He had to act like he didn't know anything about Dean, that he hadn't been investigating him on his own. Adam hated withholding the truth from Freya, but he knew she wouldn't trust him anymore if he told her the truth now. He hoped he would be able to tell her later on as they got to know each other better and she saw how much he wanted to protect her.

But as Adam listened to Freya's story, he became more and more angry with Dean. He couldn't deny that he desired to protect Freya from this man, because he had to admit that he cared for her.

Adam wished he could punch Dean in the throat, even though he knew it was wrong and he'd only be stooping to the abuser's level.

But maybe he could find him and make him pay by putting him in prison.

"I have to go to the restroom," Adam said to Freya. "I'll be right back."

Freya nodded.

"Here, I'll take your cup," Adam offered, picking up both of their mugs.

"Thank you."

He returned their mugs to the counter. Old memories linked his heart to this coffee shop. No one in his family knew, but he used to sneak out as a boy and come here to drink something hot at times, but mostly to read the crime novels in the basket near the fireplace. Reading fiction wasn't necessarily forbidden in Unity, but some people—like his father—frowned upon it. The crime fiction novels here were what had first sparked his interest in becoming a police officer.

Now Adam found himself at a crossroads; he thought he knew what he wanted to do next, but his soul was still caught up with that initial storm that pushed him to change his life forever. Now that he had convinced Freya to confess to his family, he had reached that level of peace he'd been yearning for.

But there was more that he had to do.

His thoughts drifted, as though riding gently on the snowflakes that had started falling slowly to the ground outside, covering the old layers of ice and snow.

His heart quickened just at the thought of Freya. He couldn't explain how it was possible that he was so drawn to her even though she had killed his brother. Yes, she was beautiful and kind, but he didn't understand how he could care for the woman who had taken his brother's life.

Yet he did.

Every time he looked into her eyes, he wasn't reminded of what she had done. All he could see were the possibilities in store for the two of them.

Adam had told her she could trust him, but he hadn't expected his family to invite her back to visit and get to know them. He expected them to forgive her, but not that. If she was going to be around his family, he needed to know who this Dean was and how dangerous he was, and if Freya seeing his family would put them in danger.

Also, he couldn't live with himself if he didn't do something to keep her safe from her violent ex. Maybe there was something he could do to help. If only she would open up to him, he wouldn't have to go behind her back like this.

He knew he was misleading her by investigating Dean without telling her, but it was the right thing to do. Along with his family's welfare, he also had her best interests at heart.

Freya had been through enough. It was now his personal mission to keep her safe. She had just done the bravest thing he had ever seen anyone do, confessing to his family like she had, but she was probably no match for the abusive man who apparently wanted to track her down and kill her.

※※※※ ※※※※

With Adam by her side now, Freya could start hoping again, maybe loving again. This cup of hot chocolate was actually the first step toward a new life for her, one where remorse and sorrow could actually be a thing of the past.

Talking with Adam eased her soul; she realized her life would never be the same after the accident, and that she would have to adapt to something else, something new. It would take time. That was for certain. Now, after her confession, a small flame of hope started burning in her heart again.

Adam returned to the table, a far-off look in his eyes as he muttered an apology for taking a while. "Sorry, there was a line. Here, I got us refills," he said, setting two more full mugs on the table.

"Thanks," she said.

He sat down at the table. "I was thinking about what just happened with your confession to my parents and Maria. I was wondering how they must feel right now," Adam said softly while gazing through the café window.

"I was shocked at how they just...forgave me." Freya shook her head, still stunned. "I mean, I don't have children, but I don't think I could forgive someone for killing my child, even if by accident."

Yes, they'd forgiven her, but it wasn't enough. Deep down, she knew she couldn't forgive herself. Not yet. Maybe in time, in many years from now, she'd be able to. But not today. Maybe she could somehow help Adam rebuild his relationship with his parents, not that it made up for what she'd done.

Adam sighed deeply. "I wasn't surprised. I knew they would. They forgave you a long time ago even though they didn't know who you were."

Freya stared at the table. This whole time she'd felt so guilty, and they'd already forgiven her? How could that be possible?

"I think my brother was their favorite, and he was the one who would always do things perfectly. I, on the other hand...left," Adam admitted.

Freya reached for Adam's hands over the table, tentatively at first, because she did not know what his reaction would be. When he squeezed her hand, she squeezed back.

"You did what you thought was right," Freya said as she tried to meet Adam's eyes, but she failed to meet them. His head turned towards the window as if he was trying desperately to spot something in the pristine snow. Nothing was there.

"Do you regret leaving them at all?" Freya asked tentatively. "Or are you angry at them for not talking to you?"

Adam finally turned to look at her, a haunted look in his eyes.

"Sorry. Those were loaded questions. I shouldn't have pried," Freya blurted, guilt filling her.

"I've asked you so many questions, and you have the right to ask me. It's okay." He sighed. "I don't regret leaving, no. I think I would have done it no matter what. I've always had a calling to help people, to fight for justice. Am I angry at them for not talking to me because of it? No. It's been mutual, really. I could have made more of an effort to speak with them, to write or leave messages on the community phone. I understood they wouldn't want to talk to me, so I didn't want to make it worse by having to face their rejection again." He shrugged. "It is what it is."

"But what if you're wrong? What if they want to talk to you now?" Freya asked.

Adam slowly shook his head. "I'm not sure even our visit would make them want to be on speaking terms again. My father made it quite clear when I left that he wouldn't speak to me unless I became Amish again."

"People say things they don't mean when they're angry. Maybe he regrets it now and doesn't know how to tell you," Freya offered.

"I seriously doubt it."

"What about your mother? What did she say when you left?"

"My mother was heartbroken, not angry. She just sobbed but didn't argue with my father, as always. If it wasn't for him, I think she would have reached out to me."

Freya's heart wrenched. "I've always longed for a real family, and if I had one, I can't imagine them not wanting to speak to me. Yet I've faced enough cruelty from my foster families to know how families should not treat each other. When families have each other, they should love each other no matter what. At least, I wish they did."

"Sadly, that doesn't always happen."

Freya put her elbows on the table, leaning forward intently as she looked into his eyes. "You brought me to face your family, Adam, and I'm grateful for that. But now it's time that you face your family."

"What?" Adam leaned back in his chair, shaking his head. "You don't understand. I can't just go knock on the door and expect them to forgive me."

"Why not? They forgave me for killing their son. Why wouldn't they be able to forgive their son for leaving?" Freya asked.

Adam looked at the floor.

"Don't you want to at least try to be on speaking terms with your father again? You never know how much longer your family will be on this earth. Don't waste one day not telling them how much you love them. You, of all people, should know that. What if your parents died tomorrow, and you never mended your relationship? I know that's a harsh thing to say, but it needs to be said."

He slowly looked up and met her gaze.

"You pushed me out of my comfort zone, so I want to help you do the same," she added.

"You're not going to give up, are you?" Adam asked, furrowing his brow.

"No." She shook her head.

Adam heaved a heavy sigh, placing his hands on the table. "Fine. I'll try, but I don't know if it will work."

"If you try, then that's all you can do. The rest is up to them."

Chapter Eighteen

Adam and Freya trudged through the snow once more to the Lapps' house, but this time, it was Freya who led the way, encouraging Adam when he lagged behind.

"Just remember all the things you said to me when I spoke to your parents," Freya said. "This is best for everyone. Remember saying that?"

"Yes," Adam said, catching up to her reluctantly. "And I know you're right, but it will still be hard."

"I'm sure you've been through worse, and maybe after this, we can visit your family under nicer circumstances." Freya bit her lip at the implications of what she'd just said. She hadn't meant that they'd be together long enough to be visiting his family. Had he taken it the wrong way? "I'm sorry. I mean you. Or me. You or me, not necessarily at the same time. You know, if they ever want to still see me after this. I know they said they want to get to know me, but that still seems too good to be true."

"If they said it, they meant it. Trust me." Adam tugged on the collar of his coat.

"I've never met anyone like them," Freya murmured.

Adam chuckled.

They approached the house. Freya heard Adam take a deep breath behind her.

"You were here for me; now I'm here for you," Freya told him, briefly grabbing his hand. She hoped she hadn't been too forward, but she didn't know what else to do to comfort him.

"Thanks." He gave her a meager smile, then knocked on the door. A moment later, Hannah opened the door.

"Well, what a nice surprise!" she said. "Aaron? Adam and Freya are here." She gave them each a warm smile and welcomed them inside.

Adam's father met them in the entryway. "This is a nice surprise," he said. "Come on in."

"I hope you will stay for dinner," Hannah said. "I made chicken and dumplings, and I always make too much."

"Well, if you are sure, *Maam*," Adam said meekly. "And if it's okay with *Daed*."

"Of course." Aaron nodded to both of them politely.

Hannah waved her hand. "Of course, I am. Come sit in the living room."

Adam's heart thundered in his chest like stampeding horses. It was only his parents, but they were the most important people in the world to him, and he wanted to do this right.

As they all sat down, Adam's fingers fidgeted in his lap. "I have something to say to both of you." He took a deep breath and went on before he could change his mind. "I know you are disappointed, maybe even angry with me, for leaving the Amish, and I don't blame you for that. I'm sorry I never called or wrote. It was just too hard, and I thought maybe you wouldn't want to talk to me, anyway. It was easier to not write at all than to have you not reply to any of my letters. I wasn't sure if you would."

He paused, watching his mother, who gave him a sympathetic look. Yes, he knew she would have secretly written to him without his father knowing.

"I'm not sorry I left. It was what I wanted to do, and I'm glad I did it. You might think that I broke my oath to God when I left, but that's not how I see it. The oath I made was to maintain my relationship with God above all else, and I hold that true in my heart to this day. I know God called me to be a police officer, even if it wasn't to get justice for Robert's death, but to help people. I'm sorry I didn't try harder to mend our relationship after I left. Please, if you can, I hope you forgive me, and I hope we can put this behind us."

"First of all, we aren't angry with you, son," Aaron said. "We were heartbroken."

Adam blinked in surprise. His father was speaking to him directly? Was it because he had apologized?

"We know you wanted to follow your dream, but we were sad to see you go," his mother said. "When you didn't make contact with us, I didn't know how to reach you. I didn't know what to do. We thought you wanted to stop speaking with us," Hannah said, tears already escaping down her cheeks. "It's a relief to know this now."

"We forgive you, Adam. I just wish you would have said all of this sooner." Aaron got up from his chair and walked over to Adam, who stood up, and they embraced. Crying, Hannah joined them.

Adam glanced over to see tears coursing down Freya's cheeks as she smiled.

"We love you, Adam," Hannah said softly as her shoulders shook with a sob.

"I love you too," Adam said.

Suddenly feeling like an outsider who was looking at a family through a window, Freya stood and crept out of the room. She went to the kitchen, grabbed a clean glass off the counter among a stack of clean dishes, and was surprised to see a faucet with running hot and cold water. She filled her glass, tipped her head back, and gulped down the cool liquid.

When she lowered her head, Maria was standing in the kitchen, staring at her, her arms folded across her chest.

"What are you doing here?" she asked in a quiet voice.

"I'm here with Adam. He wanted to speak to his parents."

"I think you've done enough." Though the tone of her voice wasn't menacing, the words still cut through Freya's heart.

"They're making amends," Freya stammered, feeling as though she needed to defend herself. *She has every right to be angry at me, to hate me,* she thought.

"That's good," Maria said softly, looking toward the living room. "Aaron and Hannah have missed Adam."

"I know you said you forgive me, but I understand if you don't want to," Freya blurted out. "I mean, I know Aaron and Hannah said it, so maybe you felt pressured—"

"You're right. I was going through the motions. I don't forgive you," Maria said, uncrossing her arms. Her voice cracked as she spoke, stepping closer to Freya. "I'm sorry, but I just can't. Please don't tell them. They'd be devastated, and they've been through enough. I shouldn't even be saying this to you. It's the Amish way to forgive, but I think when that rule was made, no one ever imagined their husband being murdered."

Freya's heart felt like a block of ice that had been shattered. "I didn't murder him."

Maria just looked at her, her eyes empty and cold. "He's gone. My son is fatherless, and I'm a widow. My husband is dead, whether it was an accident or not."

Freya shivered, guilt weighing on her and seeping into her bones. "I know there's nothing I can say to make it better, but I want you to know I'm so incredibly sorry, and I'd give anything to go back and change it."

Just then, Adam, Hannah, and Aaron came into the kitchen. Hannah pulled Freya into a hug. "Thank you, Freya, for encouraging Adam to come speak with us." She grinned at her son.

"It was all him," Freya said, shifting her feet awkwardly. She felt Maria's eyes on her.

"I'm not sure I would have mustered up the courage to come alone," Adam said. "She convinced me, reminding me family is the most important thing in the world."

"She's right. It is." Maria turned around, walking down the hall and up the stairs.

Everyone glanced at each other, awkwardness thick in the air.

"She's still struggling," Hannah said softly. "I think in time, the two of you will be friends."

Freya seriously doubted that.

Throughout dinner, Maria avoided Freya completely. After they ate, Carter tugged on Freya's sweater, holding up a wooden puzzle.

"*Spiele?*" he said, asking for her to play with him in Pennsylvania Dutch.

"Sure. I'll do a puzzle with you, Carter," Freya said. She followed Carter to the floor in the living room, where they sat down and dumped out the pieces. She noticed Maria glaring at her out of the corner of her eye, but how could Freya tell Carter no now?

Before Freya could figure out what to say to the boy, Maria pivoted on her heel, yanked on her boots, and fled out the door.

As Freya was playing with Carter on the floor, Adam followed Maria out to the barn. Once again, she'd walked away from the group.

He found her with the horses, stroking their soft noses. Adam pulled his coat tighter around himself and cleared his throat as he entered the barn. "It's freezing out here."

Maria shrugged, not even wearing a jacket. "I don't feel the cold anymore."

Adam didn't know what to say as he stepped closer. "She's trying, Maria. Freya doesn't expect you to forgive her, but if you did, maybe it would help you find closure."

"I told her I forgave her, remember?"

"Sorry if I'm wrong, but it seemed like your heart wasn't really in it."

"No. It wasn't. How can I forgive the woman who killed my husband, even if it was an accident? I'll never be able to. How can you forgive her? She killed your brother."

"It was just something terrible that happened. It's not her fault. Of course, I forgive her."

"Didn't you leave the community to arrest her?" Maria demanded.

"Well, yes, originally, but my heart changed when I met her," Adam said. "I saw her as a terrified, abused woman, not the cold-blooded killer I imagined. She's a wonderful person, Maria. I just hope one day you'll see past your anger and realize that. Unforgiveness will only eat at you."

"I don't care if it burns a hole in my heart. I just don't care. My life is over anyway," Maria said, her voice void of emotion. "Robert is gone. I have nothing."

"Your life isn't over!" Adam cried. "You have an amazing son who needs you and a family who loves you."

"I'll never be the mother he needs me to be, not without Robert. He completed me."

"God completes you, not any person. People will let you down, and people have flaws. There's no one on earth who can complete you."

"Who are you to tell me that? You left the church."

"I never lost my faith in God. I will always be a believer, Amish or not," Adam told her. "You know, I thought I could never forgive Freya either, but now that I've gotten to know her, I'm realizing she has such a good heart."

Maria turned and glared at him. "It almost sounds like you have feelings for her. How could you, Adam? I've seen how you look at her, but I thought I was imagining things. How could you fall for the woman who killed your brother? You're betraying him."

"Betraying him?" Adam blurted. Maria's words cut Adam's heart like a knife. "My brother would want us to forgive her, and he'd want all of us to be happy, especially you. Maybe you'll even find love again."

Maria scoffed. "Robert was my soulmate, the best man I've ever met. I'll never love another man for the rest of my life." She turned and stroked the horse's nose again.

Adam sighed. How could he get through to her?

"All I'm saying is I hope you give Freya a chance. Maybe one day, after you have more time to heal, you could—"

Maria whirled to face him. "Don't you dare say maybe we could be friends. I will never be friends with that woman, and I want her to stay away from my son. He doesn't realize she killed his father. I wish she'd never been born. Then my husband would still be alive." She turned and marched out of the barn in a huff.

'I wish she'd never been born.' She can't mean that, Adam thought.

This was not the Maria he knew. The Maria he knew had always been so vibrant and full of life, kind to everyone she met. Robert's death had shattered her heart, and clearly, it hadn't begun to heal yet.

Chapter Nineteen

As Adam and Freya left, Freya had mixed emotions. She was happy for Adam and his parents, but she felt sick at the thought of Maria being unable to forgive her.

If Freya was in Maria's place, would she be able to forgive the person who had killed her husband? Freya wasn't sure.

How could she even guess what that would be like? She'd never had a real family, and the only man she'd ever let into her heart had abused her, so what did she have to gauge her reaction? How would she feel if someone had killed Victor, her sweet neighbor? Could she forgive that person?

What if someone had killed Adam? How would she feel? She had no idea where the thought came from, but she guessed from the stab of instant rage and panic at the thought of it that she understood a sliver of how Maria must feel towards her. The thought scared her on so many levels.

The fact that she was the cause of so much rage and pain in another human being filled her with shame and regret, and she had a burning desire to do something, anything, to make it better and soothe Maria's soul.

She needed to pull back and protect herself. She was getting caught up in a family that wasn't hers. They had no reason to accept her, and they had every reason to hate her, even if they said they didn't.

And then, underneath it all, there was the fear that she was letting herself fall for a man whose brother she had killed. A man who couldn't possibly feel anything for the woman who had killed his brother.

"What's wrong, Freya?" Adam asked.

"I'm not really sure I should tell you," Freya said, not wanting to make Maria sound bad.

"Is it about Maria?" he asked.

"How'd you know?"

"I talked to her in the barn. She just needs time. Don't feel discouraged."

"I don't blame her for not wanting to forgive me. It seems almost unreasonable to ask it of her."

He reached for her hand and said, "I know she's hurting, but she will come around in time. And if she doesn't, I guess that's her choice."

Stunned by the sensation of his fingers wrapped around hers, all she could do was smile at him. Why was her heart beating so fast?

"Thanks again for going with me. I'm hoping I'll be able to rebuild my relationship with my parents now. They want us to keep visiting, to come for family dinners," Adam added, letting go of her hand. Disappointment bubbled up inside her, but why?

His parents want us to keep visiting? She thought, gulping. Had her two visits with Adam given his parents the wrong idea about them? Did they see them as a couple?

"Unless you don't feel comfortable seeing Maria again," Adam said. "You seem unsure about it."

Freya squirmed in her seat, unable to deny she would be uncomfortable facing Maria again.

How could she keep on facing Maria and act like everything was fine between them? Maybe she shouldn't visit for a while.

Freya realized she was even less comfortable admitting that wasn't her biggest concern. Her biggest concern was being around Adam more, which she now realized could result in her falling for him. Yes, she barely knew him, but there was something between them—a spark. Or were all the emotions from recent events getting to her head?

Right now, all she could do was focus on hiding from Dean. What if she had to suddenly move again? She could never be in a real relationship until Dean was out of her life forever, but would that ever happen?

"I'll be with you, Freya," he said. "It might be hard, but I do think once she gets to know you, she will love you."

Freya smiled at Adam. Where had this kind, caring, handsome man been all her life? Butterflies danced in her stomach.

I'll be with you, Freya. She rolled the words around in her mind—they sounded so good coming from his lips, even if they weren't in the context she desired.

Yes, she'd felt tied to this place before, but now she felt as though she'd never be able to leave for so many reasons.

A few minutes later, Adam pulled into the driveway of Freya's house, and the car stopped.

"So, now that I'm speaking with my parents again, I'll be going to church Sunday. They asked me to go, and they want you to go, too. Do you want to come?" Adam asked, scratching the back of his neck.

"To the Amish church?" Freya asked. "What should I wear?"

"Just wear what you would normally wear to church. They won't expect you to show up in a long dress and *kapp*," Adam said.

"Really? I mean, I don't want to stand out or offend anyone."

"You won't offend anyone. I'll be wearing my normal clothes, too. The Amish families here have many Englisher friends, and when they go to church, they wear their normal clothes too. Don't worry about it."

"Okay, sure. I'd love to go."

"I'll pick you up at eight-thirty," he offered. "It starts at nine and goes until noon."

Freya's eyebrows shot up. "Three hours? Wow." She nodded. "I'll be ready."

Freya got out of Adam's car and watched him drive away. What had she just agreed to? She would be going to an Amish church full of people who knew or would soon know she had killed one of their own.

What would they think of her? How could they possibly welcome her? Would they speak nicely to her, then turn around and talk about her behind her back?

More importantly, while the family had said they wouldn't turn her in to the police, could she really trust the entire community to stand by that decision? What about Maria? Should she leave and go back to Canada?

Please, God, show me what to do, she prayed.

Wrought with anxiety, Freya got in her car and drove downtown to the coffee shop. There was no payphone around that she knew of, so she asked the manager if she could quickly use their phone, and she was surprised when he agreed.

She dialed Victor's number. It was time to give him an update. She hadn't spoken to him in months.

The phone rang, and Victor's groggy voice answered.

"Victor, it's me."

"Oh, Freya, I was getting worried. Where are you? Are you okay?"

"I'm in Unity."

"Unity? After everything that's happened? Did you find the family?"

Freya told him everything. "I don't want to leave. I want to see where things lead with Adam, and I want to try to mend things with Maria. I have to stay."

"You shouldn't stay anywhere too long. He could track you down."

"I'm being careful, and Adam is a police officer."

"That might make things more dangerous for you if Dean really does have connections."

"I can't leave, Victor."

"Are you interested in this Adam, Freya? Is that why you don't want to leave?" He paused. "That name sounds familiar."

Freya hesitated. "He's Robert's brother. I barely know him. I only care about his family."

"You need to think about your safety first," Victor reminded her.

"I know. I've been careful all this time. For the first time, I feel like I can begin a new life here without Dean's shadow hanging over me. I'm going to try to find a place here." Would Adam be part of that future? Freya considered that possibility as a little smile crept across her face.

"Well, if you think you should, then I wish you the best. It's good to hear from you."

"Thank you, Victor, for everything you've done for me. I'll be in touch."

Freya ended the call, a feeling of hope rising within her. She knew without a doubt it was worth the risk to stay here, but how could she ever make amends with Maria? And how exactly did Adam feel about her?

***

After staying at the Millers' Bed and Breakfast for a few nights, Freya found a nice little house to rent out near the community, and she got a job at the local diner that was willing to pay her in cash under the table. Fortunately, there was a bed and all the essentials, but she found some used furniture at the local thrift store along with some décor pieces to make it feel like her own. It felt so good to have a place all to herself.

On Sunday morning, Freya awoke with panic rising within her. She looked around the room, seeing the bed she was in, the bookshelf, and a closet with a few pieces of clothing hanging in it. Where was she? Then it all came back to her—she was in Unity.

"Maybe I shouldn't go to church today," she muttered. "Maybe it's not worth the anxiety."

Yet, she knew this was the least she could do. She would face these people sooner or later, and she might as well not put it off any longer. One day soon, she hoped to ask for their forgiveness.

For now, she could go to church and meet them.

She got showered and dressed in a turtleneck and the longest skirt she owned, which reached her ankles. The Amish didn't expect her to dress like them, but she wanted to be respectful with her attire and blend in as much as possible, even though she knew she'd stick out. She tied back her red hair in a French braid.

This is as good as it's gonna get, she thought, looking in the mirror.

Soon Adam arrived to pick her up. As she got in the car, her stomach quivered.

"You ready?" Adam asked. "You look nervous."

"I am nervous." She took in a deep breath.

"Who wouldn't love you?" Adam asked with a smile. "You have nothing to worry about."

Her stomach flipped at his words. *Who wouldn't love you?*

There was that word again coming from him. Love. Did that mean he was starting to care for her? In a godly love-thy-neighbor way, perhaps. But surely, he couldn't think of her that way, could he? Not after what she'd done. "Let's go before I change my mind," she said.

"How do you like the new place?" Adam asked.

"I love having a place to call my own," Freya said. "I do miss Shirley's house sometimes. At least, I miss it the way it used to be when we shared it together."

Adam gave her a smile. "Maybe you'll get the house to yourself again one day."

Freya shrugged, looking out the window. "I won't get my hopes up. If I did, I'd sell it. I couldn't live there after all the horrible memories Dean created there."

Adam nodded slowly, and a comfortable silence settled around them. A few minutes later, Adam drove down a dirt lane that led to a lane in the woods, then they pulled into a dirt parking lot filled with buggies. Amish families were walking into a sturdy, two-story wooden building.

Freya sucked in a deep breath and almost forgot to let it out. "We're the only non-Amish people here."

"They have visitors sometimes who aren't Amish."

"What if they take one look at me and figure out what I did?" she asked, then realized how ridiculous that was.

"No one knows except my parents and Maria. They won't tell anyone. It'll be okay." Adam patted her hand, sending sparks up her arm, straight to her heart, combining with her anxiety. "Besides. I'm the black sheep who left. If people will be focused on anyone, it'll be me."

"Let's go." She turned and got out of the car, and he walked with her to the church. Feeling him just walking beside her brought her comfort, and she knew she couldn't have done this without him.

As soon as they walked through the door, everyone stopped to stare at them for a brief moment. Several men came up to Adam, greeting him and hugging him.

"Good to see you, Adam," a man named Elijah said. "We've missed you."

More men joined in, and Freya was glad to see so many men greeting Adam so enthusiastically after he'd been gone so long. Adam introduced her to them, and she smiled, trying to remember all their names. Once the crowd around him thinned, Adam turned to her.

"Let's take off our jackets."

"That was quite the welcoming committee. I'm so glad everyone is happy to see you."

"Me too." He leaned in closer and whispered, "I wasn't sure what to expect."

There was a table in the back of the large, open room that was covered in jackets, hats, and scarves. Freya followed Adam over and they removed their coats.

Freya looked around the large room, realizing the back half was a schoolroom and the front was the church sanctuary, where long, backless benches stood in rows facing the front wall.

"When there are big groups or weddings, we cover this entire floor with benches," Adam said softly near her ear. Not wanting anyone to see the blush that crept up her neck at his nearness, she ducked away.

Aaron and Hannah walked up to them.

"You made it," Hannah said, hugging Freya. "I'm so glad you came."

"It's good to see you in church again, son," Aaron said, shaking Adam's hand. He turned to Freya. "We thank you for bringing him back to us and getting him to come to church."

"Thanks," Freya said, seeing Maria on the other side of the room, watching her. Then Maria turned to a group of women beside her and began speaking with them in what looked like hushed tones. Maria glanced over at her every few seconds as she talked to them.

Was she talking about Freya? *Of course, she's not talking about me. Don't get paranoid,* she chided herself silently.

Then one of the women turned and began talking to another group of women, and they also glanced at Freya.

She felt the blood drain from her face as she watched them. When they made eye contact, she turned away.

"Are you well, Freya?" Hannah asked, peering into Freya's eyes.

"Oh, yes, I'm fine," Freya stammered, trying to swallow, but her throat felt like a ball of dry wool was lodged there.

"Let's go introduce you to some of the ladies and then get a seat," Hannah said, looping her arm through Freya's and leading her away. Freya glanced back at Adam, who shrugged and smiled.

"Ella Ruth, this is Freya," Hannah said, introducing Freya to a pretty young woman.

"Hi," Ella Ruth said with a wide smile. "It's nice to meet you. Are you from around here?"

"I just moved here," Freya said.

Two other young women came over. "This is Liz and Leah," Ella Ruth said. "Ladies, this is Freya."

Several other women came over and introduced themselves, and soon Freya's head was swimming with all the different names as she tried to remember them.

"Church is starting in a minute," Hannah said, taking Freya's arm again. "Let's go sit down. The women sit on one side, and the men sit on the other. You can sit here with Maria, her mother Mary, and me." As they sat, Hannah gestured to a woman sitting on the bench. "This is Mary Mast, Maria's mother."

"Oh, it's nice to meet you," Freya said, shaking her hand.

I killed her son-in-law, she realized grimly.

"Nice to meet you, Freya," Mary said as they all sat.

Maria sat next to her mother, quickly glancing at Freya, then looking away with a downcast look.

Will she ever stop ignoring me? Freya wondered.

The service started at nine with an hour of slow, German hymns from the *Ausbund,* the Amish songbook. Freya didn't understand one bit of the words, but she tried to follow along, mispronouncing many of the words and losing her place often. Then there were three sermons by three different speakers. While they spoke in German, Hannah whispered the English translation in Freya's ear, for which she was grateful.

In the third hour, Freya's back was aching, and she fidgeted in her seat. How did they sit on these uncomfortable benches every Sunday?

Even though Hannah translated for her, Freya's mind began to wander. She looked around at the congregation and was struck by their attentiveness and serenity—even the children.

She began to listen intently to the words, the slight cracks in Hannah's voice. The songs about forgiveness reached into her fractured soul and pulled something to the surface that she'd been packing down deep for two years now. She touched her face and felt something wet, not even realizing until then that tears were flowing from her eyes.

Could she really forgive herself and let go of the guilt and shame, like the speaker said? Freya glanced over at Maria, who was staring at her in horror and disgust. No, how could she forgive herself when Robert's widow wouldn't?

Yet, despite her discomfort, the words of the sermons that Hannah whispered into her ears reached deep into her heart—words of God's unconditional love and how believers should always encourage each other and build each other up. Most of all, Hannah whispered words about how God would always forgive, no matter how bad the sin was.

When Freya started going to church with the woman who lived on her street in Boston, she'd heard this message then. Now, it meant even more to her than it had then.

God, can you really forgive me for just leaving Robert there in the road and not telling anyone until now? It was a despicable thing for me to do, even if I was afraid for my life. Even so, I hope You forgive me, God.

A warm feeling of peace washed over her, and she smiled where she sat. Before she knew it, the service was over.

Chapter Twenty

"Now we go downstairs to have a potluck lunch," Mary said, leaning toward her.

"Oh," Freya said, her heart dropping. "I didn't know. I didn't make any food."

Hannah waved her hand. "You're a guest. You don't need to bring anything. Besides, there's always more than enough food."

After they made their way downstairs, Freya was stunned to see long tables covered in all kinds of food ranging from cookies, pies, casseroles, bread, soups, cinnamon rolls, pasta salads, and tossed salads. There were even jams, jellies, and pickles—all homemade.

"This is incredible. Is it like this every week?" Freya asked.

"Yes," Hannah said with a smile. "Maybe we take it for granted more than we should, but we do eat well around here." She gestured to two young women. "Ella Ruth makes the best seasoned popcorn, and Marta is known for her pot roast. We all love to make many different foods. Let's get in line."

As they were making their way to the line, two teenage girls met Hannah's eye—Laura and Lydia. Laura waved and bounded over, followed by a reluctant Lydia.

"Hi, Freya," Laura said. "So nice to see you again. Are you going to be staying with us again?"

"Nice to see you too." Freya smiled. "Actually, I found a place to rent, a small house just down the road."

"That's great! So will you be staying a while?"

"I would like to," Freya said.

"Come on, Laura," Lydia muttered, tugging her sister's sleeve with an annoyed look on her face. "Let's get some food."

"It was nice to see you again," Laura said before the two girls walked away.

Hannah chuckled. "That Laura is a funny one. She loves to read, and she has an adventurous spirit, a lot like Damaris." Hannah motioned to another young woman. "Damaris is always reading. She bakes, too."

"There are so many names to remember," Freya said, her head swimming.

"You're doing great." Hannah patted her arm, "Now, we really should get in line before all the food is gone." A twinkle in Hannah's eye told Freya she was joking.

"Yeah, right! This could feed an army."

As they stood in line, Freya caught Maria's eye again. Standing on the other side of the room, Maria was speaking to another group of women, who were now also looking at Freya. They whispered to each other, glancing at her, and memories of high school flooded back to Freya.

Was that disdain in their eyes, or was she imagining it?

"See that woman over there?" Maria leaned closer to her group of friends and lowered her voice.

"Who is she?" Samantha asked. "Is she from around here?"

"She's from Boston." Maria looked at Samantha, Debora, and Lisa, who were watching her with wide eyes. She had their attention. "She is the one who killed Robert."

"What? No," Lisa whispered. Deborah and Samantha gasped.

"It's true. She came to our house to tell us what happened and to apologize."

"So, it truly was an accident?" Lisa asked.

"Well, yes," Maria said. "But she still killed him."

"You've forgiven her, right? I'm sure Hannah and Aaron did," Deborah said, and the other two nodded in agreement.

"They did, yes." Maria glanced at Freya. "I'm trying to."

"You might need some time. That's understandable. But you will, won't you?"

Annoyance bubbled up inside Maria, and she plastered on a fake smile. Freya had no business being here, in Maria's church, acting like she was one of them. Why wouldn't she just leave already?

"Of course, I will. Eventually."

Freya's blood pumped in her ears. Was Maria telling them that she killed Robert?

"Freya, are you unwell? You look pale," Hannah said, touching Freya's shoulder.

"I... I need some air," Freya stammered, ambling toward the back door. She pushed it open, taking in deep breaths of the frigid air. The cold didn't bother her but actually felt good on her heated face.

As her breathing began to return to normal, she heard voices around the corner of the building.

"Do you think she is Adam's girlfriend?"

"I don't know, but Maria told me about her just a minute ago. Her name is Freya, and she's the one who killed Robert."

"What? No. Really?"

"Ja. Maria said Freya ran him over with her car and just left him there in the road to die. Now she's back to apologize. Hannah and Aaron already forgave her."

A few voices began to murmur.

"How sad. At least they know now how he died. Was it an accident?"

"That's what she says, but who knows?"

Freya's face heated again, burning despite the snow flurrying around her. She clutched at her stomach, feeling it churn, threatening to heave the little amount of food she'd eaten for breakfast. Leaning against the side of the church for support, she took in deep breaths through her nose, trying to ward off the dizziness that had suddenly hit her.

Maria had told them. How many people had she told? Did everyone know?

All Freya knew was she couldn't be here one second longer. She turned and ran down the hill, toward her house, not caring about walking there in the cold without her jacket.

***

After church, several of Adam's friends approached him. He'd played with all of them when they were boys and had been friends with them for as long as he could remember.

"Who on earth is that beautiful redhead?" Dominic asked.

"Shh. Someone will hear you," Gilbert said, swatting at Dominic's arm playfully.

"Anyone can see she's a beauty," Luke added, looking around. "No one can hear us."

"So, are you going to tell us?" Isaac asked.

"Ohh," Elijah teased. "I think Adam is finally falling in love. Look at his face. She's your girlfriend, then?"

Adam's face burned. "Her name is Freya. No, she's not exactly my girlfriend."

"She either is or she isn't," Elijah said.

"Well, I can't deny I have feelings for her."

The group of young men snickered and laughed, clapping him on the back.

"I'm not sure how she feels about me. It's hard to tell with her sometimes. Things are very…complicated," Adam said, kicking a pebble in the parking lot. "You have no idea."

"Complicated? Now you have to tell us," Gilbert said, leaning in.

"Well, I can't say. When she's ready, she wants to make it known, so you'll know soon enough."

"Now I'm hanging in suspense." Elijah tilted his head. The others agreed.

"I'm sorry. It's not my secret to tell." Something caught Adam's eye, and he turned to see Freya running away from the parking lot and down the hill, toward the road, her long red braid streaming behind her.

"Uh, there she goes," Isaac remarked. "Didn't you ride here together?"

Why was she leaving without him?

"Something must have upset her," Adam said, turning to leave. "Sorry, I have to go!" he called over his shoulder.

"Adam!" his mother called, hurrying across the lot toward him. "I just saw Freya running away. What happened?"

"I have no idea," Adam said, opening his car door. "I'm going to find her and ask her."

"Well, here's her jacket. She left it behind. She must be freezing." Hannah handed it to Adam.

"Thank you. I'll give it to her."

Behind his mother, he saw Maria stepping out of the church, crossing her arms and watching them with a vacant look on her face. He'd seen Maria speaking to several groups of women in hushed tones, but he hadn't thought anything of it until now. Maria was acting so unlike herself lately.

Sometimes grief made a person do things they would otherwise never do.

No. She wouldn't have... Would she? he wondered silently.

Hannah peered at him, her eyes wide with questions.

"Don't worry, *Maam*, I'll make sure Freya is okay," Adam said.

"Tell her you are both welcome to come over to our house, if she's up for it," she added.

"Thank you. I'll let her know. If she wants to, we'll come over." Adam turned and got in his car, backed up slowly while watching for children, then drove out of the lot. He drove down the hill, toward the main street, then saw Freya walking down the long stretch of road. He slowed the car and pulled to the side.

When she heard his car, she stopped and turned to him. "I'm sorry I left like that."

"What on earth happened? Are you okay?"

She looked away, her bottom lip trembling and her eyes reddening, threatening tears.

"Get in," he ordered. "You look freezing without your jacket."

"I left it at the church."

He held it up. "I have it for you. Come on, Freya, get in the car. I won't take no for an answer."

Instead of arguing, she opened the door and got in the passenger seat. He drove a bit more and pulled over near some trees, away from the road. He turned to her.

"Tell me what happened." He took her hand, slowly rubbing her knuckles with his thumb.

She took in a shaky breath. Whether it was her trying to stop crying or the effect of his touch, he didn't know, but he hoped it was the latter.

"I heard... I heard some women talking about me. They know everything, Adam. One of them said Maria had just told them a minute ago, and I saw her talking to a group of women, whispering and looking over at me." She groaned. "I knew I shouldn't have come today."

Adam scowled. How could Maria have done this? His parents would have never told anyone. This was not the Maria he had known all his life. "I'm sorry, Freya. Did you enjoy the service?"

"Actually, I loved it. While I was listening to Hannah translate, I felt so at peace. I want to let go of the past and forgive myself, but how can I when Maria won't?"

"You can still forgive yourself," Adam said. "That's all up to you."

"Look, I know one of them said Maria had told them about me, but it is hearsay. I don't know if they actually heard it from her," Freya said.

"I don't see who else could have told them," Adam admitted. "She was only one of five people who know, and I know my parents would never say anything until you're ready. I'm so sorry, Freya."

Freya nodded, wiping a tear away. "I wanted to so badly to tell everyone and apologize to the church on my own terms. Now everyone knows."

"We don't know that. Either way, you can still apologize to everyone."

Freya shook her head, a tear falling into her lap. "I don't know if I could do that." Just thinking about standing up in front of all those people and apologizing made her insides quiver.

"I promise, Maria is normally the kindest person. I've known her all my life, and I've never seen her do anything like this before. I think the grief has changed her," Adam explained. "Please don't think this is her true personality."

"It's all my fault." Freya took in a deep breath, then let out a sob.

Feeling helpless, Adam rubbed her back while she cried. "I'm guessing you don't want to go back there for lunch. My mother invited us over. Do you feel like going?"

Freya wrapped her arms around herself. "Maria will be there, right? I'm not sure I can face her right now."

"Maybe it's time we get this out in the open. This isn't like her, Freya, but she's being unkind to you."

"And I deserve it. She has every right to be unkind to me."

"No. It's not the Amish way. God calls us to forgive, to love each other, no matter what. So, what do you say? Do you want to go talk to her about it?"

"Ugh, this is so hard," Freya groaned, running a hand through her hair. "I hate confrontation. But yes, I suppose so, but I doubt she will want to talk about it."

"As always, I'll be there to support you."

That made her feel a little better, but her insides still filled with dread.

"How about we go to a nice restaurant? No one will know us there. Do you feel like eating though?" he asked.

She looked up at him and smiled through her tears. "That sounds nice. Actually, I'm starving."

"I know just the place. Do you like Italian food?"

"It's my favorite." Her smile slowly got wider.

Adam put the car in drive. "Let's go."

About twenty minutes later, they arrived at a classy Italian restaurant two towns over.

"I feel kind of weird wearing this here," Freya said, looking down at her long skirt. "I was trying to fit in."

"You look beautiful in anything," Adam said, flashing a grin. "And you don't need to try to fit in."

She gave him a shy look, then he got out of the car and hurried to her side, opening the door. The whole time at the restaurant, Freya tried not to think about speaking to Maria, and she tried to focus on the meal. After they finished eating, they headed back toward the Lapps' house.

A few minutes after they arrived, the buggy pulled into the driveway. Freya's stomach twisted like it had the day she had met them and made her confession.

Adam reached over from the driver's seat and grabbed her hand. Warmth spread up her arm and rushed through her whole body, making the anxiety subside, but only for a moment. Once he let go, the anxiety returned. "You can do this," Adam said. "What's the worst that can happen? I'm sure you've faced more difficult things than this in your life."

Freya sighed. "I sure have. I guess the worst that can happen is she tells me she hates me and never wants to see me again, which I'd understand."

"Still worth a try."

Chapter Twenty-one

They got out of the car and walked up the front steps, going into the house along with Hannah, Aaron, Maria, and Carter. Hannah pulled Freya back onto the front porch as the others went into the kitchen and living room.

"I'm sorry about earlier," Hannah whispered. "I think I know what happened, and I just want you to know that Maria has not been herself lately. I hope you'll forgive her."

"Of course, I do. Adam told me the same thing. I completely understand."

Hannah smoothed her apron with her hands. "You looked very upset. Are you well now?"

Freya nodded. "I'm doing better, thank you. We had lunch at the Italian restaurant down the road. Sorry we didn't go back to the church. I was upset and didn't want to go back for the potluck. I feel bad I left like I did."

"So, what happened?"

"I heard a group of women talking about me." Freya lowered her head, staring at her hands in her lap. "One of them said Maria told them what I did. I felt like everyone knew, and I felt like everyone was looking at me, talking about me. I was so claustrophobic; I just ran away. I was heading for home when Adam found me and picked me up."

"It's true." Hannah sighed heavily. "I was standing behind her and heard Maria tell several women that you killed Robert. That was not her place, and I deeply apologize. She has not been the same person since his death, and ever since you came here, she's been acting erratically. It's not your fault. Grief and anger make people do horrible things."

"I know she's angry with me," Freya said, her eyes stinging with tears. "I just wish she would get to know me." She waved her hand as if trying to ward off the tears. "I shouldn't be asking that of her. She has every right to hate me."

Hannah leaned forward and took Freya's hand. "It is the Amish way to forgive, not to hate, no matter what a person does. She knows God wants her to forgive you, but she can't yet. She needs some time. Still, what she did today was wrong. I hope you can forgive her. I know you were planning on apologizing to the entire church and telling them your side of the story. I tried to speak to her about what happened today, but she wouldn't talk with me about it. I'll try again."

"Thank you, but I don't want her to get in trouble with the church or anything."

"I hope it won't come to that. Everyone knows, including the elders, how much she has been through. They might speak to her about what she did, but I don't think they will go beyond that."

Hannah's eyes darted to the door. She looked back at Freya. "When you're ready, come join us in the living room."

Freya turned and glanced at Maria, who was talking to Carter, bent down to his level. Her eyes flitted to Adam, who nodded. Gulping, she walked over to Maria as Carter ran to the other end of the room to play with blocks.

"Maria, can I talk to you in private?" Freya asked in a shaky voice.

Maria stood up to her full height. "Anything you need to say to me can be said right here in front of everyone."

Hannah, Aaron, and Adam sat down in the living room. Hannah and Adam busied themselves by playing on the floor and talking with Carter while Aaron picked up a book.

Freya clasped her hands in front of her and took a deep breath to calm her pounding heart. "I heard some women talking about me and the accident when I was walking out of the church, and one of them said you told her about it just a minute before. I saw you whispering with some of the other women just a minute before that. Did you tell them about me?"

Maria threw her hands up. "Why would I do something like that?"

Freya shrugged. "I mean, I'd understand if you did. What I did was horrible."

"I think your guilt is making you paranoid," Maria said, her eyes narrowed. "You might think I was talking about you to those women, but I wasn't."

"Then how else would they have known? Only the five of us know."

Maria threw her hands up again. "You're a stranger, and maybe one of them made it all up."

"What are the odds of that?" Adam interjected from where he sat on the floor with Carter. "The church gets *Englisher* visitors every now and then, and the accident was two years ago. What are the chances of someone making it up?"

"People make up rumors all the time!" Maria snapped.

"Maria, I heard you," Hannah said, setting down the blocks she was holding and getting up off the floor. "I was standing behind you. I heard you telling Lisa, Deborah, and Samantha about Freya and the accident. I wanted to give you the chance to tell the truth, but you're lying to Freya right now."

Maria's face went pale as her eyes darted between each person. "You... You heard that?"

Hannah nodded.

"Well," Maria sputtered, crossing her arms. "How can you blame me after what she did to me?" She pointed an accusing finger at Freya. "You killed my husband, and we're all expected to forgive you. I tell a few people what you did, and now I'm the villain?" She let out a frustrated groan.

"I was hoping to apologize to the entire church before rumors got out," Freya said, taking a step backward. "Now I'm not sure people will believe what I have to say. You have every right to be angry with me, Maria."

"We are called to forgive and to love one another," Aaron said, setting his book down. "Maria, that was not how we are supposed to do things."

With an exasperated growl, Maria stomped her foot, turned, and marched out the door.

"Where's *Mammi* going?" Carter asked.

"She's just going outside for a bit," Adam said as he helped Carter build a tower. "She'll be back soon."

"I'll go talk to her," Hannah said, getting her coat on and grabbing another one for Maria, then going outside.

"I'm going to walk home," Freya said, headed toward the door.

Adam scrambled to his feet. "Let me drive you."

Freya held up her hand. "No, that's okay. I want to walk. I need to clear my head. It's not that far. Please, I need some time to think."

"If you're sure."

"I'm sure. Thanks. Bye," Freya said, putting her coat and boots back on before walking out the door.

Maria looked out the barn window to see Hannah following her, jacket in hand, as Freya walked down the driveway. Good. Maria was glad she was gone.

"Maria," Hannah said, entering the barn and handing her the jacket. "How could you treat Freya that way?"

Maria took the jacket, throwing her hands up. "How could I not talk to people about what she did? I had to talk to someone about it."

"So you told people what happened? She was going to tell everyone herself."

"I don't think I did anything wrong. Everything I said was the truth. I wasn't spreading rumors. She did kill Robert, so I told my friends. I just needed to talk about it to someone. Why am I the villain here?"

Hannah sighed. "I see what you're saying, but now rumors might spread because of what you told them before she had a chance to apologize."

Maria looked out the window at the snow, emptiness weighing on her. "That might be true, I guess."

"Will you apologize to her? She went home, but you should next time you see her."

"I don't know. I still don't think I did anything wrong."

"Maria, I love having you and Carter live with us, but I'm afraid if you don't change your attitude, we will have to ask you to move out." Hannah put her hands on her hips. "I'm sorry. I can't have so much negativity in my house. I think Aaron would agree."

Maria's mouth fell open. "You're asking me to leave because of this?" How could she? Freya was the villain here.

"You have changed into someone I do not recognize, Maria. I've known you all your life. You have always been a kind, caring, compassionate person until now. Ever since Freya came into our lives, you have been cold and bitter." Hannah reached out and touched her arm. "What happened?"

"It wasn't when Freya came here for the first time. It was when Robert died." Maria turned away to stare out the window at the snow-covered fields. "After Robert died, I became angry with God. I don't understand why He took my husband away from me. He was such a good man. Why would God let him die?" Maria shook her head slowly. "I'm sorry to tell you this now. When Freya came along, I stopped trying to hide how I felt. Something inside me snapped."

"You need to talk to God about this, Maria, and examine your heart. You won't be able to heal and move on if you refuse to forgive. Your heart will become even more bitter. Choose forgiveness, Maria, so you can become free of this."

Maria turned to her mother-in-law, tears in her eyes. "I don't think I can do it."

"With God's help, you can." Hannah patted Maria's arm. "I don't want you to move out. I know you can do this."

With that, Hannah walked out of the barn and headed back to the house.

Adam turned and walked back toward Carter and his father. "Wow. That was intense."

"Maria hasn't been the same person since Robert died. She has become very withdrawn. Ever since Freya showed up, she's just been angry." Aaron slowly shook his head.

Adam sat down on the floor and continued to play blocks with Carter, who stacked more blocks to make the tower taller. Adam laughed when it toppled over, and Carter clapped his little hands.

"Okay, let's build another one," Adam said. He looked up at his father. "So, do you think she forgave Freya?"

"No, I don't think she's forgiven Freya," Aaron said from his chair. "She acted like she did, but I can tell she's angry with Freya. She thinks we don't know. It's quite obvious."

Adam nodded. "It's understandable."

"No. She should have forgiven her."

"Like how you've forgiven me for leaving?" Adam retorted without looking up. When he lifted his head, he expected to see anger on his father's face, but there was only sadness.

"You did what you thought was right. I'm coming to realize that now, Adam." Aaron's eyes reddened with tears. "There is nothing to forgive."

Adam sat up taller, wondering if he'd heard him correctly. "Really?"

"*Ja*." Aaron leaned forward in his chair. "I am the one who needs to be forgiven, son. I'm sorry. I was wrong not to welcome you back, to tell your mother she couldn't contact you if you wrote or called. I see now why you didn't. You didn't want to put her in a difficult position." He swatted away a tear that had fallen on his wrinkled cheek. "I'm sorry, Adam."

Adam pushed himself to his feet and knelt beside his father. "All that matters is that we're together now. Of course, I forgive you, *Daed*. We were just both doing what we thought was right."

"But I was the one who was wrong. I was stubborn and blind."

Adam threw his arms around his father. "I love you, *Daed*."

"I love you, son."

Adam squeezed his eyes shut, barely able to believe this was happening. This was so unexpected—an unexpected miracle.

His father pulled away. "There is something else I have to tell you."

"What is it?" Adam stood up and sat on the couch beside his father as Carter continued to play.

"The night Robert was killed, I regret not going outside to help him look for Robin. He didn't want me to get sick with bronchitis, but still, I could have insisted on going. He said he'd be right back, so I didn't think…" Aaron looked away, sniffling.

"None of us thought that would happen to him," Adam rushed in, patting his father's arm. "I should have gone with him."

"You had the flu," Aaron said. "No one could blame you for not going out in a blizzard with the flu."

"And you could have gotten bronchitis."

"I've been so full of guilt and regret since that night." Aaron leaned back against the couch. "I feel like it's partly my fault."

"Me too. I didn't know you felt that way."

"I think we all feel that way for not trying harder to stop him from going out into the storm," Aaron said. "But you know how stubborn your brother was. There was nothing we could have done to stop him."

Adam chuckled. "Definitely not. He loved that horse. He never would have left him out in the storm."

"Never," Aaron agreed. "I guess there's nothing any of us could have done, was there?"

Adam shook his head. "We've been blaming ourselves for no reason. It wasn't anyone's fault. It just happened."

"We need to accept it and move on," Aaron said. "It's still so hard after two years."

"I do regret not being here for all of you during the hardest two years of your lives, but I thought if I caught Robert's killer that the hole in my heart would mend. I thought I'd feel better. I had no idea it would be someone like Freya. I could never turn her in." Adam let out a deep breath. "Now I have a new mission. I have to find and arrest her ex. He's an abusive criminal who belongs behind bars. He gambled away her inheritance, you know."

"That's terrible," Aaron said.

Adam nodded. "He's living in the house she inherited from a good friend, and he took her money, then abused her. He is the scum of the earth."

"I don't understand how some people can be so cruel and evil." Aaron slowly shook his head. "This world needs Jesus."

"He's the reason she was driving through that blizzard in the first place. If I arrest him, then the person who is ultimately responsible for Robert's death will pay," Adam said with determination.

"Don't get caught up on seeking revenge," Aaron said.

"I know. Vengeance is the Lord's."

"Do it, but do it for the right reasons—to protect Freya. I see how you look at her." Aaron gave a wry smile.

"How do I look at her?" Adam chuckled.

"Like you're falling in love with her. It's okay, you know, even with what happened. I can tell she has a good soul. Robert would want you to be happy, and we want you to be happy too."

Adam smiled. "She is wonderful. I want to keep her safe." He pushed a hand through his brown hair. "I never thought I'd fall in love with the woman who killed my brother, but I am."

"God works in mysterious ways, son. It would be nice to see some good come out of such heartbreaking circumstances."

Adam nodded. "It would. The thing is, I'm not sure she's ready to trust someone again. She's been hurt so much, and she's never had a real family, so she doesn't even know what real love is. That's why she was so shocked when you welcomed her into your lives."

"So, show her real love," Aaron said. "If there's anything I've learned in all my years, it's that life is short, son. Tell her you love her because you never know what could happen at any time."

Adam knew that all too well.

Chapter Twenty-two

Dean sat in his car, parked across the street from Adam Lapp's apartment as he opened a protein bar and a bottle of water. He stretched, kneading out a cramped muscle in his neck, stiff and sore from sleeping in his car. The last remnants of night were fading fast, chased away by pink and yellow hues of the rising sun. As a bounty hunter, this was not the first time he'd slept in his car.

He'd been here doing the exact same thing a year ago after his friend had told him about how Adam Lapp was investigating him. He'd watched him and followed him for a week but soon figured out that Freya was long gone.

Now, Dean had been alerted that Adam was investigating him again, and this time if Freya was here, he wouldn't let her slip through his fingers. Hopefully, Adam would leave his apartment at some point in the next day or two. When he did, Dean would follow him.

A few hours later, after dozens of smooth jazz tracks, Dean sat up straight when Adam walked out of the apartment building and got into his car. He drove out of the driveway and down the street, and Dean followed from a distance.

About forty minutes later, Dean followed Adam into a rural area of Unity that looked like a separate world from the little town not very far away. Vast fields sprawled out on either side of the road as Adam slowed then turned down a long, winding dirt lane. Some of the houses had buggies in the yard, and he noticed some of the people were dressed in Amish clothing. Was this an Amish community? Was this where Adam was from? Dean had no idea there were Amish in Maine.

Finally, he reached a large, gray house with a barn and a buggy parked in the driveway.

Dean's eyebrows shot up. The Amish sure had big houses. Dean parked on the other side of the lane behind some trees, hoping to remain invisible as he watched Adam go inside the house. Through the large window, he could see Adam hug an older man and woman. So, were these his parents?

His grip around the steering wheel tightened until his knuckles were white. He reached for his gun in his holster, feeling the smooth metal against his fingers. It would be so easy to go in there and kill them all—better yet, kill Adam's mother and father right in front of him, then kill Adam last. Dean could feel power surging through him, the pent-up anger infused with adrenaline that pumped through his veins.

If he did kill them, he wouldn't find out where Freya was. No, he had to wait this out. Better yet, he could make Adam pay by playing with his head a little. And if Freya was around here, then she would find out, and he would make her pay, too.

He had to be careful, though. He could mess with them, but it had to be something that Freya wouldn't suspect him of doing. If she suspected even for a moment that he was here, she'd leave town before he could find her.

He wouldn't let her slip through his hands again.

Adam walked up to Freya's door and knocked. The night sky was full of stars, and even though it was freezing cold, the night was perfect for their date. He wouldn't care if they were going to a restaurant in the Arctic as long as he got to spend time with her.

Freya opened the door. Her red hair was curled and pinned back on one side, and she wore a red knee-length dress and black heels.

"You look gorgeous," Adam murmured, taking her hand and bending to kiss it.

"Why, thank you, sir," she said, grinning.

"You're welcome, my lady," he said, offering her his arm. She looped her arm through his, and they walked to the car. "I just can't believe I get to take you out on a date."

They drove to the restaurant and were seated at a table in the corner, away from everyone else.

Unable to focus on the menu, he squinted as the words swam before his eyes. He had so much to say to her about how he felt, and he searched for the right words. They ordered their meals, and even by the time the food had been served and they began eating, he still wasn't sure what to say to her, let alone where he would find the courage to say it.

"This alfredo is amazing," Freya said as she finished her plate of food. "Thanks so much for bringing me here. This was exactly what I needed."

He couldn't wait any longer.

"Freya, actually, I need to tell you something." He reached for her hand. "I'm not great with flowery words, so I'm just going to say it. I'm falling in love with you, Freya," he blurted, anxiously waiting for her reaction.

She squeezed his hand, and his hope soared.

"Dean is probably still looking for me. I don't want you caught up in all of this. I don't want you being put in danger because of me," she said, her voice faltering with emotion as her eyes searched his.

"I know you're running, and you're scared, but I'm not scared. I'll be with you, and I'll protect you. I promise I will do everything in my power to arrest him and get him to pay back everything he stole from you, even if that won't erase all the abuse. You shouldn't have to do this alone." He tenderly stroked her hand with his thumb.

Freya shook her head vehemently. His heart fell.

"I can't do that to you, Adam. If something ever happened to you, I'd never be able to forgive myself. If Dean finds me, he'll know if we're together, and he will hurt you." A tear fell from her eye. "I'm sorry, Adam. I want to be with you more than anything. But until Dean is no longer a problem in my life, I can't be with anyone. I don't want you to have to wait for me, either. I have no idea how long he will look for me."

"So, you do have feelings for me too?" Adam managed to choke out.

"Feelings for you?" Freya smiled through her tears. "I love you, Adam. You're the kindest, best man I've ever met, and I'm astonished you could love me at all. I'd give anything to be with you, but I love you too much to put you in danger just to be with me."

Now Adam was crying, and he swiped away the tears. "I'd rather die than to not be with you, Freya," he whispered, now clutching her hands with both of his.

Freya looked away, suddenly unable to meet his gaze. "I do want to be with you, but I'm trying not to be selfish here."

"Then say yes to us, Freya. We will face this together. Even if I wasn't a police officer, I would want to protect you. Let me love you, and let me protect you. I want to do that more than anything."

Freya let go of his hands, covering her face. "We should talk about this somewhere else," she said softly. Outside, it began to rain.

Just then, their waitress came over. She noticed they were having a moment. Awkwardly, she acted as though she didn't notice either of their teary eyes. "Are you interested in any dessert?"

"No, thank you. The food was wonderful. I'll take the check, please," Adam said. A few minutes later, after he paid the bill, they returned to his car.

Silently, they drove back to Freya's house. He kept the car running after he pulled into the driveway, turning to face her.

"Please don't do this to me, Freya. Don't say no to me just because you're scared Dean will hurt me," he pleaded with her.

"I'm afraid he will kill you, Adam," Freya told him. "You don't know him; how jealous and violent he can be."

"I can handle it," Adam said. "I've been trained to take down men like him."

"But he's been trained to take down men like you. He's a bounty hunter, Adam. He's fast, strong, and most of all, he wouldn't think twice about hurting you, maybe even killing you. He's evil and vile while you're good and honest. He's sneaky, so he might even lay traps for us," Freya said. "He loves mind games."

"You're worth the risk, Freya," Adam said, looking deep into her eyes.

Freya took in a shaky breath, smoothing out imaginary wrinkles in her skirt. "What you said about you rather dying than not being with me..."

"I meant every word." He leaned in close to her, so their foreheads were touching. "You can't push me away now. My heart is linked to yours." He reached up and cupped the back of her neck, wanting so desperately to kiss her but not wanting to go too fast.

He knew in his heart he was waiting for his future wife. So, for now, he would have to wait for their first kiss.

"You are hard to say no to," she whispered.

"Then don't." He gave a wry smile.

"I love you, Adam. I love you more than I ever thought I could love someone." She leaned back just enough so she could look him in the eyes.

Relief and elation filled him, and he wanted to get out of the car and run around like a child.

"I just hope I don't regret this," she said glumly.

"Life is too short to worry about regrets. There is one thing I need to tell you," Adam said. "And I should have told you before, but I didn't want to say it in the restaurant. I have been researching you and investigating Dean since we first met at the cemetery. I found your house and reviewed all the police responses to your home for possible domestic violence. I spoke to your neighbor, Victor Johnston, and asked him for more information about the calls he made when he reported Dean abusing you."

"I knew it. You lied to me?" Freya asked, looking at him, flabbergasted.

"You didn't want to tell me much about him, and I don't blame you. I want to protect you, so I went behind your back. I knew you would get upset and maybe even run if I told you the truth. I'm sorry I kept that from you, but it led me to find out more about Dean."

"I can't believe you lied to me when I confronted you about it!" Freya snapped. "How could you go behind my back?"

"I didn't want you to panic and run again. I want to protect you, Freya. How could I have done that if you had left? I didn't want to lose you, and I didn't want to lose your trust. I've made progress that I couldn't have made if I had told you about my investigation. I just don't have enough evidence to arrest him yet. And even if I did, I don't know where he is."

"So, you know where my house is," Freya said, her hands visibly shaking. "And Dean isn't there?"

"He wasn't there when I went looking for him."

"He's probably on a job, unless he's out looking for me." Freya tugged at her hair, which partially covered her face—it was a nervous habit she'd developed while in foster care.

"We don't know that. He could have just been out. Your neighbor, Victor, said Dean had been gone for days," Adam said.

"Victor is the one who helped me leave. He gave me money and his car. I couldn't have done it without him. He's protective of me. He told me a police officer came to his house and was asking him questions, and he pretended like he didn't know anything because he thought Dean had sent a buddy to see how much he knew."

"Smart guy." Adam raised his eyebrows, impressed.

"He also said you gave him a business card with your name on it, but he lost it and couldn't remember your name. I thought it was you, and you lied to my face about it."

"I'm sorry, Freya. I hope you see now why I lied. There is one other thing. Dean filed a missing person's report for you to make it look like he's worried about you."

"Of course, he did." Freya rolled her eyes.

"And as for your inheritance, you told me he gambled most of it away, and I believe you. However, you said you share an account, so we can't arrest him for stealing your money."

"Ugh. I never should have added him to my bank account. What was I thinking? He told me he needed to borrow money to pay off his father's medical bills. By the time I escaped and closed my account, he'd already spent so much. I had enough to get me through until I found employment and started saving a little for my next move."

"He's a liar and an abuser. He played you hard."

"Look, you know too much, Adam. This puts you in even more danger," Freya sputtered, her face reddening. "I'm disappointed and angry that you went behind my back to find all of this. If I wanted you to know, I would have told you. Also, your searches may have alerted Dean, so now I need to move again."

"Freya, no. I was careful. Listen, I did this because I want to keep you safe. To do that, I need to know as much as possible. I don't have enough to arrest him, but if I keep digging, I think I could."

"Adam, please—"

"I also found him on social media. He's been posting photos of you, asking if anyone has seen you, trying to trap innocent people into helping him find you," Adam said. "And yes, I know it's not illegal for him to do that, but it's one more thing for me to show the Boston Police Department and CPDU how corrupt he is. I already spoke with my boss, and CPDU will be searching for him and making a case against him if he does anything wrong in their jurisdiction, even a minor traffic violation. Freya, if Dean comes here looking for you, we will get him."

Freya let out a sob, covering her face with her hands.

Adam gently touched her hands, and she lowered them, looking up at him. He gazed into her eyes, running his thumb from her temple down to her jawline. "I'm so sorry for what he did to you, Freya. I wish I could undo it."

"I want to be angry with you, but you're making it really hard…" she said, her voice trailing off as his gaze dropped to her lips. Again, he wanted so badly to kiss her, but he was also afraid of pushing her away, and this wasn't the right time. He knew she didn't trust easily, and he was grateful that she even trusted him at all.

"I'm just afraid for both of us. You think you can handle him, but you're underestimating Dean's capacity for evil." She leaned back, sitting up straighter. "Good night, Adam. Thank you for dinner." She got out of the car and walked into her house.

"Freya, wait!" he called after her, but she closed the door.

Had she just decided she was going to move again? Adam wasn't sure.

Will I lose her again? he wondered.

Chapter Twenty-three

Dean sat in his car parked across the dark street, feeling as if his head was about to explode as he watched Freya and the dimwitted cop talking in his car. He'd followed Adam to Freya's house, where Adam had picked her up and taken her to a classy restaurant. He couldn't go inside without Freya possibly recognizing him, so he'd waited outside in the parking lot, and it was agonizing. What were they talking about in there?

And why does this Adam guy think he has any right to take my Freya out on a date? Dean wondered.

Now Freya got out of Adam's car and walked into the house, and Adam finally left.

Freya was inside that house, all alone. If Dean wanted to, he could walk right in there and make her wish she'd never been born. However, that would be over all too quickly, and he wanted to make Freya pay. He wanted to make Adam pay too. And to do that, he had to be methodical and precise.

A few hours later, Dean quietly picked the lock on Freya's door and slipped into the house. Freya always slept with white noise on, so even if he did make a small sound, she wouldn't hear it.

He tiptoed across the kitchen and placed a bug on the inside of a lamp near the doorway of her bedroom so he could listen in on her. Her bedroom door was slightly ajar, so he crept into her room, silently making his way to the side of her bed.

Freya's red hair was fanned out across her pillow, and though her makeup was smudged as though she'd cried herself to sleep, she looked as beautiful as an angel. He had been hard on her, always telling her she didn't look attractive, but the truth was that Freya was one of the most stunning women he'd ever seen. It was why he'd taken such an interest in her—and it was part of the reason why no one else could have her.

He reached out and traced his finger along a few strands of her hair. She was a light sleeper, so he knew if he touched her, she'd wake up. Instead, he watched her slow, rhythmic breathing for a few moments. How he longed to reach out and jolt her awake with his hands tightening around her throat, her eyes wild and pleading.

No, it wasn't the right time yet. Soon he'd have his revenge on both of them.

You're mine, Freya, he told her silently. *No one else can have you as long as I'm alive.*

With that, he turned and silently left the house, returning to his car.

❧❧❧❧❧ ❦❦❦❦❦

The next morning, Freya awoke to hear someone knocking on the door. She scrambled to sit up, grabbing her phone to see several missed texts from Adam, who had been apologizing. Now she remembered crying into her pillow last night, wondering if she should move again to be safe, and wondering if she'd ever see Adam again. She must have cried herself to sleep—she was still in her clothes from last night.

"Hold on a sec!" Freya called out. Who on earth was that?

"It's me, Adam." His voice came from the other side of the door.

Adam? What? She put her hands on her head. How could she face him with tear-smudged makeup and morning breath?

"I just need a few minutes!" she called out, then pulled on some clean clothes, brushed her teeth, and ran a makeup removing wipe over her face, rubbing off her streaked mascara. She pulled her hair into a haphazard bun and skidded across the floor to open the door.

"Hi," she said sheepishly. "Sorry. I was sleeping."

"That's okay." Adam held up a paper bag. "I brought coffee and the best bagels you'll ever have. You look adorable." He grinned.

She chuckled. "Breakfast? Wow. Okay, you are allowed to come in." She opened the door wider, and they sat down at the kitchen table.

"I'm sorry I didn't answer your texts. I fell asleep," Freya said as he handed her an everything bagel with cream cheese. "This smells amazing."

"Just wait until you try it. And don't apologize, Freya. I see now why you were upset."

Last night she'd been so disappointed that Adam had gone behind her back to get all that information, but she knew he had the best intentions.

"And I see now why you went behind my back to get information about Dean," Freya said, opening the wrapper on her bagel. "I know you're trying to help me and protect me."

"I love you, Freya. I want you to be safe." Adam reached across the table and squeezed her hand. "In order to do that, we have to be honest with each other. I see why you're guarded, but please. I hope you'll let me help and protect you."

She couldn't help but smile, admiring the sincerity in his dark eyes. "I trust you, Adam. I never thought I'd say those words again to someone, but I do. I trust you."

Adam smiled, his eyes glistening with tears. "So, you'll let me help you with this?"

She nodded, unable to speak.

Adam got up out of his chair and threw his arms around her. "We'll get through this, Freya."

She wrapped her arms around him, inhaling his woodsy scent that reminded her of Christmas trees. "I hope so."

"That's the spirit." Not wanting to make her uncomfortable, he sat back down in his chair. "You know, if you want, I could teach you self-defense."

"You're right. I should learn it. Thank you." Freya took a large bite of her bagel. "Wow, this is amazing."

"See? Told you. The café has the best bagels ever." He glanced down at his bagel, then back at her. "My parents still feel terrible about what happened with Maria at church. They've invited us over today for lunch."

Freya held back a groan. She loved going to the Lapps', but she dreaded seeing Maria. "I'm sure Maria doesn't want to see me. I mean, I killed her husband. I wouldn't blame her if she hates me."

"Actually, she wants to apologize about the church incident."

"Apologize? Are you sure?"

"Yes. She feels bad now and wants to make amends. Do you want to go see her?"

Freya could see the hope in his eyes, and it would be the right thing to do. How could she say no to them?

"Of course."

"I was also thinking maybe I could take you for a buggy ride, if you want to."

"A buggy ride?" She tilted her head to the side. That would be romantic, if she could be brave enough. "I have to admit I've been wanting to ride in one, but there's a horse involved." Her small smile faded.

"Robin is gentle, Freya. He won't hurt you."

"I think he remembers me from the night Robert died. He was in the road, looking at me while I tried to revive Robert and failed. He remembers me as the person who killed his owner, doesn't he? Do horses remember things like that?" Freya asked, scrunching up a napkin in her palm.

Adam ran a hand over his chin, and Freya was strangely drawn to the soft scratching sound of his fingers rubbing against his short stubble. "Horses are very smart animals. Even in that terrible blizzard, he may have gotten a good look at you or maybe even smelled you. I don't know. I guess it's possible that he remembers you."

"What if he attacks me?"

"Robin has never hurt anyone."

"But I'm the only person who has hurt him, right?"

Adam took a thoughtful, deep breath. "I'll be there with you. I can always calm him down. I really don't think he will hurt you. I was thinking if you could trust him and you can both feel comfortable around each other, it might help you heal."

Freya sighed. "You're right, Adam. If I'm going to forgive myself, I need everyone else to forgive me, too. Even Robert's horse. I'm still trying to get over the fact that you and your parents have forgiven me for your brother's death."

Adam nodded. "I'm glad you want to try getting near Robin. If you decide you don't want to, that's okay. We can go to my parents' house after this if you want."

"Sure. I'll just need to finish getting ready."

"You could wear a cloth sack and still look beautiful."

"Ha. Thanks." She chuckled, taking another bite of her bagel.

You could be beautiful if you made any effort at all, Freya. Dean's voice echoed in her head. *Every day I come home to see you looking terrible.* Freya closed her eyes, trying to shut him out.

"Are you okay?" Adam asked.

"I'm fine."

"Come on. We need to be honest with each other, remember? What's wrong." He reached for her hand again.

"I just remembered Dean telling me I always looked terrible. He was always talking down to me," she murmured, staring at the table. "I have a hard time accepting compliments from people because Dean criticized everything about me, from the way I smile to the shape of my eyebrows. I've never told anyone that before."

"Look at me, Freya."

Freya met Adam's eyes, which were full of concern.

"You are beautiful, inside and out. You are kind, thoughtful, brave, and strong. He only spoke lies to you. It doesn't matter what he said to you. What matters now is who you choose to be."

Freya's eyes stung with tears, and she smiled. "Thank you."

Adam leaned back in his chair. "It's the truth. And if you'll let me, I want to tell you that you're beautiful every day for the rest of our lives."

Freya's face burned. Did he really mean that?

"Sorry. Too much too soon? I just want you to know how I feel about you," he said.

"I'm not used to someone being so nice to me." She tucked a piece of hair behind her ear.

"Get used to it, sweetheart. I'm a nice guy." He grinned mischievously.

She chuckled. "Thanks so much for the bagel. I'll go change, and then we can go."

"Take your time. I'm ready when you are."

Dean strummed his hands on the steering wheel as he listened to Freya and the cop talking.

"I'm still trying to get over the fact that you and your parents have forgiven me for your brother's death," Freya said.

"What?" Dean almost leaped off his seat in the car. "How am I just finding out about this?" he muttered, mulling over everything Freya and Adam had just talked about. Had she run over the cop's brother, Robert, with her car in the snowstorm?

Dean's mouth fell open in shock. Why had Adam taken Freya out on a date if she had killed his brother? There was no way he actually could be in love with her, could he?

"Maybe he's out to get revenge on her. Maybe he's wooing her but planning to kill her," he said to himself. A hundred questions filled Dean's mind. Why hadn't he arrested Freya for killing his brother?

How had he not known about this? Apparently, no one had reported it. How had everyone just forgiven her? What about this Maria, who was apparently Robert's widow?

His mind was already working, contemplating new ideas on how to mentally torture Freya and make her wonder if he'd found her.

He remembered one time they'd been watching a movie, and Freya had mentioned how scared she was of horses. If that horse had been there the night she'd killed Adam's brother, wouldn't she be even more afraid of them now?

Dean already knew from looking around the Lapp property late at night that they had a horse named Robin. He'd already studied the barn and every way he could get in and out without being seen. He was sure he could mess with Freya by using that horse to frighten her.

It would be tricky to get the barn door open while she was at the Lapps' house during broad daylight, but he was a bounty hunter—stealth was his job description.

As Freya spoke about how Dean had talked down to her, he growled in annoyance. Of course, he had told her she was unattractive. He didn't want her to think she was too good for him—which she was.

"And if you'll let me, I want to tell you you're beautiful every day for the rest of our lives," Adam said.

Dean's blood boiled. He imagined running into the house and beating Adam to a pulp. Were they engaged? Did this man plan on marrying Freya?

No. No one else could have Freya, especially not this big-shot cop who thought he was all that.

His lips curled into a snarl as he pulled out his long knife, admiring the way it glinted in the sunlight.

By the time this day is over, things would be different.

"This should be fun."

Chapter Twenty-four

Freya clasped and unclasped her hands in her lap as Adam pulled his car into the Lapps' driveway. They walked up to the door and Hannah answered. The sound of Carter's crying carried through the door.

"Carter is having a meltdown," Hannah said, a few of her gray hairs slightly disheveled, which was unusual for her.

"Well, we were thinking of going for a buggy ride anyway, if that's okay," Adam said. "Does anyone need the buggy?"

"That would be fine." Hannah smoothed a hand over the edges of her hair that peeked out from beneath her prayer *kapp*. "No one needs it right now, and it would give us time to get Carter to calm down."

"We will just go down the road. We'll be back soon."

"Take your time," Hannah said, turning to go back into the kitchen. "This could take a while."

Adam closed the door, and they walked toward the barn. "We could go downtown. Do you need anything?"

"I was actually thinking of buying some things for my new place," Freya said. "I don't have any picture frames or anything to make it feel like home."

Adam grinned. "Well, we need to change that. It just so happens I'm an expert interior designer."

"What? No way." Freya laughed.

"No, I'm kidding. I don't know anything about decorating a house, but I'd love to go shopping with you." Adam walked through the door of the barn, but Freya hesitated.

What if Robin still didn't like her?

Adam held out his hand to her. "I'm going to help you through this, Freya."

She took his hand and walked inside the barn with him.

"Good morning, Robin," Adam said, rubbing the horse's nose. He let go of Freya's hand and turned to her. "I'm going to open his stall now and lead him out to the buggy."

"I'll go over there and watch." Freya hurried over to the other end of the barn. She watched Adam unlatch the stall door and gently lead the horse out the door, to the side of the barn. She followed them from a distance, and by the time she came close enough to see what he was doing, he had Robin hitched up to the buggy.

"See? He's a good boy." Adam ran his hand down Robin's nose again, talking to him in a baby voice. "Yes, he's a good boy."

Freya laughed at seeing him treat the animal so tenderly, like a child.

Adam shrugged. "What? He's one big baby." Robin nibbled at Adam's ear, and he laughed. "See?"

"Okay, okay." Freya came closer.

"Make sure you come around the side, where he can see you, so you don't accidentally sneak up on him."

Freya walked to Robin's side while keeping a distance so he could see her approaching. Adam held his hand out to her, and he lifted her hand toward Robin's nose. The horse sniffed her, then licked her hand, and Freya held back a squeal. "His tongue feels like sandpaper!"

Adam laughed. "Like I said, he's just a big baby. Come on, let's go to town." Adam brought her to the side of the buggy and helped her up. She loved the feeling of his warm, strong hand in hers, and she wished he wouldn't let go as he went around to the driver's side. He clicked his tongue, and the horse turned and started down the lane.

"Robert trained him to respond to sounds and verbal cues," Adam explained. "He's a very good horse."

"That's amazing," Freya said. "I don't know anything about this."

"If we got lost in town, Robin here would bring us right back home without me having to guide him at all."

"Really? Wow. Horses really are smart."

"They truly are. Sometimes I think they are smarter than some people." Adam gave her a sidelong glance, giving her a goofy grin.

Freya laughed out loud. "I believe it."

As they approached town, they got some confused looks from people who were probably wondering why two people who were clearly not Amish were riding in a buggy.

"Oh, let's stop here," Freya said, pointing to a thrift store. "I bet I could find some things for my house here."

"Sounds good." Adam secured the buggy to a parking spot outside, then they went inside the shop.

Adam reached for Freya's hand as they walked into the thrift store, and he smiled when she let him hold her hand. It was so nice to be with her, to be out doing things with her. He didn't care where they went—he just wanted to spend time with her and make her feel special, because she was.

"What about this?" Adam pointed to a bright pink lamp that was shaped like a flamingo.

Freya laughed. "I can see why someone donated that."

"What's wrong with it? I think it would actually match the color scheme in my apartment."

"What's a color scheme?" Freya asked, raising one eyebrow.

"I have no idea what that is. I heard it on TV once."

Freya smiled. "Well, I guess we are both clueless then."

Freya picked up a standard black photo frame, a white lamp, and some dishes.

"Let me get you a cart," Adam offered, and he went to the front of the store. As Adam grabbed a cart, a man with a baseball cap and a black hooded sweatshirt that partially concealed his face walked through the door. It struck him as suspicious, and Adam made a mental note to keep an eye on him.

"Here you go, my lady," Adam said, walking up to her with the cart.

"Oh, thank you. My arms are getting really full." Freya carefully set down the bowls, plates, mugs, lamp, and photo frame into the cart. "Now I need to find some silverware. Wow. Ten cents apiece. Not bad. Why do people pay full price for anything?"

Adam peered into the large boxes of forks, knives, and spoons. "Wow. That's a lot of silverware. Why do people donate so many random spoons?"

As Freya made some more jokes about the silverware and picked out several pieces, Adam noticed the man in the sweatshirt lurking at the end of the aisle, glancing at them.

"I'll be right back," Adam said.

"Okay. I'll be here."

Adam walked to the end of the aisle, and the man darted away, headed down the next aisle.

"Hey. Can I help you?" Adam asked the man. The man didn't turn around; he only walked away faster.

"Hey, you," Adam called out, his fingers brushing the end of his concealed gun.

"I didn't do anything!" The man whirled around to face him, finally stopping.

Adam had studied Dean's photo for over a year, analyzing every feature in his face so that he would know him if he ever saw him in public.

This man was not him. He was a young man in his early twenties with a skittish look in his bloodshot eyes. Adam let go of his weapon. "Oh. I'm sorry. I thought you were someone else."

"Sorry, man. I was...uh...checking out your girlfriend. She's hot," the young man said, backing away with his hands up. "You're a lucky dude."

"Women are not objects, *dude*," Adam shot back. "Every girl and woman should be treated like the treasures they are."

"Oh, yeah. Sorry, man. I'm out of here." The man turned and walked away.

Adam let out a long breath, his eyes darting to the people who had stopped shopping to watch the exchange. After the young man bolted out the door, Adam turned around to see Freya standing at the end of the aisle.

"What happened?" she asked, her eyes wide.

Adam rushed to her side. "I'm sorry. I saw him watching you. He had a dark hood and baseball cap on. I thought he was..."

"Oh," Freya said, nodding, her face going pale. "What a relief."

"Are you okay?"

"Just the thought of him being here, watching me..." Freya shuddered, and Adam put his arm around her, leading her away from the view of the onlookers.

"Let's get out of here," he said. "And I'm paying for this."

"Adam, no. You don't have to do that."

He gently touched her cheek. "You're my queen. Let me treat you like one. This hardly even counts, though. I mean, a hundred spoons would cost like ten dollars, if I'm doing my math right."

She smiled. "Thanks."

Freya took a deep breath as she let Adam pay for items she'd picked out for her house, which he had insisted on doing, no matter how much she'd argued. The sight of him accosting that man still played again and again in her head. He'd looked so strong and capable, but what if that man really had been Dean? What would have happened? It could have ended so differently.

Adam caught her eye and smiled as if knowing what she was thinking and trying to reassure her.

"You picked out some nice things. Maybe later we can go to your house and style them," Adam said, pretending to toss imaginary hair over his shoulder. "That painting and the candles will create a cozy ambiance."

Freya chuckled, feeling her mood already beginning to lighten. "I'm actually looking forward to setting it up. This is my first real place of my own. I want to make it feel like home. I plan on being here a long time, if all goes well."

Adam's face turned serious. "Of course, it will, Freya."

They brought Freya's bagged purchases out to the buggy and started back toward the Lapps' house. Freya scooted over and sat closer to Adam as he drove, resting her head on his shoulder. She pulled her jacket tighter around her, not minding the cold as long as she got to sit near him. Snow had fallen last night, creating a glittering white glaze over every branch that arched over them and every painted mailbox. They drove on the side of the road at a slower pace as cars passed them. She could feel strength and kindness emanating from Adam, and she closed her eyes, savoring every moment.

As they drove down a long, winding road, Freya looked around and took in the details. That tree—she recognized it. Was this the road where she'd hit Robert with her car? She and Adam had been talking so much on the way to town that she hadn't even noticed until now.

She grabbed onto Adam's arm, her heart rate spiking as she felt the blood drain from her face. "Is this where Robert died?"

Adam looked around and slowly nodded. "I wasn't going to say anything, but yes. It was right around here."

"I recognize that tree. That's it. It was right there." Freya squeezed her eyes shut, feeling her chest constrict as her heart pounded and dizziness and nausea swept over her. All she could see was Robert's lifeless face in the snow.

"Deep breaths," Adam said, slowing the buggy to a stop. He turned to her, taking her hands, his gentle voice calming her. "It's okay, Freya. I'm here with you. It's all over."

Freya focused on taking in a deep breath and letting it out, trying to ward off the nausea. "I still see him like it happened yesterday."

"Me too."

Freya opened her eyes. "You saw him here?"

"Well, not here in the road. When I got home after looking for him, they told me he had died. I went outside and saw Robert's body in Sid Hoffman's buggy. Sid saw the accident from a distance. He came out here and lifted Robert's body into his buggy and drove him to our house."

Freya nodded slowly, her hand on her heart. It felt as though a giant fist was around her ribs, squeezing with every breath she took.

"I went out to his buggy in total shock and disbelief. I saw him lying in the back...dead." Adam looked away, a tear running down his face. "I'm sorry. I shouldn't be telling you this."

"No," Freya said, guilt overwhelming her. "I want to hear what it was like for you. We're going to be honest with each other, remember?"

Adam nodded. "Well, then if I'm honest, I was angry. That was when I vowed to find and arrest the person responsible for killing my brother. I packed my things and left, even though my father said I wasn't welcome back until I decided to come home for good. It was a horrible day." He looked back at her. "But it's behind us. What matters is we're together now. Even though it was a devastating tragedy, it brought us together. I wouldn't have met you if that hadn't happened."

Freya didn't know what to say as her heart lodged in her throat. Her lip trembled as she gazed at Adam—sweet, caring, courageous Adam.

"I love you, Adam," she murmured, her gaze dropping to his lips, which were a mere few inches away.

"I love you, too," he whispered.

He reached up and gently touched her face, then she leaned forward, bringing her lips close to his. Their kiss was slow and sweet, yet it ignited fire through every nerve ending in her body. When she kissed him, she wanted to show just how she felt about him by intensifying the kiss.

Adam pulled away, gazing into her eyes. "That was amazing, Freya. I just don't want to go too fast and mess this up. You mean so much to me."

She threw her arms around him.

Thank you, God, for this thoughtful, caring, considerate man you've brought into my life, she prayed.

When she finally let go, Adam rubbed her arms.

"It's freezing. Let's get you in front of my parents' fireplace," Adam said and took hold of the reins, guiding Robin home.

Chapter Twenty-five

Freya looked at the road ahead. This place that had only held terrible memories now held one good memory—their first kiss.

With the way he had so sweetly kissed her and touched her face—she smiled at the mere thought, pressing a finger to her lips, still feeling the sensation of his lips on hers.

Soon, they were pulling into the Lapps' driveway.

"You go on inside. I'll get Robin back in the barn and put your bags in the car, then I'll meet you in there," Adam said, dropping her off at the door.

"Such a gentleman." She kissed him on the cheek.

He gave her a confident grin. "I try my best."

She climbed down from the buggy and hurried to the front door, where Hannah let her in.

"It's freezing. Come on inside before you catch a cold," Hannah said, ushering her in. "Did you have a nice time in town?"

"Oh, yes. The buggy ride was nice, and we got some things at the thrift shop for my new place. We got some artwork and dishes and candles to make it homey."

"That's great." Hannah beamed. "So, it sounds like you're making Unity your home."

"I'd really like to, if I can," Freya said, and Hannah nodded in understanding.

"We must trust in the Lord's plan and provision," Hannah murmured, patting Freya's arm.

"Is Carter feeling better now?"

"He's better now, yes. Thanks. He just didn't want to take a bath. Of course, once he got in, he never wanted to get out."

Freya chuckled. "Kids are so funny sometimes." She loved children, but she hoped she'd be a good enough mother. She knew without a doubt Adam would be an excellent father. At the thought, she could feel a red blush creeping up her neck.

"You'd make a good mother, Freya," Hannah said, as if reading her mind. "You want children someday?"

"Oh, definitely." Freya nodded enthusiastically. "At least four or five, maybe even six."

"Children are such a blessing from the Lord. Yes, they're a lot of work, but every minute is worth it. I wish I could have had more children. We tried for years, but after Adam was born, I didn't have any more children. We did get married in our thirties, and I was in my early forties when he was born." Hannah smiled with a dreamy look in her eyes. "I'm just thankful I had them. Those boys have brought so much joy to my life. I would sure love to have lots of grandchildren in my older years."

Guilt ate at Freya again for taking one of Hannah's sons away, but she pushed the feeling down. She couldn't let the guilt overtake her life. When she saw Hannah still grinning at her, Freya blinked.

Was Hannah insinuating that she and Adam might get married and have children? She felt her face heat again.

"I see how he looks at you," Hannah said in a low voice. "I wouldn't be surprised if he proposed to you soon. Oh, how wonderful that would be." She clasped her hands together.

Freya's heart filled with joy just knowing Hannah would be pleased if she did marry Adam. "I'm glad you think so, Hannah."

"Of course, I do. Now come on in and sit in front of the fire. I'm making some tea."

Freya hung up her coat and followed Hannah into the living room where Aaron was down on the floor doing a puzzle with Carter, which was really quite advanced for the boy's age. Yet he was putting pieces into place without much difficulty. Freya smiled at the sight of Carter and his grandfather playing together on the floor.

"You're so good at that, Carter," Freya told him.

Carter didn't acknowledge her but kept on fitting pieces together, completely focused.

"Say thank you, Carter," Maria said flatly from the kitchen, where she was washing dishes.

Freya looked over at her, noticing her glare. She turned back to Carter, biting her lip. Clearly, Maria didn't want her here. Was she really going to apologize to her?

Carter glanced up at Freya just for a moment before returning to his puzzle. "Thank you."

"You're welcome, Carter."

"He's so smart for his age," Aaron said, getting up off the floor. "So good at puzzles. How are you, Freya? How was your buggy ride with Adam?"

"It was lovely. I am scared of horses, but Adam is helping me get acquainted with Robin. He's a sweet horse."

"He sure is. He wouldn't hurt a fly."

Adam walked through the door, and the wind lifted flurries of snow into the entryway before he closed the door. He opened his arms. "Carter! How are you, little man?"

Again, Carter barely looked up as he continued working on his puzzle. Adam shrugged. "What can I say? I'm not that interesting."

"He's so focused." Freya chuckled.

"Tea is ready!" Hannah called out. "Let's have a seat at the table."

Freya's stomach churned with anxiety as they went into the kitchen and sat down. Maria refused to look at Freya, a blank look on her face.

"We invited you over today so we can talk about what happened on Sunday," Hannah began, then looked to Maria to continue.

Maria visibly took a deep breath and looked at Freya, and Freya tried not to let her eyes dart away. She wanted to crawl under the table and cover her face with her hands, but she sat up tall.

"I'm very sorry for how I gossiped about you on Sunday, and for how I told people that you were cruel. I may have exaggerated to them. I was upset. I'm also sorry for denying it after and refusing to apologize. I realize now that it was wrong, and I hope you can forgive me," Maria said flatly, as if she had memorized her monologue.

Freya bit her lip, blinking. It was obvious that Maria didn't mean any of this, wasn't it? As Freya looked around the table at everyone's smiling reactions, it was clear she was the only one who thought so. Even Adam looked happy that Maria had apologized.

"Of course, I forgive you, Maria. I see why you were upset, and to be honest, I might have done the same things," Freya said. "You have every right to be angry with me."

"But it is not the Amish way," Aaron said. "Maria, we are so happy you came around."

Freya caught a glint of fiery animosity in Maria's eyes as she looked her way. "I finally realized how wrong I've been. I should be welcoming her into the family, as all of you have."

"This is wonderful!" Hannah cried. "Now we truly are a family again."

Aaron smiled and nodded, and Adam smiled until he saw Freya's face, then he gave her a concerned look. Freya watched Maria's face turn redder and redder as Hannah went on about how they would spend Christmas as a family.

"We'd love to have you spend Christmas with us," Hannah said. "We have a huge breakfast, then we open gifts and spend the day visiting family and friends. It's simple, but a lot of fun. What do you say?"

"We'd love to have both you and Adam," Aaron added, looking at each of them.

Freya looked at Adam, unable to speak.

"I'd love to come. Thank you so much," Adam gushed gratefully. "Freya?"

Freya's eyes filled with tears, and she swiped one away that escaped down her cheek. "I've never had a happy Christmas in my life that I can remember, to be honest. It seemed like I was with a different foster family every year, and I always felt like a burden. I hope this Christmas will be my first happy Christmas because when I'm here, I feel like I'm home, like you're my family."

"We are your family now, Freya," Hannah said, reaching across the table to grab her hand. Aaron and Adam grinned.

"It's good to be home again," Adam added. "It'll be like the old days."

Freya's heart swelled with joy within her, then deflated like a balloon when she caught Maria's steely gaze.

"The old days? How can you say that?" Maria spat out. Adam's smile fell, and his mouth fell open in shock. Maria looked at Hannah and Aaron. "Robert isn't here because of her. How can you invite her to spend Christmas with us, telling her she's part of the family when she *killed* your son?"

Freya's heart fell, shock washing over her. She blinked, stunned.

Aaron started to stand up, and Hannah reached for Maria's arm. "Maria—"

"No," Maria retorted, rising to her feet. "I don't want to hear about how it's not the Amish way for me to be angry at the woman who killed my husband. I'm not just angry at her." Maria set her raging eyes on Freya, and Freya shrank back, instinctively flinching as if Maria might slap her. "I *hate* you, Freya Wilson!" Maria seethed through clenched teeth. "And I will never, ever forgive you for what you've done. You are a murderer."

Freya winced as if Maria's words had physically slammed into her, especially with the word *murderer*. Her hand flew to her aching chest, which felt as though it was being crushed by a horse's hoof.

Maria whirled around and ran to the entryway, scrambling to put on her boots. She grabbed her jacket and bolted out the door, leaving the four of them staring at each other, speechless.

Carter cried out, "*Mammi!*"

Hannah blinked, eyes wide, then finally registered Carter's cries. "*Mammi* will be back soon, Carter. Let's finish your puzzle." She sat down on the floor to play with him.

"I'm so sorry," Aaron murmured. "I truly thought she wanted to apologize. I thought her heart had changed."

Freya stared at the table, her emotions and thoughts reeling. Maria hated her. She actually hated her. How could she blame her? How could they ever spend Christmas here with the Lapps or continue to have a relationship with them if Maria didn't want her anywhere near her?

"Are you okay, Freya?" Adam asked, gently squeezing her hand. "You looked frightened."

Freya looked up at Adam. "I'm okay." It was instinctive for Freya now to expect to be hit any time someone raised their voice at her.

"I'll go talk to Maria," Adam said, standing up.

"No. I'll go. I need to sort some things out with her," Freya said, putting a hand on Adam's arm. She pulled on her boots and jacket and walked outside toward the barn, where she guessed Maria was.

Snow began to fall softly around her as Freya's boots crunched through the snow on the worn path to the barn. "Maria? Are you in here?" Freya approached the doorway.

A thunderous neighing and the sound of hoofbeats filled Freya's ears as Robin came into view. He ran to the barn doorway and stopped in front of Freya, rearing up on his hind legs and letting out a screeching neigh, as if he was frightened. His hooves stomped the ground, and Freya screamed, running to the side of the barn. All she could see was his hooves coming down on her, trampling her to death. If Robin truly did remember who she was, why wouldn't he want to kill her in revenge for killing his owner?

The horse huffed out a breath through his nose, looked at her, then galloped down the lane, leaving Freya huddled on the right side of the barn behind a wheelbarrow, covering her head with her arms like a frightened child.

Breathe in, breathe out, she told herself.

She took in deep breaths, trying to slow her heart rate, which felt as though it was racing as fast as Robin's hooves.

"Freya!" multiple voices called.

Freya peeked out between her fingers to see Adam racing toward her, with Aaron following closely behind. Hannah stood on the porch, watching with a concerned look on her face.

"What happened? I heard Robin neighing and saw him galloping out of the barn," Adam said.

"I'll ask John next door if I can borrow his buggy. I'll go after Robin. He probably didn't go far," Aaron said, hurrying down the lane.

That's what Adam told me that Robert had said right before he died, Freya thought glumly.

Maria fell facedown onto a pile of hay in the loft of the barn, and let out a scream, her fists clenched. How could this be happening? How could her in-laws pretend like everything was fine, as if Robert hadn't been killed by Freya? How could they sit at the table with her like she was part of the family?

How could Adam love her, the woman who had killed his brother?

No, she couldn't lie to herself, and she wouldn't go through the motions for them. Because of that, she was now the bad guy.

"Oh, Lord, please help me," she whispered, lifting her head. "I don't want to hate her, but I do. I can feel my heart turning more and more bitter. Please take this from me. I know she didn't mean to kill him, that she was afraid for her own life. Half of me feels so sorry for her, but half of me is so angry with her. Please, Lord, help me stop hating her."

Tears coursed down her cheeks as her feelings warred within her. This was not the person she wanted to be. This was not the mother her son deserved. He deserved a loving mother who was kind to everyone.

What had she become?

"Please, God, change my heart," she begged, taking a fistful of hay and throwing it down.

"Maria? Are you here?" Freya called out.

She was coming. Maria dried her eyes and walked toward the ladder to climb down from the loft, when a thunderous neighing filled the air, followed by Freya's screams.

She heard several voices as she climbed down from the ladder.

"What's going on?" Maria said, racing out of the barn. A few pieces of hay stuck to her dress.

"I was hoping one of you could tell me. Freya? What happened?" Adam said, gently taking Freya's hands and pulling them away from her face so he could look into her eyes.

"I was looking for Maria," Freya said. "I came to the barn doorway, and Robin was loose. He reared and then ran away. I thought he was going to trample me, so I ran over here to get away from him." She took in a shaky breath. "I thought he was going to kill me."

"He wouldn't kill you, Freya, but that was smart. The question is, why was he out of his stall? I just put him in his stall after our buggy ride, and I made doubly sure that it was latched," Adam said. He slowly stood up and faced Maria. "Did you see anything, Maria?"

"I was up in the loft." Maria rubbed her eyes, which she knew were red from crying. "I heard everything, but I didn't see it. By the time I climbed down, Robin was gone."

"You were in the loft? Really?" Freya asked, despising the ice in her own voice. "How do we know you didn't let Robin out of his stall right before I walked over here? You know I'm terrified of horses, don't you?"

Maria put her hands on her hips, anger filling her once again. *Lord, help me.* She took in a deep breath, trying to calm her raging emotions. "I know I said I hate you, but I'm not a cruel person. I would never do that."

"Freya," Adam whispered, frowning. "Let's not make accusations."

"You really don't think she did it after what she just said to me? She heard me coming near the barn and let him out, hoping to scare me. Well, it worked. I was terrified!" Freya cried, her words bubbling out of her before she could stop them. "I was coming out here to tell you that it's okay if you hate me, Maria. I did something unforgivable, and I don't know if I could forgive someone if anyone ever hurt the man I love." Her eyes involuntarily darted to Adam.

One corner of his mouth started to lift into a small smile, then his brows furrowed. "If Maria says she didn't do it, I believe her. Let's not turn this into a big deal. Maybe I didn't latch it properly, or it just came loose on its own."

"You said you made doubly sure that it was latched. No, this wasn't an accident. This was deliberate." Freya turned to Maria. "You denied talking about me at church when we first asked you about it. You lied. Maybe you're lying again now." Freya's hands clenched into fists. She hated the words that were spewing out of her mouth, but the stress and guilt were bubbling over in the form of angry words, and she couldn't stop them. They seemed to be rising higher and higher with each second.

"Freya!" Adam cried. "Please. This isn't like you. There's been enough hurtful words exchanged for today. Let's go find Robin." He reached out and helped Freya to her feet.

Freya brushed the snow off her pants, glancing at Maria, who crossed her arms and looked at the ground. Hot tears filled Maria's eyes. Well, she deserved this for how she'd behaved earlier. She'd lied about what had happened at church, and she'd told Freya she hated her. No wonder Freya thought Maria had done this.

"I understand why you think I did it, Freya, but I promise you, I didn't. I was up in the loft sobbing and praying. It's up to you whether you want to believe me or not," Maria said, staring at her.

Guilt and realization flashed across Freya's face. "I'm so sorry, Maria. I shouldn't have said any of that. I don't know what came over me. I let my emotions take over."

"It's okay," Maria said, finally meeting her eyes. "I know what it looks like, but it wasn't me, Freya, I swear."

"I believe you, Maria," Adam said, looping Freya's arm through his and leading her away from the barn and to his car. "We'll find Robin and bring him back here." Adam opened the car door for Freya.

Maria watched as they drove away, sadness overcoming her at the thought that Freya suspected her of something so cruel.

Lord, I know I was horrible to her, but please show her I didn't do this, she prayed. *How can we come back from this?*

Chapter Twenty-six

For the first few moments, the car was painfully silent as Adam drove slowly, searching for Robin. Finally, Freya swallowed and spoke up. "I'm so sorry, Adam. I really don't know what came over me. I feel like all the guilt and stress just piled on top of me at once and I let it overtake me. That wasn't like me."

"I know," Adam said calmly. "We all let our emotions take over and say horrid things sometimes. Trust me, I know. Just ask my father. We've done it to each other."

Freya sighed, staring at the snow-covered fields. "You really don't think Maria could have done that?"

"She's hurt and angry, but not capable of something that cruel and violent. She has a good heart."

"Grief makes people do things they wouldn't normally do."

"No," Adam said, a bit too forcefully. "Not Maria."

Freya flinched and glanced at him, shrinking back.

"I'm sorry. I'm just protective of her. She's my sister-in-law. I just know in my heart there's no way she could have ever done that, and I don't like to see you accusing her. I understand why you did, and I see how it could seem like she did it, but there's no way."

"So then, what happened?"

Adam shrugged. "I'll take a look at the latch. I'm sure it came loose on its own or maybe Robin figured out how to undo it." He chuckled.

"You did say horses are very smart. Maybe he did." Freya gave Adam a small smile, but it didn't feel genuine. It did nothing to hide the physical pain in her chest.

"I need to look after her. Robert would want me to. She's like a sister to me. When you accused her like that…" He sighed. "I'm sorry if I scared you. We shouldn't be pointing fingers at each other," Adam explained.

"You're absolutely right." Freya sighed, guilt washing over her once again for how she had reacted. "What I did was wrong."

"I think Maria understands."

Now she probably hates me even more, Freya thought.

"Look, there's Robin." Adam pointed and Freya looked out the window to see Robin standing on the side of the lane. "You drive the car, and I will lead Robin back to the house. I'll meet you there."

Freya nodded.

"Do you want to go get some lunch with me after?" Adam asked, reaching for her hand. "Then I could give you self-defense training. Actually, I would like to take you to the shooting range and teach you how to use a gun. What do you think?"

"A gun?" Freya shrank back. "I've never touched a gun in my life. The very thought of it is terrifying."

"Not if you know how to use it and practice until you feel comfortable with it. Please, let me just show you how with one of my personal weapons. It would make me feel better if you could protect yourself with a weapon, and you could even borrow one."

"Borrow one? I don't know about that, but I'll try it if you think I should know how to use one," Freya said. "But first, do you want to go to that sandwich place again?"

"I'd go eat out of a dumpster if it meant a date with you."

Freya laughed out loud. "Wow. You must really like me."

Adam glanced over at her as he got out of the car, giving her a handsome grin that made her heart trip over itself. "You have no idea."

Dean waited until the woman, Maria, had gone back inside with the older woman, and he watched Freya get in the car with the cop and drive away. He looked around, then crept across the yard to where his car was parked behind a small group of trees.

"That went even better than I expected," he said to himself as he started the car and waited for the heat to come on.

He couldn't have timed it more perfectly. He heard an argument in the house, then crept into the barn, letting himself into the horse's stall and hiding there. When that woman, Maria, had come in the barn crying and climbed up into the loft, he almost let the horse out, but he waited. Then he'd heard Freya calling out for Maria and approaching the barn.

That's when he'd opened Robin's stall, hitting the horse to spook him. He heard the horse rear and Freya scream, knowing he'd timed it just right. Then the entire argument that had taken place right after was like music to his ears—Freya suspected Maria and had no idea Dean was there. After everyone had left, he'd slipped out of the stall and sneaked out of the barn.

He thought he would feel disappointed that Freya hadn't recognized his genius move—how he had been trying to show her that he knew she'd killed Robert and how he knew she was terrified of the beast. No, this worked out so much better. She still had no idea he was here, which meant that he could mess with her even more, and she wouldn't be expecting it.

The heat in his car finally came on, and Dean pulled off his gloves and warmed his hands. The question was, what should he do next? He still had to be careful—if Freya suspected it was him, she would leave, and then he might never find her again. He couldn't let that happen.

What was something that might occur naturally around here? Dean eyed the barn. Didn't the Amish do barn raisings all the time? Maybe they could build one more if one caught on fire.

Dean nodded slowly, the mere thought of revenge satisfying his soul, flowing over him like warm water. What better way to get payback than by making Adam's parents suffer? Oh, the righteous, brave Adam would hate that. It would eat him up inside.

Perfect, Dean growled under his breath. The question was, when would be the right time to do it?

After returning Robin to the barn, they went out for sandwiches, then Adam took Freya to the shooting range where he taught her how to fire a pistol. Though Freya was nervous at first, she did surprisingly well for her first time shooting, and Adam insisted that they would have to return as soon as possible to practice more.

They stopped by the hardware store to get a hammer, some nails, and a stud finder to hang her artwork, then they went to her house, where he helped Freya unload her purchases from the thrift store.

After an hour of self-defense training, Freya put her hands on her knees, trying to catch her breath. "I need a break. This is exhausting."

"Now you know what to do if someone attacks you," Adam said, clapping his hands together. "You're making great progress. Sure, we can take a break."

"How about we set up what I bought?" Freya rummaged through the bags and pulled out the decorative items.

"I think this painting would look nice here," Adam said, squinting at the image of the sailboat on the water and pointing to a wall. "The blues and grays would match the sofa."

"You almost sound like you know what you're talking about." Freya walked to the sink to wash the white dishes she'd bought.

"I try to. Want me to hang it here?"

"Sure. Thanks so much."

Adam picked up the hammer. "Glad to be of assistance."

Freya glanced at the painting. "It's beautiful, isn't it? I always wanted to learn how to paint. I never had any art supplies of my own growing up, so I never really learned how. I mean, I took some art classes in high school. I was pretty good, actually. After that, I never got the chance to do it again."

"I've never learned how either. Why don't we try it together? They have classes downtown where they supply everything, and they teach you how to paint a scene. That would be a fun date, wouldn't it? I mean, I'd be terrible. I give you full permission to laugh at me." Adam used a stud finder to find a stud, and then he hammered the nail into the wall.

"Why wait for a class? Let's do it now. Are there any art stores around here?" Freya began washing the silverware.

"Sure. There's one downtown." Adam turned around and smiled.

"What?" she asked, her hands dripping with suds.

"You're being spontaneous. I like it. Does that mean you're feeling better?"

"You have a way of cheering me up, Adam. Yes, I feel a lot better, thanks to you."

"I'll hang this and your other pieces, then we can go if you want. Maybe you can teach me how to paint."

"I'm no expert, but I'll try. You know, I've heard painting can be therapeutic. I don't know... Maybe it'll help me heal." Freya shrugged. "Might as well try."

Adam turned to face her again. "I've heard that too. It might really help you. Just promise me we will do some more self-defense training when we get back, then we can start painting."

"Deal."

Maybe she could paint the images in her mind, like Robin and the buggy in the blizzard, Robert's tombstone in the cemetery. If she painted them, would they get out of her head and stop haunting her dreams?

"You okay?"

Freya blinked, brought back to reality. "I'm fine. Almost done here."

"Freya, that's incredible," Adam murmured, staring at Freya's painting that she had done after they'd bought supplies at the art store and finished their self-defense training.

She'd been furiously working on this painting while Adam had tried to paint a few different scenes, calling each one garbage. She'd tried to encourage him, but he only laughed at himself. He'd then fallen asleep on the couch while she continued painting.

Freya stared at the canvas before her. The road stretched before her, but the snow concealed how far it reached toward the horizon, blocking out the rest of the world in a wall of snow. The road was lined with tall, frozen skeletal trees that arched over the icy pavement. Hundreds of tiny snowflakes dotted the scene, and on the snowy road stood Robin, ears alert, his black body sharply contrasting the white background. The black buggy stood in the distance, its orange-red triangle the only vivid color in the entire painting.

Something dripped down her face, and Freya realized she was crying. She wiped the tears away and sniffed.

"Freya?" Adam asked groggily, stretching and sitting up on the couch. "Are you okay?"

"That's what I saw that night." She gestured to the painting. "Well, I didn't show everything, of course. I don't think I could paint the rest."

Adam stared at the canvas. "You just painted that? You said you haven't painted since high school."

"I haven't, no."

"Then how did you do that?"

Freya shrugged. "This scene has been plaguing my mind for two years. It just came from my head. I was kind of hoping maybe if I painted it, it would stop haunting me." She gathered up her paintbrushes to go wash them in the sink. "That's silly, isn't it?"

"Not at all." Adam took her hands. "It's kind of like when people make a to-do list, right? If you write down everything you have to do, your brain feels like it doesn't have to hold on to that information anymore. Maybe it works the same for images."

Freya sighed and stared at the painting. "I hope so."

Adam glanced at the clock. "Wow. I had no idea how late it was. It's almost midnight."

"Midnight?" Freya whirled around in disbelief. Time went by so quickly when she was with Adam. "No wonder you fell asleep. We did a lot today."

"I love spending time with you." He smiled, and her heart warmed at his words. "I better get home. Thanks for helping me, even though I'm a terrible artist." He laughed at himself again, pointing to his half-finished canvases.

"Oh, Adam. All that matters is that we had a good time together. Thank you for doing this with me. You're right. I feel... I feel like maybe I can finally start to move on now."

Adam pulled her into his arms. Her head fit perfectly under his chin, and she savored the way she could feel him breathing, his chest slowly rising and falling. She loved his strong arms around her, making her feel safer than she ever had in her entire life. She could stay like this forever.

Adam's phone rang, shattering the moment. "I'm sorry. Who on earth is calling me at this hour?" he muttered, lifting his phone from his pocket. "It's CPDU. This must be important. Sorry." He answered the call. "Adam Lapp." He paused, listening, then his eyes went wide as he started moving to the door. "Thanks. I have to go."

"What's wrong?"

Adam pulled on his boots and coat. "Someone called 911. My parents' barn is on fire. I have to go."

"Let me come with you. I want to help." Forgetting her paint brushes that needed to be cleaned, she rushed to get ready to go with him.

"It could be dangerous. I don't want anything to happen to you."

"Come on, Adam. I need to help. It's the least I can do. Please? I'll stay in the car if it's too dangerous." She had no intention of doing that, but she had to say something to get him to let her go with him.

"Okay, fine. Let's go."

Chapter Twenty-seven

They rushed out the door, and Adam sped to his parents' house. When they arrived, flames were engulfing the left side of the barn. His heart hammered at seeing part of his childhood home succumbing to flames.

"Are all the animals out?" Adam asked his father as he got out of the car. "Is everyone okay?"

"Yes, the animals are out and everyone is fine," Aaron said.

"How did this happen?" Hannah cried, wringing her hands.

Several of the neighbors had gathered around to help carry buckets of water from the hose, which didn't reach all the way to the barn.

"Someone called this in," Adam said, hearing sirens in the distance. "Here they come now."

"Who reported it?" Aaron muttered.

"Doesn't matter, *Daed*. At least the barn won't be completely destroyed now."

"We should rely on the Lord, not the fire department."

"What if God sent the fire department to help you?"

Aaron shook his head and walked away, grabbing a bucket and filling it with water. Hannah did the same.

"Where's Maria?" Freya asked. "Is she okay? What about Carter?"

"They're inside," Hannah said. "She didn't want Carter to see this. He woke up when he heard all the commotion and got upset."

"Poor kid," Freya said. "Let me help." She reached for a bucket.

"The fire department is here now. Let's let them handle it." Adam raised his voice, addressing all the neighbors. "Thank you all so much for coming to help. Let's all back up and make room for the firefighters so they can work." He waved his hands, directing them away from the barn.

The fire engine pulled into the driveway, and several firefighters jumped out and got right to work, stretching out the fire hose and spraying away the flames.

"I'm going to check on Maria and Carter," Freya said to Adam, putting a hand on his arm.

"That's a good idea."

Freya made her way quietly into the house, and she heard Carter crying softly. She followed the sound to one of the bedrooms, where Maria held Carter, sitting with him on the bed.

"What are you doing here?" Maria asked.

"I was checking to see how you're both doing. Is he okay?"

"He's shaken up, but he'll be fine. He's been through worse. So have I." Maria narrowed her eyes at Freya.

Freya shrank back a bit, putting her hand on the doorway. Of course, Maria had been through worse. "When I was a kid, my foster family's home burned down."

"Really?" Maria looked up with wide eyes. "How old were you?"

"About ten, I think. I'm not really sure. My entire childhood was not a happy time, so all the years blur together. I try not to remember it."

"You never knew your parents?" Maria asked softly.

Freya shook her head. "Apparently, my mother was a drug addict who couldn't take care of me. She probably didn't want me. My father walked out on her, so she gave me up."

"I'm so sorry. I didn't realize."

Freya shrugged. "It is what it is."

"What happened with the fire?"

Carter nodded off, half asleep. Freya came closer and sat down carefully on the other end of the bed. She kept her voice quiet as she spoke. "I actually liked the family I was staying with during that time. Diane, my foster mother, took her children and me out to go shopping for a surprise birthday gift for my foster dad. They were all really nice. We were going to throw him a little surprise family birthday party. I remember we picked out a big bag of popcorn for him and some funny socks. He loved those. They had pizza and hot dogs on them. He used to wear mismatched ones all the time. He was funny."

Maria chuckled. "Socks with hot dogs and pizza on them? That does sound silly."

"He was silly. He made the house fun. Anyway, when we got back to put up the decorations, the house was on fire. Diane had forgotten to blow out a candle before we left. They thought maybe the curtain in the kitchen caught fire." Freya shuddered at the memory of seeing her temporary home go up in flames. Unlike most of her other foster homes, that home had made her feel safe. They'd shared so many fun, happy times there together. "After the fire, the family had to relocate. They couldn't take care of me anymore and sent me back into foster care. I got sent to another family that was…not so nice."

Maria shifted Carter in her arms. "How many families did you stay with?"

"I don't know. Like I said, it all blurs together. Maybe dozens. I think I blocked some of them from my memory, or I was too young to remember. That's probably a good thing."

"Did they hurt you?"

Freya paused, glancing at Carter, who was clearly asleep now. "It wasn't just the parents. It was their children, too. They'd taunt me, play cruel tricks on me, and blame me for things they did so I would get punished. They often told me no one wanted me, not even my real parents. One night I got out of bed to get a drink of water, and…" She paused, memories assailing her as she shivered. "I was caught. It didn't end well. No child should ever have to endure what I endured at such a young age. No one loved me."

"I'm so sorry, Freya." Maria had genuine concern in her eyes along with tears. "No child deserves that, not ever."

"I don't know if the Amish make wills, but if I have one piece of advice to give you, I'd say you should make a will and make sure that if anything ever happens to you, someone you trust will take care of Carter for you. If you don't, he could go into the system, even if relatives wanted him."

"Really?"

Freya nodded.

"I knew you grew up in foster care, but I had no idea how terrible it was for you," Maria said slowly.

"There are some specific stories I could tell you that would make your skin crawl or make you weep," Freya said. "But I'm not going to tell them to you. I don't want them to stay in your head like they stay in mine."

"I don't think I want to know," Maria said. "I don't understand how anyone could ever hurt a child. I'd easily give my life for Carter."

"You're right. There are some sick people out there. I wish there was no such thing as child abuse. Every child should be loved and cared for always."

A long silence fell over them, and they listened to the sounds of shouting outside. Through the window, Freya could see that the fire was almost completely gone.

"I'm so sorry for how I reacted yesterday," Freya said softly. "I shouldn't have jumped to conclusions and blamed you. It wasn't right."

"I forgive you, Freya. I know how it looked. I would have blamed me too. You have to know even though I get angry, I am not a malicious person. I would never hurt you like that."

"I believe you, Maria."

A look of relief crossed Maria's face, and she smiled down at her sleeping child. Freya's heart was touched by the tender sight.

"I have something to confess, Freya," Maria said, and Freya's heart lurched. She wasn't about to admit to opening the horse stall, was she? Freya had changed her mind about that and no longer suspected Maria.

"I ran to the phone shanty down the lane with Carter and called 911 to report the fire," Maria whispered. "Don't tell anyone, please." She glanced down at her son. "I just hope he doesn't mention it."

Freya let out the breath she'd been holding, relieved. "Why? Why keep that a secret?"

"The Amish here don't report crimes," Maria said. "Not even fires."

"Why?"

"We believe we should leave all things to the Lord. We don't like involving the local police force or fire department. Well, at least, that's what we've been taught. I have personally always disagreed with that. I believe God put police and firefighters here to help us. I don't see why it would be wrong to report a fire so they can come put it out. It could save lives," Maria explained.

"I absolutely agree." Freya's eyes went wide. "I don't want you to get in trouble. I won't tell anyone."

"Thank you. I just feel like I had to tell someone and get it off my chest. And after you told me those stories about your childhood..." Maria cleared her throat, tilting her head to the side, as if in deep thought. "I don't know why I told you that, I guess."

"You can trust me with your secret, Maria."

"You know, Hannah and I are going to town tomorrow to get some supplies, and we were planning on going to a diner we like for lunch. Do you want to come with us?" Maria asked.

Freya's mouth fell open in shock, her eyes wide. "Me? You want me to come?"

Maria gave a small smile. "*Ja*. It could be fun."

"That would be great. Thanks, Maria." Freya wanted to shout and jump up and down with joy. Maria had invited her to do something fun with her—she was in total disbelief.

"Meet us here at noon tomorrow." Maria nodded. "It'll help take our minds off all of this."

The front door closed and footsteps sounded in the hallway. Adam appeared in the doorway. "The fire is out."

"Thank the Lord," Freya said, getting up off the bed.

"That's great news. Is the damage extensive?" Maria asked.

"The left wall of the barn will need to be completely rebuilt. *Daed* said they're going to have a work day." Adam turned to Freya. "Most of the community, if not everyone, will show up to help rebuild it. I wouldn't be surprised if they rebuild it in one day."

"That's incredible," Freya said.

"I better get him to bed. Drive safe," Maria said, setting Carter carefully down on his bed.

Adam and Freya walked toward the door, a small smile on Freya's face.

"What happened in there?" Adam asked as they walked outside. By now, many of the neighbors had gone home.

"I told Maria about a time when I was young, and my foster home burned down. It was such a tragedy because I really liked that family and couldn't live with them anymore. They were one of the few families who loved me."

"What did Maria say?"

"She sympathized with me. She was really nice. I think she saw me as an actual human being for the first time." Freya shrugged. "I don't know. It just seemed like she had some type of realization."

"Maybe she did," Adam said, taking her hand.

"She invited me to go to town with her and your mother tomorrow and to go to a diner for lunch," Freya gushed, not bothering to hide the excitement in her voice. "Isn't that wonderful?"

"Wow. That's huge progress, Freya!" Adam gave her a quick hug. "I'm so happy to hear that. Whatever you said to her must have helped her see a different side of you."

"Yeah. Maybe you're right."

As they approached Aaron and Hannah, Freya wrapped Hannah in a hug. "I am so sorry this happened. I hope they can rebuild it quickly."

"At least no one nor any animals were hurt," Aaron said.

"Thank you, Freya," Hannah said, pulling away. "You're both welcome to come to the work day. We will need help serving food and drinks." She turned to Adam. "And if you want to help with the building, we'd appreciate it. It will be all day this Saturday."

"Of course," Freya said. "I'll be there."

"Me too."

"Thank you both," Aaron said. "How did you get here so quickly, Adam?"

"A coworker from CPDU called to alert me that this had been called in."

"I woke up to Robin neighing loudly, so I came out here and saw the flames. You got here soon after, so I guess someone reported it right away," Aaron explained. "Maybe it was one of the *Englishers* down the lane."

"Maybe. All that matters is that everyone is safe now," Adam said, and Freya nodded in agreement. She knew who reported the fire, but she hoped to gain Maria's trust by not telling her secret.

"Come on. Let's get you home," Adam said, putting his arm around Freya's shoulders and guiding her to the car.

Dean watched the fire debacle from his car, which was parked in the shadows behind a cluster of trees. He fiddled with a match, turning it over in his fingers.

Dean hadn't expected the neighbors to show up so quickly and help put the fire out with their measly buckets, and he hadn't expected someone to report the fire so quickly. In his recent research, he'd read that the Amish do not usually report crimes, depending on the district. If someone hadn't called 911, then that fire would still be raging right now.

He watched with clenched fists as the firefighters put the fire out. No one had even gotten hurt. He'd hoped that at least it would have killed the Lapps' horse and other animals in the barn, but the old man had gotten them out in time.

No, this had been a failure. He would have to think of something else.

He watched as Freya and Adam spoke with his parents, talking and hugging like it was a happy family reunion. They hardly even seemed rattled by what had just happened. What would it take to break up this love fest?

He needed to do something more direct, more drastic. Freya had even gone inside to talk to the widow. Were they pals now? That wouldn't do at all.

Dean wanted to rip apart every relationship she had made in this town until she was cut off from their little society. How could he turn the blame back onto her, making her feel isolated and alone? If he could achieve that, maybe he could charm his way back into her life, convincing her that this little adventure hadn't worked out, and he was the only one who truly cared about her. Maybe he could even convince her that the cop didn't love her.

Yes, Dean had to convince her that she needed him, that she was nothing without him. If he couldn't have her, then no one could.

※※※※

The next day, Freya drove to the Lapps' house to meet them. Adam would have gone with them, but he had to work.

"Good morning!" Hannah called as she, Maria, and Carter walked out of the house and made their way to the buggy.

"Good morning," Freya said. "Would you like to take my car instead? I could drive you. Are you allowed to ride in cars?"

"Oh, yes, we are allowed to ride in cars; we just can't own one. There's a local man who often drives us places." Hannah looked at Maria. "Would you like to ride in her car, Maria?"

"I would be fine with it," Maria said. "I have a car seat for Carter in the barn for when Bob drives us in his car. I'll go get it. I got a new one after the fire."

Freya raised her eyebrows, impressed that she had a car seat. She felt as though she was learning something new about the Amish every day. Soon, Maria walked out of the barn with the car seat and quickly had it secured inside Freya's car.

"I have no idea how to do that," Freya said. "I'm glad you do."

"They aren't too hard to figure out," Maria said, lifting Carter into the car seat. He bounced a red ball on his lap. "Thanks so much for the ride. It'll go much quicker this way."

"Of course. Glad to help." Soon they were all buckled up and headed down the lane toward the main road that led to town. "So, what supplies do we need to get? Or are we going to lunch first?"

"Let's go to lunch first, so Carter doesn't get too hungry," Maria said. "If everyone is fine with that."

"Certainly. We don't want a cranky Carter." Hannah turned and smiled at Carter from the front seat, then turned to Freya. "We just need to go to the supermarket and get some flour, sugar, rice, pasta, things like that. I do like to get my produce at the farmers' market, but it's too cold, so I will get some there."

"I have to admit I was surprised to see you in the grocery store," Freya blurted out. "I didn't think that the Amish went to grocery stores. I guess I assumed you grew or made everything from scratch."

Then Freya realized what she'd said, and she felt the blood drain from her face. Would they notice her slip up?

"When did you see us at the grocery store?" Maria asked after an uncomfortable pause.

Freya glanced at the rearview mirror to see a confused look on Maria's face. "I, uh... Before I officially met you, I was in the grocery store to buy some roses for Robert's grave, and I saw the three of you. You were talking about Robert and how much you missed him." Freya glanced at Hannah. "You were holding Carter."

"I remember that," Hannah said. "You were there?"

"I'm sorry if that seems creepy or weird," Freya rushed to explain. "You see, I asked around town where you lived, and I went to your house. I was going to walk in and apologize, but I got too scared and didn't do it. I saw you through the window, so I saw what you looked like and then later recognized you in the store. I'm sorry. That sounds so strange when I say it out loud."

Hannah patted Freya's arm. "That's not strange, my dear. You were trying to tell us the truth. It's okay if you were scared. What matters now is that you faced your fear and told us what happened."

"It wasn't until after I met Adam that I had the courage to face all of you. It was because of him. I couldn't have done it without him," Freya added.

"If I were you, I couldn't have done it," Maria murmured. "I would have been too scared. What you did was brave, Freya."

Freya glanced at Maria in the rearview mirror again. "Thanks."

Thank you, Lord. It seems like maybe she's starting to see me as someone other than a soulless criminal, Freya prayed.

They soon arrived at the diner, and they all got out of the car. As Maria unbuckled Carter from his car seat, Freya pointed, standing near the drivers' side door that faced the street. "This is the diner where I work. Is this where we're going?"

"Oh, yes. I didn't know you worked there," Hannah said from the sidewalk on the other side of the car. "We love it there. They have the best burgers."

Freya chuckled. She didn't know the Amish ate burgers. "I just started."

Maria came to join Hannah on the sidewalk, and Carter held on to her jacket. "What did you say? You work at Molly's Diner? That's our favorite. I didn't know that either."

"She just started," Hannah told Maria.

As they continued to talk about their favorite foods to order, Freya watched Carter. He dropped his red ball, then let go of his mother's jacket and dashed into the street after it. Freya instinctively dashed after him, snatched him up without even stopping, then darted back toward the sidewalk with him in her arms. A black car veered out of the way, just barely missing her and Carter. Freya's heart pounded in her ears, almost blocking out Carter's cries and his mother's screaming, but she didn't slow down until they reached the sidewalk.

"Carter!" Maria called, taking the wailing boy from Freya's arms and holding him close. Maria looked at Freya, her eyes filled with tears. She reached one hand out toward her. "Freya, you saved his life."

Chapter Twenty-eight

Freya blinked, frozen, as the realization of what had just happened washed over her.

Maria comforted Carter, patting him on the back. Hannah touched Maria's arm, giving her a look, as if telling her to thank Freya.

Maria turned to Freya. "Thank you so much, Freya. How can I ever thank you?"

Freya couldn't read her expression. Was she truly thankful, or was she just saying that to be polite? Freya shook her head rapidly, lifting her hands. "No, no. You don't have to do anything to thank me. I just did it without even thinking. It happened so fast."

"It was incredible," Hannah reflected in awe. "You moved so quickly."

Maria let out a sob. "I don't know what I'd ever do if..." She wiped her eyes. "Let me at least buy you lunch."

"No, please, you don't have to do that. Actually, I do know what you could do." Freya shook her head, realizing how ridiculous her request was. "Never mind."

"What? Please tell me," Maria pleaded.

Freya sighed. She might as well say it. What was the worst that could happen? "I would love it if you reconsider how you see me as a person. If you would reconsider forgiving me, maybe even consider us being friends. I know, that sounds like too much to ask. You don't have to do it." She shook her head. "Never mind. I'm sorry. Please forget I said anything. Let's go inside." Freya's cheeks burned with embarrassment as she moved toward the diner.

"Freya," Maria said, handing Carter to Hannah, who had now calmed down enough to go inside the restaurant. Maria turned to face her, putting her hands on Freya's wrists. "It's not too much to ask. I will try. It's hard for me, but miracles happen every day," Maria said, wiping another tear from her eye.

"I think we just witnessed a miracle," Hannah said with a knowing smile, and Freya suspected she wasn't talking about Carter being pulled from the street.

Freya had taken Robert away with a car, but she'd saved Carter from another one—it was almost as if she'd balanced the scales.

She shook her head, dismissing the thought. No, there was nothing she could ever do to make up for Robert's death, even if it wasn't her fault. But this was a start to building her friendship with Maria. It was a small start, but it was something.

"Come on," Maria said, tugging on Freya's arm. "Let's go get those burgers. They have the best fries here."

"They sure do," Freya said, grinning.

"Ball!" Carter cried as they started to move away.

"Oh, his ball went across the street. I'll go get it," Freya said, then hurried to retrieve it. She handed it to Carter, who beamed at her.

"Thank you," he said.

"You're welcome." Freya touched his nose, and he giggled.

After they walked through the door of the diner, Molly, the owner, waved to Freya. "Hi, Freya. Oh, you know Hannah and Maria?"

"We're great friends. She might even be my daughter-in-law one day!" Hannah called out to Molly, and Freya felt heat creep up her neck.

"*Mamm!*" Maria said, playfully batting at her mother-in-law's arm. "Don't embarrass her."

"What? It might happen sooner than you think." Hannah winked at Freya. "My son doesn't just fall in love with anyone, you know. I tried to encourage him to date many young Amish ladies, but he was never interested in anyone. You, my dear, are special."

Freya looked away shyly. "Thank you, Hannah." She wasn't used to so much kindness and so many compliments, and she didn't even know what to say.

"You ladies can come sit over here," Molly said, then smiled at Carter. "And I have some special crayons and coloring pages for you, sir." She set a package of crayons and some paper down on the table. She took their drink orders then said, "I'll give you some time to look at the menu."

"Now before any of you say anything, I'm paying for this. It's my treat," Hannah announced as Molly walked away. "So, I want you three to order whatever you'd like."

"Oh, Hannah, you don't have to do that," Freya said.

"*Ja*, that's too generous," Maria added.

"Nonsense. Indulge an old lady and please let me treat you to a nice lunch," Hannah said, opening her menu. "As for me, I am going to order some of those delicious fries. People think the Amish don't eat food like fries, but they're wrong." She chuckled.

Freya laughed, then met Maria's eyes. They exchanged a brief smile before Carter tugged on his mother's arm, asking her to open the package of crayons.

While they waited for their food, Hannah told several stories about Adam's childhood, which had Freya laughing out loud.

"He was such a rambunctious child," Hannah said. "One time, I found earthworms in his bed. When I asked him why he'd put them there, he said he wanted to keep them warm and dry because it was raining."

"Oh, that's too funny. Thank you for telling me all those stories," Freya said with a mischievous smile. "Now I have something to tease Adam about when I see him."

Freya looked at the people around the table, and her soul was filled with warmth and gratitude.

Is this too good to be true, Lord? Is Maria finally warming up to me and seeing the real me? Please, Lord, let it be genuine, Freya prayed.

***

Maria smiled at Freya, who sat across the table from her, as if seeing her for the first time. Freya laughed with Hannah, and Carter also laughed at something she'd said.

She'd meant what she said. She wanted to give Freya another chance. Maria realized more and more what a kind soul Freya had, and she was realizing how wrong her first impressions were.

I was so quick to judge her. Why have I never realized how kind she is before? Maria prayed. *Have I really been so blinded by my anger and hatred, Lord? She just saved my son's life without even thinking for a second about her own safety. She could have been hit by that car too. Please help me see the good in her. Please soften my heart towards her. And maybe...*

Was it possible? Could Maria forgive Freya someday?

"Maria?"

Maria blinked, looking at Hannah. "I'm sorry, what did you say?"

"Remember when Carter pulled down my bag of flour and got it all over himself and the kitchen a few months ago?" Hannah laughed out loud. "It took us all day to clean up."

"Oh, yes," Maria said, chuckling, poking her son playfully. "You silly boy." She looked up and caught Freya smiling at her, and Maria smiled back.

"I can't thank you enough, Freya, for saving his life," she said.

"Please. You don't have to thank me." Freya's eyes lowered to the table.

"I'd like to get to know you better," Maria said.

"Really?" Freya looked up, hopeful.

"Yes, I would," Maria said, and she meant it. As she smiled, warm peace washed over her. Maria wasn't sure what was happening, but she felt as though the darkness was slowly being peeled away from her heart to reveal the joyful person she used to be.

Could she be that person again? Could she truly give Freya a second chance?

Dean drove down the main street of the little town of Unity, approaching a diner. He almost slammed on the brakes in shock when he saw long, fiery-red hair blowing in the frigid breeze. Was that Freya?

It was her, standing on the drivers' side of her car, mere feet from where cars drove past.

Dean let out a sinister chuckle. "Let's rattle her a bit and remind her of the car accident. Shake things up." He veered his car to the right, coming dangerously close to hitting her with his car. He wouldn't try to kill her now, only scare her.

Suddenly, a little boy ran out into the street, chasing after a red ball. Dean slammed on the brakes, veering away from the toddler. In the same instant, Freya darted after the child, grabbing him and returning him to the sidewalk with lightning speed.

Dean blinked, impressed at her quick rescue. He continued down the street, slamming his fist on the steering wheel in frustration. Well, that hadn't worked at all.

"I'll get you, Freya, and when I do, you won't see it coming," he growled under his breath.

※※※※※

Early on Saturday morning, Freya drove to the Lapps' house for the work day, and Adam showed up right after her. She lifted a cinnamon coffee cake out of her car that she had made to share with the group.

"What is that?" Adam asked, leaning forward to get a good whiff. "Wow, that smells amazing."

"It's just a box mix," Freya whispered. "Shh, don't tell. I'm sure all these ladies make their desserts from scratch."

"You might be surprised." Adam shoved his hands into his pockets and leaned back on his heels. "My mother has been known to use a boxed cake mix in a pinch."

"Really? Well, now I don't feel so bad."

"Just don't tell her I said that. Everyone keeps asking for her chocolate cake recipe, but she won't give it to anyone because she doesn't want anyone to know." Adam grinned. "She'd be so embarrassed that I told you."

"Aw, she shouldn't be. Besides, she's an amazing cook. I bet she could bake anything." Freya had assumed the Amish always made everything from scratch.

"Thanks so much for coming," Aaron said, approaching them. "Adam, you can join us for the carpentry work. Freya, you can help the ladies with serving breakfast. We'll be serving meals all day today, and there will be a lot of setup and cleanup work."

"Well, I'd be useless doing carpentry, so I'm happy to help with the food."

"The women don't do carpentry here," Adam whispered in her ear as Aaron walked away. "It's not exactly banned, but it's just not something that's done."

"That's good with me," Freya said as they walked toward the barn. "I'd just stand around wondering what to do. I'm sure I'll be busy helping the other women all day."

"Have fun." Adam winked then joined the other men. Freya turned to the large group of women who were setting out food on long picnic tables.

"Here goes nothing." She took a deep breath, hoping she wouldn't feel too much like an outsider. Her face burned with embarrassment when she realized these women had probably already been here for hours and she was just now getting here, but Hannah hadn't mentioned a specific time.

"Good morning." Maria came to Freya's side and walked with her the rest of the way. "What do you have there?"

"It's just a coffee cake." Freya shrugged, pleasantly surprised by Maria's warm greeting. "I probably should have brought more."

"No, I'm sure everyone will love it." Maria gently took it and set it down on the table with the other breakfast dishes.

"What can I do to help?"

"You can start by setting the table with plates, silverware, and cups. To make it easier, the women will serve all the men down the line, dishing food on their plates and filling their cups. Afterward, we clean everything up, and they go back to work."

"Sounds like a good plan."

"Freya!"

Freya turned to see Laura bounding toward her, followed by the always reluctant Lydia. Laura wrapped her arms around Freya. "So good to see you. How have you been?"

"It's nice to see you both, too. Things have been…" She glanced at Maria, who raised her eyebrows with a small smile. "Chaotic. But I'm well."

"That's great. Come on; I'll help you with setting the table." Laura took her hand and led her away, showing how to do each place setting. Soon they had a system going and finished the task. Every once in a while, Freya paused to watch the men work, fascinated at how quickly they were rebuilding the side of the barn. Perhaps they would be done before dinner.

It was time for breakfast, and the men all came over to sit at the table. Hannah came out of the house with an enormous dish of scrambled eggs that she had made, followed by Marta Miller, who had grilled a tall stack of toast on the woodstove in the house.

"Here, Freya, you can dish out the scrambled eggs," Maria said, taking the dish from her mother-in-law and handing it to Freya.

"I'll be handing out our famous donuts," Laura said with a grin. "Lydia has the cinnamon rolls. We took your coffee cake over to the men, and it's already almost gone."

"Really?" Freya's eyes shot up. "They liked it?"

"Of course! They said it was delicious."

Even though it was a box mix, a sense of pride washed over her. She leaned forward and whispered in Laura's ear, "It was a box mix."

Laura laughed out loud. "Trust me, they wouldn't have cared. What does it matter as long as it tastes good?"

Freya nodded. "True."

"You should come over and bake with us sometime if you want."

"Wow, that would be great. I would like to learn some Amish baking recipes. Thanks so much."

"Of course," Laura said. "Oh, it's time to start. Let's get this food served."

They made their way down the line, and Freya put a scoop of scrambled eggs on each plate for every man who wanted some. When she reached Adam, her heart started pounding harder. Why did she feel this way every time she was near him?

"Scrambled eggs?" she asked.

"Oh, yes. Thank you. Your coffee cake was a hit, by the way." He grinned up at her, and for a moment, she got lost in his warm brown eyes. Her spoon tilted, and she accidentally dropped eggs onto his lap.

He chuckled, wiping them off, attracting glances from some of the other men who sat nearby. She felt the heat of embarrassment creep up her neck, reaching her cheeks. "I'm so sorry."

"It's okay," Adam said. "Please, don't worry about it."

"Adam here was one of the clumsiest kids growing up," Isaiah said. "Always dropping his lunch at school and tripping over his own feet.

He's been talking about you nonstop, you know."

"Have I?" Adam asked, feigning innocence.

"*Ja*, he sure has," Dominic added. "I've never seen Adam so smitten."

Freya's face flamed even hotter, and she noticed the other women behind her. "I'm holding up the line. Sorry." She quickly scooped more eggs onto Adam's plate. "Would you like some eggs?" she asked Dominic, who was next.

After breakfast was served, Freya crossed her arms, looking out over the massive group of people who had gathered together to help Hannah and Aaron rebuild their barn. What would it be like to belong to a community of people who helped each other and cared about each other so much, to feel like you belonged?

"Amazing, isn't it?" Maria asked, coming up beside Freya. "This is one of the best parts about being Amish. No matter what happens, you always know your community will help you."

"The rest of the world isn't like that," Freya reflected. "Trust me, I know firsthand. People can be so selfish and greedy."

"Not here. Here, we're all one big family." Maria turned to Freya and grinned. "So, do you still plan on speaking in front of the church?"

"As in asking for forgiveness? I want to, if I could just summon the courage." The mere thought of standing in front of all these people made her stomach do backflips, and queasiness swept over her.

"You should speak with the bishop today if you really do want to do it. You could even ask for permission to speak before the church tomorrow."

"Tomorrow?" Freya gulped. "What would I say?"

"I'm sure the right words will come to you. Just ask the Lord for strength. He always provides it, especially when you need it most. I know that firsthand." Maria sighed, looking over at the barn.

"I'll try to talk to him if I can," Freya said. "I know I have to do this as part of my healing process."

"You can do this, Freya. I know it." Maria reached for Freya's arm.

"Thank you." Freya studied Maria, trying to read her. Was she truly being supportive, or was she only pretending? Freya wanted to trust that she was being genuine, but after what had happened between them before, Freya struggled to believe what she was seeing.

Please, Lord, let Maria's kindness toward me be real, Freya prayed. *And please let me trust her.*

Several hours later, after lunch, the day finally came to a close and the side of the barn had been completed. The day had gone by so fast because they had been so busy, and the other women were so kind, including her in their conversations.

She finally started to feel like she belonged.

"That was incredible!" Freya cried as Adam walked over to her. "The barn looks great."

"Teamwork makes the dream work," Adam quipped, leaning closer. "How did it go today?"

"Everyone was so nice. So many women talked to me, telling me stories and exchanging recipes. They really made me feel included, and Maria spent time with me. This was a really good day, one of the best. I think she's starting to see me for who I really am."

"That's so great to hear, darling, especially after how you saved Carter's life." Adam grinned at her, and Freya's heart warmed at the sound of him calling her such an endearing name. Freya had called Adam already to tell him all about how Maria was going to try to give her a second chance.

Freya caught sight of the bishop walking alone toward his buggy, his long white beard flowing in the breeze. "I have to go speak with the bishop. I'm going to ask him if I can stand before the church tomorrow and ask for forgiveness."

"You're amazing, Freya. Do you know that?"

His comment caught her off guard. "What?"

"You've come so far since you arrived here, conquering so many of your fears. You're incredible," he marveled, watching her closely.

She gazed into his eyes, smiling. "Well, thank you."

"You better hurry before he leaves."

"Oh, yes." Freya turned and hurried toward the bishop.

"Freya," Bishop Byler said with a warm smile. "I hope you had a pleasant day today."

"Yes, I did. I loved working with everyone. It's wonderful to see how everyone worked together to get the barn repaired."

"We always come together in times of need." He clasped his hands together. "Is there anything I can do for you?"

"You may have heard about what happened with me and Robert Lapp," Freya said hesitantly.

"Yes, I'm afraid I have." He nodded.

"I was wondering if tomorrow I could explain what happened to the church to correct any rumors that may be floating around. Also, I want to apologize and ask for the church's forgiveness." She bit her lip, waiting for his reply.

"I think that's a very good idea. I have heard some people talking about it, and I worry that some parts of the story may have not been told accurately. It would be good if you could tell what really happened, and I think it's good that you want to apologize and tell your side of the story."

"Thank you."

"I will open the service tomorrow, then I will invite you up. How does that sound?"

"That would be great. Thank you so much."

"You're welcome. See you tomorrow." The bishop climbed up in his buggy and drove away.

"What did he say?"

Freya jumped at the sound of Adam's voice. He was standing right behind her, but she hadn't noticed him walking up to her.

"He said I could at the beginning of the service tomorrow. I don't even know what I'm going to say." Freya ran her hands through her hair, tugging at the roots. "Ugh, what if I can't do it?"

"Of course, you can do it," Adam said, reaching for her hand, not caring who was watching. "I've seen you overcome so many fears. This is just one more. You can do this, and it will help you heal and forgive yourself. You'll be so happy afterward."

"That's true. It will be nice to get it over with. I'm not sure what people have heard about what happened. I wonder if parts of the story were exaggerated."

Adam chuckled. "They don't have cell phones here, but word sure does spread fast. Sometimes people resort to gossip, even though everyone knows it's wrong. The Amish are human, too."

Freya nodded slowly. "Will you come over and help me practice what I'm going to say? You can be my pretend audience."

He smiled. "Of course."

Chapter Twenty-nine

The next morning, Freya walked into the church with Adam, pushing down the feeling of anxiety that was building in her chest.

"Remember, you can do this. You've been through worse. What's the worst that can happen?" Adam reminded her.

"I might completely stumble over my words or freeze up completely." Freya wrung her hands in front of her long dress. Despite the cold, her hands felt clammy.

She could do this.

I can do this.

They walked into the church, and soon Hannah, Aaron, and Maria joined them.

"How are you feeling?" Hannah asked. "You look a bit...terrified."

"I am terrified." Freya gulped, her heart racing.

"If you forget what you were going to say, just speak from your heart. Just say what happened and apologize. If you want, it could take only thirty seconds," Maria said, touching her arm. "Then it will all be over."

"The congregation is very understanding. They will be gracious, no matter what happens. You'll do great." Aaron smiled at her.

"Thank you all," Freya said. "I better go sit down."

Adam escorted her to the front row of the women's side of the church. "You okay?"

Freya nodded as she sat down. "I'm fine. Thank you for all your help."

"If you get nervous, just look at me." Adam gave her a smile that made her heart soar.

"I will."

With that, Adam turned and walked over to the men's side, where he talked with his friends. More people milled into the room, taking their seats and speaking in hushed tones. Freya didn't try to make conversation with anyone, trying to go over what she was going to say in her head. When people spoke to her, she gave a polite greeting, but her brain couldn't handle small talk at that moment.

The bishop went up to the front of the room. "Good morning. First of all, thank you all who went to the Lapps' yesterday for the work day. Thankfully, the barn was fully repaired." He went on with a few more announcements, then looked to Freya. "Now I want to invite Freya Wilson to come up for a moment to share with us."

Freya swallowed, but her throat felt as dry as sand as she stood up and made her way to the front of the room. She faced the congregation as all eyes were on her. Her heart rate surged as adrenaline flooded her system.

"Good morning," she began, trying to remember the speech she'd practiced with Adam. "First of all, I want to thank you for welcoming me. I feel at home when I'm with you, and for me, that's really saying something. I think some of you have heard about what happened on the night Robert Lapp died. I want to tell what really happened from my perspective."

Adam nodded, encouraging her to go on.

She explained how Robert had died, speaking quickly before she lost her nerve. Perhaps she'd spoken too fast—she was just trying to get the words out before she was too afraid to go on. She glanced down at the floor, then at Adam, who was giving her an encouraging smile. It gave her the strength to continue.

"Hitting him was an accident, but I'm sorry that I left him there. I didn't call the police because I was afraid my ex would find out where I was and kill me. So, I drove away and fled to Canada. I know he would have killed me if I'd reported the accident, but that doesn't make it right. I finally got the courage after two years to ask the Lapp family for their forgiveness, and they went above and beyond—they've made me feel like a part of their family. I don't expect you to do the same because I don't deserve it, but I am so sorry, and I want to ask you all for your forgiveness."

Freya closed her eyes for a moment, too afraid to see everyone's reactions. Suddenly, she felt arms wrapping around her, and she opened her eyes to see several other people coming over to her, and the women wrapped their arms around her.

"Of course, we forgive you," Laura said.

"Amen," Mae Miller said.

Everyone else spoke their agreements, nodding and smiling. Their words blurred together in a sweet symphony in her mind, and she could barely distinguish one voice from the other because they were one.

Lisa, Deborah, and Samantha, the women who had talked behind her back, approached Freya.

"We want to apologize for how we gossiped about you that one time," Lisa said.

"We are very sorry. It wasn't our place to talk about it before you told everyone what really happened," Samantha added.

"We hope you can forgive us," Deborah said.

"Of course, I forgive you. That seems like such a long time ago." Freya smiled.

They shook her hand, nodding and welcoming her, then moved aside when Hannah and Maria walked up to Freya. Maria threw her arms around her. "You did it, Freya."

"See? Everyone wants to welcome you into our community," Hannah added.

"I didn't expect this." Freya grinned, her emotions overwhelming her as hot tears spilled down her cheeks and gratitude filled her heart.

They spent a joyful afternoon having a potluck lunch at church and then playing board games at the Lapps' house. Freya was surprised to see how competitive Adam's family was at Dutch Blitz, Pictionary, and Scrabble.

As Maria put Carter to bed, Freya sat with Adam on the couch.

"Today was so wonderful." She sighed, briefly resting her head on his shoulder. "It's nice to feel like part of a family."

"You *are* part of the family," Adam said. "So, can I take you out to dinner?"

"I don't think I'll ever say no to that."

"Well, I'm going to go to bed early," Maria said. "I have a headache. Today was really fun. I'm glad it went so well at church."

"Thank you. Me too. It's a huge relief."

Maria went to bed, and Adam and Freya said their goodbyes to Hannah and Aaron before leaving for the restaurant.

Maria went to her room and closed the door, leaning against it as emotions swirled through her.

What is wrong with me? she wondered. *Lord, the entire church accepted her today. We had a great afternoon all together, and Freya forgave me for outright lying to her. I want to forgive her more than anything, but something is holding me back. What is it? Pride? Stubbornness?*

She collapsed on her bed, sinking her face into her pillow.

"Please, God," she whispered. "Please take this bitterness from my heart. Please make me the person I used to be. Please help me forgive Freya and accept her into our lives. She might very well be part of the family soon, and I have always wanted a sister."

She rolled over on the bed. What would it be like to have a sister-in-law, someone to share secrets with?

In order to be that close to someone, Maria knew she had to accept every single flaw that person possessed. She knew she had to forgive her every wrong. Sisters fight, but they also forgive.

She'd give almost anything to have a sister. Sure, she was close to Hannah, but she was her mother-in-law. She longed for a woman her age who understood her, who accepted her for who she was, who shared every secret with her, someone she could be herself with.

"Help me be that kind of person. Help me become the person I want to be, Lord. Please, please, change my heart."

***

After dinner at the local Italian restaurant they both loved, Adam and Freya drove to Freya's house. Their bantering and laughter quickly ended as they stared at the front of the white house, which had been vandalized.

Someone had painted the word *Murderer* in shocking red paint.

"Who did this?" Freya cried, feeling her hope sink like a stone in water.

Had this entire day been a lie? Were there some people who really hadn't forgiven her and were just faking it? It couldn't have been Dean—he didn't know about the accident because it was never reported, and this wasn't his style. If he were here, he would come right after her.

"I don't know, Freya. I'm so sorry. I don't know anyone who could have done this."

Freya's mind reeled, playing over every detail of the day in her mind. After they'd left the church, anyone other than the Lapps could have come here and done this. But would they really have done this in broad daylight? It probably happened while they were at dinner, after dark. Here, it got dark quite early in the winter, and there were no street lights in her neighborhood.

Freya froze as she remembered Maria saying she was going to bed early because of a headache.

"What? What are you thinking about?" Adam asked.

"Maria went to bed early."

"So?"

"She could have sneaked out without your parents knowing. She could have done this while we were at dinner." Freya covered her eyes with her palms. Oh, how could she have been so naïve?

"Freya, no. Maria wouldn't do this. Remember how you blamed her for letting out Robin? Don't make that mistake again," Adam warned. "Your relationship with her is finally mending. You are friends now, and she's forgiven you. If you accuse her of this, she may never trust you again. Do you really want to hurt your relationship with her over something she most likely didn't do?"

"It was all an act, wasn't it? What if she pretended to like me and forgive me just so I would let my guard down and she could get revenge on me?" Freya wrapped her arms around herself.

"Trust me, she would never do that."

"Why are you always taking her side? What if she really did let out Robin? We don't know for sure that she didn't," Freya blurted, guilt instantly setting in. What was she saying? She hated how untrusting she was, how she was so quick to blame and accuse. What had she become?

"I love you, Freya, but you have to stop doing this," Adam said. "You could ruin relationships. Once you break trust, it takes a long time to earn it back, if ever."

"Ugh," she groaned, knowing he was right. "I hate this about myself. I just don't know what to do." She stared at the crimson letters marring her house, telling the whole town she was a murderer.

"Before you do anything, you need to calm down and think this through. Don't make any rash decisions when you're angry."

Freya took in a deep breath and let it out. "I need to scrub that off right away."

"Let me help you." Adam unbuckled his seat belt.

"No, that's okay. I want to clear my head."

"It's freezing out. I can't let you do this alone."

Freya shook her head. "No, I want to do it on my own. It won't take that long. I just need to be alone." She needed to think and pray.

"I'll call you later to check in."

"Thanks." Freya got out of the car and grabbed a scrubbing brush and bucket from the garage while Adam drove away. She filled it with hot, soapy water and walked to the front of the house and began scrubbing. Within seconds the water seeped through her mittens, making her fingers even colder.

"Why is this happening, God? I thought that everyone here forgave me. I thought they wanted me in their lives. Was it all an act? Who was lying to me? Was everyone lying to me?" she prayed as she scrubbed. "I thought for the first time in my life I was part of a community, part of a family. I knew it was too good to be true."

She scrubbed even harder, and the paint turned the water pink as it dripped down into the snow below. She stepped back and squinted at the cleaned wall. It still looked a little pink. She'd have to call her landlord about it tomorrow and would probably have to paint over it.

"Good enough for now," she muttered, grabbing the bucket and hurrying to the door.

Freya walked through her front door. So many emotions were running through her, and her mind felt like a jumbled mess.

Freya washed her hands under warm water, trying to regain the feeling in them. Freya lit a few candles, taking in a deep breath, trying to remove the stress from her mind. She changed into some sweatpants and a sweatshirt, then grabbed a book off her dresser, ready to curl up and get lost in its story. Picking up a throw blanket, she headed for the couch.

Before she could sit down, there was a knock on the door. Hesitantly, Freya peered out the window to see a buggy. Who was here?

Freya opened the door to see Hannah. Her eyebrows shot up. "Oh, hello, Hannah."

"I'm sorry to just show up like this," Hannah said.

"Come in, please," Freya said, ushering her in. She put some water in the tea kettle and set it on the stove, then sat with Hannah at the table.

"Tea?" she asked. "I was going to make some, anyway."

"Yes, thank you. That would be lovely."

Had Adam gone to his parents' house and told them about the vandalism?

"You know, this is the happiest I have seen Adam since..." Hannah looked up at the ceiling. "Well, for a very long time. Even before Robert's death. When he's with you, joy radiates from him."

Freya gave a small smile.

"Has he spoken to you about his intentions?"

Freya felt heat creeping up her neck, and she smiled into her mug.

Hannah laughed out loud, leaning back in her chair. "I can tell he's deeply in love with you."

Freya looked up. "When did he tell you?"

"He didn't have to. It was all over his face whenever I saw him with you," Hannah said. "My son has never been interested in any of the girls in this community, not like he is with you. Not even close. Girls have been interested in him, though." Hannah chuckled, sipping her tea. "He was always oblivious."

Freya wrapped her hands around her mug as silence fell around them.

"Adam came by to tell us about what happened to your house," Hannah said softly. "I'm so sorry to hear that. It looks like you got it cleaned up."

The tea kettle whistled, and Freya brought it to the table along with tea bags, spoons, honey, and two mugs.

"I couldn't let it stay like that for everyone to see tomorrow." Freya poured hot water into mugs for both of them.

"I want you to know that no one in our community would ever do something like that."

Hannah chose a tea bag and plopped it into her mug, blowing on the steaming liquid in her cup.

"He told you my suspicions?" Why would he do that? Now the Lapps probably thought she didn't trust them.

"No, he didn't say anything about that, actually." Hannah tilted her head. "He just said you were upset and could maybe use a friend."

"Oh." Freya sipped her tea again, feeling like a complete jerk. "I feel terrible for even saying this, but I was afraid someone at church did it. My whole life, I've never had a real family, and I've never been part of a real community. I guess today it all seemed too good to be true, and then when I came home and saw those red letters, I thought maybe someone at church had been faking their kindness toward me." She shook her head slowly. "I'm a horrible person. I wish I didn't have so many trust issues. I'm so sorry."

Hannah reached for Freya's hand. "I can see why you have a hard time trusting people, but if you stick around, you will learn how to. I know without a doubt no one here would have done this. Their reactions to you today were genuine. They care about you. We all do."

"So..." Freya was going to ask if Hannah knew for sure if Maria had really gone to bed or not, but she couldn't bring herself to say it. "Never mind."

"Maria was in bed the whole time, Freya. Carter woke up because he had wet the bed, and Maria changed his sheets and gave him a bath. She was home the entire time. There was no way she would have had time to do this while you were out to dinner with Adam. I have seen her heart change toward you, and now I know without a doubt it is true. She is becoming more and more like her former self. She used to be such a joyful person. It's taking some time, but she will become that person again, and I do think one day soon she will forgive you."

Freya covered her face with her hands. "I'm so sorry, Hannah. I feel awful. She's been so kind to me, and here I go suspecting her because of our rough start." She scrubbed a hand down her face as realization set in, and she felt the blood drain from her face.

"Freya, are you alright? You look pale."

Freya blinked. "I'm sorry, Hannah. I just realized something. I need to call Adam."

"What's wrong?"

Freya felt the blood drain from her face. "I think Dean is here. I think he did this. I didn't think it was his style at first, but now I understand. He's trying to drive a wedge between me and everyone I trust..." Freya scrambled to grab her phone.

"You think Dean is here, in town? Maybe you should come home with me. Adam is spending the night with us before heading back to work early tomorrow morning. You can call him and let him know. I don't think you should be alone."

"If you're sure, I would appreciate that. I'm going to pack right now and will meet you there in a few minutes."

"I'll see you there. Please let me know if you need anything else. I'll be praying for you." Hannah gave her a hug, said goodbye, and drove off in her buggy.

Freya watched her leave, grateful that Hannah had stopped by and checked on her. She called Adam, and he answered right away.

"How are you?" he asked.

"Adam, I think it was Dean who did this. I think he has found me."

"How would he know about the accident?"

"He probably asked people in town. I think he's trying to alienate me from everyone I've grown close to because he's trying to make me think I need him."

Adam paused. "You may be right. That means he knows where you live. Can you come here? I'm at my parent's house. I feel like such an idiot for not staying with you. I shouldn't have left."

"I made you leave. And yes, I'm leaving right now. See you soon." Freya set her phone down on her dresser and grabbed a change of clothes.

Though she knew she had to leave, she just wanted to crawl into bed, feeling so emotionally exhausted. The wind outside picked up, shaking the branches outside her window.

Before she could comprehend what was happening, a loud crash came from the closet as it burst open, and something incredibly large and heavy fell on her, knocking her to the floor and pinning her there.

Dean had found her.

Chapter Thirty

Her nerves on fire, she leaped for the gun in her nightstand drawer, yanking it open. The gun was gone.

"Oh, yeah, I found that." He lifted his jacket to reveal the pistol Adam had given her.

She felt the blood drain from her face. Did he plan to shoot her?

"I thought that woman would never leave, then you went and called that cop. I've been in here waiting. Did you think you could leave me and hide from me forever?" Dean's voice enveloped her. He sneered at her, his hot breath stinging her face. "Didn't you know I'd find you?"

Panic surged within her, flooding her veins with adrenaline as she kicked and fought against him with everything she had, but he had her wrists pinned to the floor and she couldn't move her arms. She tried using her legs to get him off her, to kick him, but he only laughed.

"I thought you learned a long time ago that's it's useless to try to fight me," Dean growled in her ear. "You'll just end up hurting yourself."

He lifted one hand to slap her in the face, and while ignoring the sting, she used that second to lift her hand and attack his eyes, pressing them with her finger and thumb as hard as she could. Memories of all the self-defense training Adam had given her came flooding back to her mind as she used what he had taught her.

Dean screamed in rage, heaving her off the floor and lifting her to her feet. She kicked him in between the legs, and he howled while thrashing her into the dresser behind her.

Out of the corner of her eye, she saw the candles teeter, then one of them tipped and rolled off the dresser. The flames caught onto a sweater that was on the floor, which then traveled to a throw blanket.

Dean clicked his tongue. "You were always such a messy person. Now it's going to cost you your life."

He grabbed her by the shoulders and threw her across the room.

Dean wrestled her to the floor. Her mind flashed back to all the times she'd been in this situation before. The instinct to curl up in a ball and protect her face and vital organs was almost overpowering, but since then, she'd learned to defend herself, how to use his size against him. Instead of freezing in fear, she felt a quiet sense of relief that Dean felt the need to gloat and to punish her for trying to leave him. Otherwise, she would be dead by now.

His arrogance was saving her life. Now she needed to do something to get away before he took more of his revenge out on her body.

"How long have you and the cop been together?" Dean asked in a seething voice. "Did you think I didn't know about him? I'll be taking care of him next. And before I do, I'm going to tie him up and take him to his parents' house and make him watch while I burn their house down. I want them inside when I do it. That's why I waited for little old Hannah to leave."

"No," Freya choked out.

Dean laughed, a vile and heinous sound. He wrapped his hands around her neck. "Oh, yes. And it's going to be delicious. Too bad you won't be around to watch along with Adam."

Freya reached behind her, grabbing the handle of an umbrella. It wasn't much, but she shoved the pointed end of the umbrella toward his eyes as hard as she could, drawing blood. He loosened his grip for only a moment, and Freya coughed and sputtered, fighting for air. She stabbed at him again, and this time, her grip was stronger and she hit her target dead on. He finally let her go, tilting to the side. She used that moment to roll and grab a small side table, which she struck him with, using as much strength as she could muster.

He faltered, rubbing his head, blinking rapidly, slumping. Freya gripped the legs of the table even harder, scrambling to her feet. She stood, feeling as though she was towering over him.

"No matter how many times you try to kill me, no matter how long you look for me and try to ruin my life, I will fight you. I will never go down without a fight again." Not even knowing where her sudden strength came from, she didn't even recognize her own confidence and voice.

"This will be the last time you fight me," Dean snarled, blood seeping through his pointed teeth and from his wounded eye socket as his adrenaline heightened. "Because you're about to die, Freya."

"See you soon."

Adam was about to hang up the phone when he heard another voice in the background. Clearly, Freya hadn't hung up the phone.

"I thought that woman would never leave, then you went and called the cop. I've been in here waiting. Did you think you could leave me and hide from me forever?" a gravelly voice growled.

Dean. That was Dean.

Adam's adrenaline spiked and his fingers shook as he put Freya's call on hold and called CPDU dispatch on another line, giving them Freya's address. He identified himself and requested immediate backup from any officer available. "This is a domestic violence situation, and the suspect is dangerous and possibly armed."

As Adam rushed to the door, Aaron and Maria followed him.

"What's wrong?" Aaron asked.

"I have to go right now. I think Dean found Freya." Not explaining any further, Adam barely had his shoes on as he scrambled out the door, sliding on the ice to his car. He drove down the road, going as fast as he could without sliding on black ice. He had switched the call back to Freya's call, and he could hear her trying to fight off Dean. With every passing second, the anger and fear within Adam built higher and higher until he thought he might explode.

"Why did I leave? I should have never left her!" he screamed, pounding the windshield. Couldn't this car go any faster?

Snow began to fall, and within moments, it was pelting his windshield, limiting his vision so much that he could barely see anything in front of him. Adam's car sped down the road, and he swerved to avoid another car he'd barely seen.

The reality of what that night must have been like for Freya, running scared for her life in similar weather, hit Adam full-force. Even though he'd forgiven her, up to this point, he realized he'd still felt on some level that it was her fault, that she should have done something differently, even if he hadn't admitted it to himself.

Now, racing through the night to save her life, he understood—she couldn't have done anything differently.

He just hoped he would get to tell her that.

Finally, Adam rounded the corner and approached Freya's house, seeing the orange glow of flames through the onslaught of falling snow. He pulled into the driveway, stopping the car with a skidding halt. He jumped out of the car and threw on his vest. Not caring that the engine was still running and the car door was hanging open, he ran toward the flames.

He got there before the fire department or CPDU, who were on their way and would be there any moment, but he couldn't wait for them—he had to get Freya out that very second. As he sprinted toward the door, he saw the orange flash of fire through the window.

A scream came from inside, unmistakably Freya's.

He tried opening the door, but it was locked. He kicked the door down, hearing it splinter as it broke. Luckily, the lock was old and weak.

He stumbled into the entryway, then ran into the living room and kitchen area.

"Freya! Freya!" he called. Flames were now engulfing the curtains, the walls, and the couch. A loud crash came from the bedroom.

Adam stumbled in to see Freya holding a small table, standing over Dean Hamilton, who then lunged at her, wrapping his hands around Freya's neck. They were only a few feet away.

Adam drew his gun and screamed. It was an animalistic, raging sound that he didn't even recognize as his own voice.

"Let her go, or I'll shoot!" he shouted, his finger on the trigger.

Dean immediately let Freya go, his cold, dark eyes locking with Adam's. He stood up and lunged at Adam, and in the scuffle, the gun was knocked out of Adam's hands as he was trying to shoot.

Dean had already been so close to him, and it happened so fast that Adam was unable to shoot him without possibly hitting Freya.

Instead, Adam attacked Dean with all the anger and indignation he'd been storing up inside him, releasing it through his pounding fists.

Freya fell back on the floor and coughed, her legs giving up on her. She finally realized how much her lungs were burning now that Dean was finally away from her. The flames and smoke were devouring the room, and the roar in her ears was making it hard to comprehend what was happening. And the heat... The heat seemed to be enveloping her, scorching her skin.

She watched in a daze as Adam attacked Dean. They rolled and punched at each other, and Freya wanted so desperately to do something to help Adam, but all she could think about was how hard it was to breathe and how tired her body felt, as if she was drowning. If she could just rest her eyes for a moment, maybe she could think more clearly.

"Get out, Freya!" Adam called to her. At first, the words seemed garbled, but as he kept on repeating the words, they became clearer.

Get out. Get out.

"Go!" he screamed.

Dean weakened, slumping to the floor, then his head dropped, his eyes closing. Was he...unconscious? She felt her own vision tunneling, darkness creeping into the corners of the room. Freya willed herself to stand, for her feet to carry her out of the burning house, but then her legs gave out, and she found herself staring at the ceiling.

Suddenly Adam was leaning over her. His strong arms swept under her body, lifting her off the floor. Her eyes closed as she felt him moving her, but she couldn't figure out where he was taking her.

Adam suddenly jerked.

"Let her go!" That was Dean's voice.

"Back off!" Adam commanded, and his body jerked again as if he was kicking. Then they were moving again. She hoped he was taking her somewhere nice, but maybe if the darkness overcame her, she could just sleep for a while…

"Hang in there, my love," Adam whispered in a raspy voice—he must have inhaled too much smoke…and it was all her fault.

Cold, frigid air hit her face, but it was a warm welcome compared to the smoky, sweltering house she'd been in. She coughed again, sputtering to get air into her lungs. She felt like she could again open her eyes, but somehow, she wasn't.

***

Adam carried Freya out of the house. CPDU and the fire department were still not there yet. He wanted to curse under his breath. It felt as though he'd been there for an eternity, when in reality, it had only been a few minutes. Hopefully, they'd be here soon. His lungs burned from inhaling smoke, but that was the least of his worries.

While he'd been carrying Freya out, Dean had opened his uninjured eye and grabbed at Adam's leg, trying to stop him. Adam had kicked Dean in the head, knocking him unconscious. He'd had to do it in order to get Freya out of there.

Now he gently set her on the back seat of his car. She was slipping in and out of consciousness as her eyes fluttered partially open and closed. He wanted to stay with her, but if he did, Dean might die in the fire. Adam wanted Dean to pay back everything he owed Freya, and he wanted Dean to go to prison for everything he had done to her.

But Freya needed him now, and he needed her to live more than anything. He coughed from the smoke, but she'd been inside longer than him. Guilt tore at him for possibly letting Dean die, but if Freya didn't make it, he'd never forgive himself for the rest of his life. He didn't even want to imagine it.

"Come on, sweetheart, wake up," Adam murmured as he checked her airways. She was breathing, but still slipping in and out of consciousness. Finally, after several heart-crushing moments, she coughed, and her eyes opened fully.

"Adam?" she rasped.

"Oh, thank you, Lord in heaven," Adam prayed out loud, taking her hands. "You're safe now."

"Dean?" Freya rasped, a look of fear overtaking her lovely face.

"He's still in there," Adam said. "I have to go get him out."

"No!" Freya screamed, looking past him at the burning house as she grabbed his arm. "Please, don't. I can't lose you."

"He has to go to prison and pay for everything he did to you."

"I don't care about that." She grabbed onto his shirt, pulling him closer. "If I lose you because of him, he will have won. He will have taken everything from me. He tried to kill you. And if he dies in the fire or is already dead, then he has paid the ultimate price. It is in God's hands now."

Adam searched her piercing green eyes as sirens sounded in the distance. "I took an oath to protect and serve, even if the person I'm serving doesn't deserve it. The fire department will be here any second. Until then, I have to try." Without wasting another moment, he wrenched from her grasp, as hard as it was to leave her, and turned toward the house. Before he could even take a step, a deafening boom came from the house, an explosion rocking the ground as flames shot in the air. Adam was knocked back into the rear of the car, the door protecting him from most of the heat. He got in the driver's seat. Without a word, he drove down the long driveway.

"What happened?" Freya cried from the back seat.

"That explosion had to have killed him," Adam said. "I don't want you anywhere near there. It's too dangerous."

A fire truck and ambulance rounded the corner, sirens blaring. "Finally," Adam muttered. As the trucks pulled into Freya's driveway, Adam slowed the car, stopping at the end of her driveway.

"I'll go talk to them and tell them what happened. The EMTs will put you on oxygen and take you to the hospital. I'll meet you there soon. You inhaled a lot of smoke," Adam said, getting out of the car. "I'll meet you there to be with you as soon as I can."

"Adam," Freya said, and he opened the back door. The sight of her was so wonderful, and even with her smudged and swollen face, disheveled hair, and fearful eyes, she was the most beautiful woman in the world to him. "Thank you," she whispered. "Thank you for saving my life."

"I love you, Freya Wilson," Adam said in a low voice, taking her hands in his. "When I thought you might die, I..." The mere thought of it caused his voice to crack with emotion, his heart constricting in his chest. "I knew more than ever that I want you by my side for the rest of my life."

Freya's eyes went wide.

"This is not my idea of the perfect proposal, so I'm not officially proposing now, but I just want you to know that I meant everything I said earlier. I would die for you, Freya, and I hope I just proved to you that you can trust me." Adam swallowed, suddenly finding it hard to breathe. "I just hope you know that I truly love you, and I want to cherish you every day for the rest of our lives. I want you to know I'm nothing like Dean."

Freya smiled. "No, you're nothing like him. He would have never risked his life to save mine. Now I know that there are good, honest, caring men in this world, and I meant what I said earlier too. You're the best man I've ever met, and I love you too."

"So, does this mean—"

"Lapp!"

Adam whirled to see the fire chief jogging over to him. The fire truck was already dousing the house with the water hose. "I need to talk to you," the chief said. "And you need to be checked out."

Adam nodded, then turned to Freya. "We need to give our statements to the fire department and police, so they know what happened. I need to go talk to them now, and you need to be taken to the hospital." He gently ran his thumb down her cheek and smiled. "We will continue this conversation later."

"You have a visitor," the perky nurse told Freya. "A very handsome one." Her eyebrows went up and down.

Freya chuckled, then regretted it when pain shot through her ribs. "Thanks. Send him in."

A moment later, Adam walked into the hospital room, carrying the most enormous bouquet of red roses she'd ever seen and a box of chocolates. She loved roses, but she'd always thought getting cut flowers as a gift was silly because they died so quickly. She'd rather plant flowers herself that she could tend to and nurture long term, but Adam didn't know that about her yet. However, she'd take chocolate any day of the week.

She smiled when he set the massive bunch of blooms on her bedside table. "Thank you. That is so sweet of you."

He shrugged. "I would give you the moon if I could."

"Actually, roses are my favorite because they remind me of people. I love them because even though they have sharp thorns, they're still beautiful. Even though people have flaws, we can still see all the ways they are good. I don't know of any other flowers with thorns."

Adam tilted his head. "Wow. I never thought of it that way."

He gave her a smile that made her heart flutter, and suddenly she was self-conscious of her bruised face and the bandage around her head.

"So, how are you feeling?"

She groaned. "Terrible." She coughed again, holding her side. "Smoke inhalation, a broken rib, and a concussion are no fun. Not to mention all the bruises. I know it's not really funny, but if I don't laugh, I'll just cry." Her expression turned serious, and she was dying to be updated. "So, tell me everything."

"The fire department found Dean's body, and they positively identified him. He's dead, Freya. He will never bother you again," Adam said, tears reddening his eyes.

Freya let out a half-laugh, half-sob. She didn't know whether to be elated at her newfound freedom or feel guilty that her abuser was dead. "Dead? He's... He's never going to hurt me again," she whispered.

"Never again. You're safe now." Adam took her hand in his, careful not to disrupt the IV.

"But what about his police friends? What if they want to take out revenge on me now that Dean is dead? What if they think I caused his death?" Panic rose within her, squeezing her chest.

"CPDU checked his phone records, and they had enough other intelligence to arrest the two corrupt officers who helped Dean not get arrested for domestic violence against you. During that process, CPDU also discovered several other felonies they committed, including stealing from evidence. In order to avoid a lengthier prison sentence, the officers readily plead guilty to several felonies and are now in prison. They won't be bothering you. You're free, Freya."

"I'm free from Dean." Freya let out a long breath. Even though she was saying the words out loud, it still seemed too good to be true. Peace and relief washed over her. "He's really gone."

Adam nodded. "He's gone, Freya."

"So, I'm free from Dean, but am I free from my own guilt?" She looked away. "Not yet."

"You need to forgive yourself," Adam murmured.

"I thought I did, but the guilt keeps returning. I don't feel as tortured as I did before now that I know you, your parents, and Maria have forgiven me."

Adam nodded. "That's a good start."

"I remember the sermon in your church. It was about forgiveness. The speaker said that forgiveness is not only for the forgiven but also for the forgiver. Maybe now I can move on since Maria has finally forgiven me. I hated to see Maria torturing herself and knowing it was because of something I did."

Adam squeezed her hand. "I'll help you every step of the way."

The nurse came into the room again. "You have two more visitors, Hannah and Maria. Want me to send them in?"

Adam and Freya looked at each other. "Oh, yes, of course. Thank you."

The nurse ducked out of the room.

"Anyway, it's not your fault," Adam continued. "I understand now. When I was driving through that snowstorm to get to your house, I could barely see. I was panicked, and I almost hit another car. You must have been terrified during the accident."

Freya nodded solemnly, tears welling up in her eyes. *He understood what it felt like for me,* she realized.

"He shouldn't have been in the road to look for his horse, especially in that weather. I know that horse meant a lot to him, but he shouldn't have risked his life like that. I should have gone with him to help him. Sometimes bad things happen, and we just have to deal with them. Maybe if I had gone with him, I could have saved his life," Adam said, squeezing her hand as tears glistened in his eyes. "But then I never would have met you."

A slow smile spread on Freya's face as her heart filled with warmth.

Hannah and Maria came into the room. Hannah rushed to Freya's side while Maria glanced at Freya sheepishly.

"I am so sorry this happened to you," Hannah said. "Adam told me it happened right after I visited you. He was waiting in the closet until I left?" She shivered. "The mere thought frightens me to my core. I thank our heavenly Father you are alive."

"It's true," Freya said with a nod. "I don't know how long he was in there, waiting to attack me. He wanted me alone, probably because he was a coward. I'm just glad you weren't there when he did show himself."

Maria awkwardly stood in the corner, her eyes darting between them and the floor. For the thousandth time, Freya's heart ached at the thought of all she'd taken from her.

Hannah patted Freya's hand. "At least it's over now. You know, when we were walking in, we overheard what Adam was saying. Robert's death wasn't your fault. We don't blame you."

"It was easy for me to blame you because you survived." Maria finally spoke in a timid voice, daring a glance at Freya. She took a tentative step closer. "If Dean's death in the fire taught me anything, it was that sometimes the one left standing isn't the one at fault."

Freya's hand flew to cover her mouth as she stifled a sob, hope rising in her chest. Was this a sign that she was truly trying to move toward a relationship with Freya? Friendship still seemed too much to ask for.

"I don't blame you anymore, Freya. A terrible thing happened, and you were in a life-threatening, impossible situation. Your fight or flight kicked in, and you were just trying to survive. You're here now, and you make my brother-in-law very happy." Maria smiled through her tears, then her expression turned serious. "Again, I am so sorry about what I did at church. It was wrong of me to tell people what happened. My heart was bitter, but I've had time to think about it and now I truly regret it. I have prayed day and night, asking God to change my heart." She glanced at the floor, then looked up. "To be honest, you are starting to feel like a sister to me. Sisters fight and can hurt each other deeply, but they also forgive each other."

Now there was no holding back the sob that escaped Freya's mouth. "I always wanted a sister," she choked out, feeling Adam squeeze her hand again.

"Well, me too." Maria gave a small smile. "I was so blind before, Freya. I was so blinded by my grief, anger, and hatred. I don't hate you now—not at all. I forgive you, Freya. I want you to be a part of our community and our family." Maria smiled at Adam. "As *Mamm* said, maybe that could be sooner than we think."

Freya's elation bubbled over in the form of a laugh, and she wiped away her tears. "I'm so happy to hear you say that."

"I'm so sorry for everything, Freya. I just hope you can forgive me for being so awful to you," Maria pleaded.

"Of course, I forgive you, Maria." She grasped Maria's arms, who now had tears streaming down her face. "This means the world to me. I think this is the happiest day of my life."

"There will be many more to come." Maria hugged Freya again, wiping a tear from her eye. "Welcome to the family." They held each other tightly for a few moments, then Maria pulled away.

"I'm so happy," Adam called out, hugging Freya, then Maria. "I'm so happy to see all the women I love getting along so well and caring about each other so much."

Hannah and Maria eyed Adam. "So, anything you two want to tell us?"

Freya turned to Adam, who was beaming at her. For the first time in years, she felt the tension she'd been holding onto melt away in the warmth of Adam's smile. Even all the fear, stress, grief, confusion from Dean's death seemed to evaporate like a snowflake on her skin. Yes, she felt shocked that Dean had died, but it was eclipsed with the knowledge that he would never haunt her life again.

Now that Dean was gone and Maria had forgiven her, Freya was truly free.

"Well, Freya, you know I'm in love with you, and I know you love me too. Can I tell them this is official, that we are together?" Adam asked, leaning closer to her.

She felt her soul take flight, soaring higher than a butterfly migrating from cold winds. "Yes. In fact, let's tell the whole town. I want to shout it from the hospital window!"

They all laughed, and Freya's heart soared when Adam gently caressed her hand with his thumb.

"That's exactly how I feel," he said.

Chapter Thirty-one

After Freya was released from the hospital, Hannah and Aaron let her stay at their house until she felt strong enough to go back to work and find a new place to live. Winter was finally coming to an end, and the first signs of spring were beginning to show, but it was still chilly.

Freya called Victor and told him everything, explaining how Dean had found her but that she was safe now. She also told Victor that Adam had been the one who had questioned him at his house before.

A few nights later, Adam came over to the Lapps' house for dinner. Freya had made the dinner with Hannah, wanting to make herself as useful and helpful as possible so she didn't feel so guilty for living with them. Hannah gently instructed her through the entire dinner, even the pie they'd made for dessert. Freya stumbled through, but in the end, the meal turned out delicious, thanks to Hannah.

"I do like to cook, but I'm not the best, I guess," Freya said, slicing cucumbers for a salad. "I would like to learn some Amish recipes."

"Oh, I'd love to show you some!" Hannah said with a smile.

Her mind wandered back to one night when Dean had been living with her. She'd made chicken parmesan, and the pasta had been slightly overcooked, but definitely still good.

"Can't you do anything right?" Dean had screamed, grabbing his plate and flinging it across the room like a frisbee. The red sauce had splattered all over them, the walls, and the white carpet.

Freya had been frozen with fear, sitting in her seat, her mind racing. What should she do?

Dean got up from his chair and marched around the table to lean down and growl into her face. "I work all day, and I expect to come home to a good, home-cooked meal. You call this good? This is terrible. Now clean this up." He gestured to the red-stained room, and her eyes widened in horror. It would take hours to get it as clean as he expected it to be.

When she hadn't cleaned it as well as he wanted, he'd thrown her across the room. She'd sprained her wrist that night, and his concern that her swelling would cause trouble for him had taught him to be more careful, more devious in the ways he hurt her after that. Even then, Freya had been too scared to go to the police.

One day, she hoped these memories would stop harassing her, especially now that Dean was dead and would never hurt her again. But she still had the nightmares.

Freya shivered at the memory, and the knife nicked her finger. "Ow!" she muttered.

"Are you okay?" Hannah rushed to her side, inspecting her finger. "Oh, it doesn't look too bad. I'll go get the bandages."

Just then, Adam walked through the door, immediately noticing that something was wrong. "What happened?" he quickly yanked off his boots and hurried to Freya's side.

"I wasn't paying attention, and I cut my finger. It's no big deal." Heat rose in her cheeks at his nearness. "Don't mind me."

Hannah brought the first aid kit into the kitchen and set it on the table. "Hello, Adam. How are you? Freya cut her finger."

"I see. That looks like it hurts. Here, let me bandage it up for you, Freya," Adam said, giving his mother a quick hug.

"I need to go get Aaron to come inside for dinner. He's in the barn," Hannah said, scurrying out of the room.

The immediate silence that followed the closing of the front door weighed heavily in the air.

"Here. Rinse it under the water," Adam said, turning on the faucet. He took her hand gently and held it under the cool water, then dried it with a towel. "Come sit at the table."

"Bossy, bossy," Freya chided him with a smile.

"You should know I am an expert at putting on bandages," Adam boasted, sitting at the table next to her. He moved his chair even closer to hers, and her heart rate spiked.

"Why is that?" she stammered.

"I got hurt all the time as a kid," Adam said, unwrapping a bandage. "My brother and I got into mischief all the time. We'd skin our knees practically every day in the summer running up and down that dirt lane." He dabbed some ointment on her cut. "Many Amish communities ban bicycles, but not here. We had bikes as kids, and we'd ride them so fast that when we crashed, we'd go flying into the fields."

Freya laughed out loud. "Did you ever get seriously hurt?"

"I fractured my wrist once," Adam said, placing the bandage on her finger.

His words made her shiver again, remembering her sprained wrist and wondering if it had been fractured, would she have received medical attention? Would she have escaped that first time, and never have lived through that nightmare? And if she hadn't, would she ever have met this amazingly wonderful, caring man? When she realized how sweetly and tenderly Adam was touching her hand, holding it still while he wrapped the bandage around her finger, her heart stuttered and her stomach flip-flopped at his nearness.

"Have you ever broken a bone?" Adam asked, not taking his eyes off her finger.

Good. He won't see the pain in my eyes, she thought glumly.

"Yeah, but not as a kid."

Adam stopped what he was doing and looked up into her face. "Dean?"

She nodded solemnly.

His grip around her finger tightened slightly, causing her cut to sting, and she pulled her hand away, breaking the moment.

"Sorry. Just thinking about him hurting you makes me so angry," he murmured, realizing his mistake. "I didn't mean to hurt your finger."

"It's okay. Thanks for bandaging it," she said, giving him a weak smile.

Aaron and Hannah came through the door, taking off their shoes.

"It smells delicious in here, as always," Aaron said. "Glad you could come tonight, Adam. Maria should be here any moment."

A moment later, the buggy pulled into the driveway, and Maria and Carter came inside after running errands in town.

"*Fweya!*" Carter cried as he ran through the door, replacing the *r* sound with a *w*. He held up paper and crayons.

"I would love to draw with you," Freya said, ruffling his blond hair. His bright smile lifted her spirits.

"Glad to see you are doing better," Maria said, pulling Freya into a hug. "Dinner looks great."

"It was all Hannah," Freya said, then chuckled. "I probably just slowed her down."

"Nonsense." Hannah waved her hand. "You are an excellent student, Freya, and you're better at cooking than you think. Next time you'll be able to make a dinner like this all on your own."

Freya laughed again. "That could end up a disaster if I use a woodstove. Amish cooking is different than what I'm used to."

"Just stick with us and we will teach you everything we know," Maria said with a wink.

They all gathered around the table. After the silent prayer, Adam spoke up.

"I'd like to go visit Robert's grave together, now that we are all united. We've learned and we've overcome so much together, and I feel like we need to mark this by going there together. What do you think?"

Everyone nodded around the table.

"I think that is a wonderful idea," Maria said. "For the first time, I will be able to go there without bitterness in my heart." Her voice cracked during her last few words, and Hannah reached for her hand.

It felt as though a hand was grabbing Freya's heart and squeezing, but not as hard as before.

"Absolutely," Aaron said.

"Maybe tomorrow after church?" Adam asked.

Everyone nodded again.

"That sounds wonderful," Hannah said.

Freya couldn't even think of what to say. She glanced over at Carter, who seemed as though he was pretending to not know what was going on, but Freya knew he was so much smarter than that.

Would Maria one day tell her son that it was Freya who had killed his father?

"Freya?"

Freya blinked, coming out of her deep thoughts. "I'm sorry, what?"

"Do you want to go with us?" Adam asked.

"Yes, of course. I've also changed so much since coming here, and I would like to go with all of you," Freya said.

"Good. Let's plan to meet there tomorrow after church then," Adam said.

During church, Freya listened intently as the speaker spoke about not being overcome by evil, but overcoming evil with good. Once again, Hannah whispered translations in her ear, but Freya was already picking up several Pennsylvania Dutch words from her time there so far.

Do not be overcome by evil, but overcome evil with good, she told herself. Her mind wandered as she remembered everything that had happened to her since coming here, from meeting Adam, to when he'd rejected her, then when he'd forgiven her. Then she remembered how her heart had shattered when Maria had been so bitter toward her, but now they were miraculously becoming friends.

Then the terrifying day when Dean had attacked her in Boston, then the fire—it all came rushing back to her. Most of all, the forgiveness of the Lapp family was what resonated with her. She still marveled at how Adam's parents had so readily forgiven her, just as Jesus had forgiven her of all her sins. Though it had taken longer for Adam and Maria to come around, they'd also forgiven her, and that alone astounded her.

She glanced over at Adam, who was sitting on the men's side of the room. His eyes were set on the speaker. As if Adam felt her eyes on him, he turned and his gaze met hers. They shared a fleeting connection, then each turned away respectfully.

I can't believe Adam chose me, that he loves me, Freya thought. *How is it possible?*

Then a small, quiet voice spoke in her heart.

Your heavenly Father loves you despite your mistakes, the voice told her. *Jesus died for you so you can have glorious, eternal life.*

It was all so wonderful, so surreal. She was loved by Adam, the Lapp family, this church, and God—how could it all be possible? Her heart felt as though it might overflow with joy at this realization.

Before she knew it, the service was over, and everyone went downstairs to share the potluck meal together. She spoke with everyone confidently and joyfully, yet in the back of her mind, she thought about how later on, they would go to the cemetery.

Not very long ago, this would be something she would dread. Now, somehow, she was looking forward to it.

"Ready to go?" Adam asked after the meal ended.

She nodded, and together, they walked out to his car and drove to the cemetery.

"It'll take longer for them to get there, so how about if we go for coffee first?" Adam asked.

"Sure. Sounds good," Freya said. They drove to a local drive-through coffee shop, got two cups of coffee, then drove to the cemetery.

"Let's park here," Adam said, parking a distance away from the grave. "We can walk the rest of the way." He drained his coffee cup and stashed it in the cupholder.

Freya glanced at him, thinking that was odd, but didn't say anything as they got out of the car. Freya also finished her coffee and put the empty cup in the car before shutting the door.

They walked across the field to the small cemetery, where Freya could see Aaron, Hannah, Maria, and Carter waiting.

The other two times she'd been here, the ground had been frozen underneath encrusted snow. Now that spring was coming, the snow was melting, revealing patches of budding green grass—a symbolism of her new life. Her pain and regrets had finally thawed, and the promise of a new life to come had broken through.

"I hope we didn't make them wait too long," Freya murmured under her breath.

As they came closer, Freya saw something red strewn across the ground in two lines, as if marking a path.

"What on earth? Are those…rose petals?" she whispered, then her heart galloped like a thousand wild horses.

What was happening? Was this what she thought it was?

As they came closer, Adam reached for her hand. Now Freya could clearly see a path marked out, framed by red rose petals, that led to Robert's grave. Her eyes stung fiercely with tears, and no matter how much she tried to keep them from spilling, they poured down her cheeks as she looked up at Adam.

"Did you do all of this?" she whispered just loud enough for him to hear.

"They all helped me," Adam murmured, taking both of her hands and leading her to Robert's gravestone. "We wanted a special place for this occasion, and it was Maria's idea to do this here."

Freya looked at Maria, who was beaming at them with her hands clasped together. "There's not a better place on earth for this."

Aaron and Hannah stood close together, and Carter hugged Maria's legs. They were all smiling at Freya and Adam, watching them expectantly.

To do what? Is this really happening? Freya wondered, too stunned to speak aloud.

Adam got down on one knee, pulling a small black box out of his pocket. Freya's heart felt as though it might burst from joy as she watched him open it.

"Freya Wilson, you are the bravest, strongest, most amazing woman I've ever met. When I first met you, I thought I would never like you, let alone love you, but I've fallen more deeply in love with you than I ever thought could be possible. You've pushed me to grow, to love, to care more deeply about people. You've shown me what grace looks like, and you taught me to live life to its fullest. I think we know most of all that it can all be gone in an instant." Adam took in a deep, shaky breath. "So, I want to ask you a question. Will you, Freya Wilson, be my wife and let me love you for the rest of my days?"

Freya's hands covered her mouth. She could hardly believe this was happening, here of all places, but as she looked around, she realized how perfect it all was. This was where she'd met Adam, where it all began. Even though Robert's death was the greatest tragedy Freya had ever known, if Robert hadn't died, they would have never met.

She looked to Maria and Carter, who were still smiling at her. How could they be fine with this happening here? How could they still love her? But yet they did, and they were even happy for her to be with Adam.

You are forgiven, Freya, a voice whispered in her heart.

And in her heart, she felt peace. Freedom. Clarity.

"Yes, Adam. I will marry you. I love you!" she cried, pulling him to his feet and throwing her arms around his neck. Since Amish couples here did not show physical affection in public, she knew that they would have to wait until later to share their first kiss as an engaged couple.

Adam hugged her tightly, conveying how happy he was. "I love you too," he said. "More than you know."

"So," Freya said, pulling away. "You all helped with this?"

"We came over and did it while you were getting coffee," Aaron said.

"And you were all okay with Adam proposing to me here?" Freya said, turning to Maria. "Are you sure?"

"Of course," Maria said. "I wanted Robert's grave to have a happy memory tied to it. Besides, this is where you met, right?"

New tears threatened to fall from Freya's eyes, and she hugged Maria. "Thank you."

Carter clapped his hands. "Yay!"

Freya grinned, and she bent down to hug the boy. "This is a happy day, isn't it?"

"You could get married here," Maria said, clasping her hands together. "What do you think?"

Freya stood up, looking at Adam. "Well, what do you think, my love?"

Adam smiled. "I've never heard of a wedding in a cemetery before, but I think this is the perfect place to get married. I think Robert would approve."

Maria nodded. "Yes, he would."

Later on, as everyone began to leave, Adam and Freya walked back to his car hand in hand. Freya held up her hand in the sun, admiring how the diamond on her finger caught the rays, sparkling.

"It's beautiful, Adam. Thank you. This was perfect." She squeezed his hand.

"Growing up, I never thought I'd give the love of my life a ring," Adam said. "The Amish here don't wear jewelry. But as I got older, as I started thinking about leaving, I dreamed of the day when I'd propose and give my fiancée a diamond ring." He chuckled. "And here we are."

"This will be a beautiful place for our wedding," she murmured. "I'm sure it's beautiful here in the summer and fall."

Adam nodded. "It sure is. I'm thinking September. The foliage is incredible. People travel for miles to see it. It's truly spectacular. What do you think?"

"September sounds perfect," Freya said as they reached the car. "But honestly, I'd marry you tomorrow if I could."

"Oh, really?" He looked around to see if anyone was around, then pulled her close to him. "You know, I believe you owe me our first kiss as an engaged couple."

Her heart soared as she savored the way she felt in his arms. Warmth spread through her like hot soup on a winter day.

She stood on her tiptoes, and when his lips softly touched hers, sparks ignited in her heart.

When they pulled away, she sighed in contentment.

"It's amazing how God takes the most broken people and situations and uses them for His glory, isn't it? He took our tragedies and used them to bring us together forever," Freya whispered.

Adam slowly shook his head. "Looking back, I never thought this would be possible." He bent down so their noses touched. "You know, you remind me of Robert. He always pushed me to do things that scared me, to be better. You do that, too."

"Well, Adam Lapp, before I met your family, I never had a true family. I never knew what real love looked like. You showed me what love is," Freya said softly.

"I guess God has taught us both things that we will never forget," Adam said, pulling back to look into her eyes.

Freya reached up and put her arms around Adam's neck. "Yes, He has, and He will for the rest of our lives."

Chapter Thirty-two

Freya sighed as she stepped out of the house she had inherited from Shirley. She rested her hand on the doorframe, letting out a breath. Though she'd thought she'd be more devastated about selling this house, she mostly felt...freedom. A young couple with three children had bought it, and she was happy to know that the house would be filled with happy memories again.

Selling the house felt like opening a new chapter in her life. It had been so tainted by horrible memories with Dean, literally stained by smatterings of her own blood that she'd had to scrub out of the walls and floors.

She never got the money back that Dean had spent, but she realized she didn't need it.

"What a beautiful house. So full of character," the realtor said. "And it went for even higher than what you were hoping for."

Freya grinned, looking up at her fiancé. "More than what we needed to buy our house in Unity." The house was right next to the Amish community, and Hannah had already insisted that they come over for family dinner every Wednesday night. "Let's go see Victor now."

They drove across the street, since they would be driving straight home after, and went to see Victor already waiting for them on his front porch step. When he saw Freya, he ambled over to her as quickly as he could and threw his arms around her.

"I'm so glad to see you safe," he murmured in her ear, and her eyes pricked with tears at the thought of all he'd done for her.

"Thank you so much, Victor. It's been quite the journey."

"And your journey is just beginning." Victor pulled away and looked Adam up and down. "So, you're the officer who was here grilling me about Dean and Freya? I thought you were one of Dean's goons. Freya called me and explained everything. I'm sorry I didn't tell you anything. I was just trying to protect her."

"Oh, I understand now," Adam said. "Freya did say you're very protective."

"I sure am." Victor stood up a little taller and hiked his chin.

"Victor, this is Adam Lapp, my fiancé," Freya said. "Adam, this is Victor Johnston."

"Nice to meet you." Victor shook his hand, then furrowed his brow. "Freya has told me all about you on the phone. She thinks the world of you. I just have to say I'm glad something good came out of such a tragedy. I'm very sorry about your brother."

"Thank you, sir," Adam said.

"It's just so ironic that you're his brother and how you met and fell in love." Victor stepped back and smiled at them both. "It's almost as beautiful as the story of how my wife and I met, but that's for another time." He waved his hand dismissively, then gave Adam a stern look. "You better take care of her, you hear?"

Adam put one hand up in mock defense. "You have full permission to come after me if I don't, but I promise I will take very good care of her." He planted a kiss on Freya's cheek.

Victor chuckled, pointing a thumb at Adam. "I like this guy. Congratulations on your engagement. I'm just glad to see Freya happy after all this time." He grinned at her, then motioned for them to follow him. "Come on in and have a seat."

"I wouldn't have found Adam without your help," Freya said as they followed him into the house and sat down in the living room where hundreds of books lined the built-in shelves. "Did you get the wedding invitation?"

"Absolutely, and I will be there," Victor said, gesturing to the invitation hanging on his fridge. "Wouldn't miss it for the world."

Freya squeezed Adam's hand and took a deep breath. "Would you walk me down the aisle along with my future father-in-law, Victor? I never had a father, but you've cared for me as if I were your own daughter."

Victor placed a hand on his chest. "Oh, I would be honored, my dear. That makes me so happy. I can't wait."

"Oh, good," Freya said. "Thank you. Also, I have something else to ask you. Because I'll be moving to Unity, I won't get to see you as much anymore. I know you have lived alone now since your wife passed, so we were wondering…" Freya glanced at Adam and smiled. "We were wondering if you'd like to move in with us in Unity." Freya was worried about him and wanted to take care of him, but she knew if she told him that, he would just insist he was fine. "We would really love to have you there, and there's plenty of room for you to have your own space."

Victor blinked, then took a deep breath, looking around his home. "That is a very generous offer, and I do appreciate it so much. My wife and I bought this house right after we got married, and we shared fifty wonderful years here. We raised our daughter here." He turned to Adam. "Did Freya tell you about our daughter?"

Adam nodded solemnly. "Yes. I'm very sorry."

"She would have liked you two," Victor said, shifting his weight on his chair. "This is my home. I lived the best years of my life here, and I'll die here. I feel like if I left, I'd be leaving the memory of my wife behind. I know they say you hold the memory of loved ones in your heart, but I'm a very sentimental old man, and I love this house. I'm sorry, and I thank you, but I can't leave this old place."

"We understand," Freya said. "Please, if you ever change your mind, will you please let us know?"

"Like when I get so old they'll want to put me in a nursing home?" He chuckled. "Well, if I have to choose between a smelly old nursing home and living with you, then yes, I will come live with you. For now, I'm staying here."

Freya smiled, relieved. So maybe there was some hope he'd change his mind one day. Freya opened her purse and pulled out an envelope filled with cash—the amount that Victor had given her the day she'd run away from Dean. "This is for you, Victor. I want to pay you back, and I want you to have the car back." Freya stood up, but Victor waved her back.

"No, no, Freya. The money and the car were my gifts to you. I have no family to give it to. Now that Dean is dead, I will sell the car to you for a few dollars to make it legal. Money means nothing to me in my old age. This house is long paid off, and I have plenty to keep me comfortable for the next fifty years. I bought and sold several properties over the years and had tenants, enough to make a nice nest egg for myself. Well, I don't need it anymore. I just want you to promise me you'll put the money to good use—maybe pay off your mortgage or save it for your kids' college funds or buy a car. Maybe go on a trip to Hawaii. Something like that."

Freya laughed out loud, her shock and gratitude bubbling over into a girlish giggle. "Oh, Victor. This is the nicest thing anyone has ever done for me—for us. I don't even know what to say. Thank you so much."

"A trip to Hawaii does sound nice." Adam grinned at Freya and put his arms around her shoulders.

"It sure does. I've always wanted to go," Freya said.

"Well, then, you should go!" Victor exclaimed jovially. "In fact, I've changed my will so that when I kick the bucket, you will inherit this house, Freya. You can rent it out if you'd like, or you can sell it—by then I'll be dead, so what will I care?" He chuckled and gave them a wide grin.

Freya sank back down onto the couch, stunned. "This house?" She looked around, wide-eyed. "Are you sure, Victor?"

"Absolutely. I can change my will so that both of you will inherit it after you're married, as my wedding gift to you."

"That is so generous, sir," Adam put in.

"I figured you wouldn't want to live across the street after being in that house with all its terrible memories," Victor said, gesturing to the house across the street that Shirley had given to Freya. "So you can do whatever you'd like with this house."

Freya's eyes filled with tears. "Oh, Victor." She got up and hurried over to him, throwing her arms around him. "I don't know how to thank you. I am so grateful."

He put his arms around her and patted her back. "Just promise me that you'll live a full life without fear and regrets. Don't let anything or anyone hold you back." He pulled away and looked into her eyes, his voice cracking. "You are like a daughter to me, and I want you to have a life full of love and happiness."

Freya let out a sob, tears of joy running down her cheeks. "I will. I promise."

"Now, you two have a new life to go live," Victor said. "I will see you at the wedding soon."

As Freya and Adam left the house and got in their car, she turned around to look at the two houses one last time as Adam drove away.

"Do you want to stop somewhere for lunch, or are you ready to go home?" Adam asked, reaching for her hand.

She faced the road ahead, taking a deep breath. "For the first time in my life, I'm finally going to have a true home. I can't wait to make it ours." She looked over and smiled at her fiancé. "So yes, I'm ready to go home."

EPILOGUE

The autumn foliage was truly stunning. Vibrant shades of flaming red, orange, and yellow colored the woods of Unity on Adam and Freya's wedding day.

Freya waited with Aaron and Victor behind a cluster of trees near the cemetery, out of sight from the guests. Since Freya never knew her father, Aaron and Victor were the only two father figures in her life. Even though he was Amish, Aaron had been honored when she'd asked him to walk her down the aisle. Freya didn't care if it wasn't traditional to have two men walk her down the aisle—they meant the world to her.

"It's time to go," Aaron whispered, offering her his arm. "I know we're not supposed to comment on outward appearances, but you look beautiful, dear. I am so happy and grateful to call you my daughter-in-law." He gave her a wide smile.

"Well, I'm allowed to comment on appearances, and you look as beautiful as my wife did when we got married," Victor said, patting her arm.

Freya's red hair was curled and braided into a half-up style with tiny white flowers tucked into the strands. Her long-sleeved white gown was covered in lace from the tips of her fingers to the hem, and it buttoned all the way down the back. A long white veil draped down her back.

"Thank you both." Her cheeks heating, she took their arms. As they walked out from behind the trees and the music changed to a love song that she and Adam had chosen, the guests rose from their seats.

Since Freya didn't have family or friends outside of Unity, all the guests were people she had met since leaving Boston—both Amish and *Englisher,* but mostly Amish. She'd been surprised to find out they had no problem with attending an *Englisher* wedding.

They are all here for Adam and me, she thought, her heart nearly bursting out of her chest with thankfulness as she walked down the aisle, tears spilling down her cheeks.

She quickly scanned the faces of all the guests—Mae Miller, Lydia, Laura, Hannah, Leah, Damaris, Dominic, Ella Ruth, Gilbert, Mary and Gideon Mast, Belle, Adriana, and so many more new friends she had made since coming here. Then her eyes met Adam's.

His eyes were already red with the tears that coursed down his face. He looked incredibly handsome in his black suit, looking at her with love and devotion in his eyes. At that moment, Freya's eyes stung with more tears, and a few escaped down her cheek.

On Adam's left stood Gilbert, Elijah, and Dominic, his best friends and groomsmen. On the right of the altar stood Freya's bridesmaids, Laura, Lydia, and Maria, who were watching her tearfully. Even the normally stoic Lydia shed a tear.

Aaron patted her arm, then released her, then Victor did the same, smiling at her. They turned to sit down in the front row as Freya joined hands with Adam.

"You're beautiful," he mouthed to her as the pastor conducted the ceremony. She tried to listen, but she kept getting lost in Adam's eyes, watching the way he looked at her so attentively, so tenderly, as if he wanted to kiss her right then and there before the vows were done.

Finally, after the vows were spoken, the pastor announced them husband and wife, and they shared a brief kiss. Though it was quick, it still sent heat through her body like warm honey. When Amish couples were married in Unity, they didn't even kiss at the wedding, so it was kept very brief out of respect for their guests.

Afterward, they held the reception at the Amish church and a potluck lunch. Everyone brought a dish to share, ranging from pies, casseroles, salads, sandwiches, and pastries.

"This day couldn't be more perfect," Freya said to Adam when they finally had a moment together without someone congratulating them.

Hannah, Aaron, and Maria walked over to where Freya and Adam were standing in the corner of the church.

"We are so glad to have you join our family," Hannah said, hugging Freya.

"Thank you. I've always prayed to be part of a family, and I couldn't imagine a better one," Freya replied, feeling a lump forming in her throat.

Maria took her hand. "I always wanted a sister, and I am so glad you're my sister now."

Freya threw her arms around Maria. "I've never had a sister either, so this is a dream come true."

Maria pulled away and looked at both Freya and Adam. "Now that you and Adam are married, I have something to ask you. This might not be the best time to ask, but I'm just so full of happiness, I'm afraid I can't keep myself from asking. Would you be Carter's guardians if anything ever happened to me? One thing I've learned through everything we've been through is that life is so short and can end in an instant. It would bring me peace knowing that you would raise my son if anything ever happened to me." Tears swelled in Maria's eyes, and she swatted them away. "You two will make wonderful parents someday."

Deeply touched, Freya put a hand over her heart. "Oh, Maria." She glanced at Adam, who was nodding, clearly giving his approval. "We'd be honored."

"Oh, thank you," Maria said, leaning in closer to Freya. "This is one of the happiest days of my life."

"This is by far the happiest day of *my* life," Freya said with a laugh.

After lunch, the women and girls formed an assembly line and hand washed all the dishes in the downstairs sink and also in large containers of soapy water to save time, then they dried and stacked them. Several hours later, after a day full of food and fellowship, families started to leave one by one.

"You two go on," Hannah said, shooing them away. "We will clean the rest and take care of everything." Since the guests had already done most of the cleaning up, there wasn't much left to do.

"You don't have to ask me twice," Adam said, grinning as he grabbed Freya's hand. "Come on, my lovely wife."

Freya laughed and followed him. "Bye! Thank you!" she called to their family before letting him lead her outside.

As soon as they stepped outside, Adam looked to see if anyone was around, then brought his lips down to hers in an earth-shattering kiss. He wrapped his arms around her so tight, he lifted her off the ground.

She pulled away, her heart fluttering, not wanting to open her eyes.

"Now that you're my wife, I get to do that every day," Adam said, tucking a curl behind her ear.

"Don't you forget it," Freya teased. She leaned into him, and as he held her, she gazed upon the land that surrounded her, from the woods to the cluster of homes at the bottom of the hill to the expanse of farm fields that seemed to never end. "I've lived in a lot of places throughout my life, but this place by far has changed me the most," she murmured.

"It has a way of doing that to people," Adam said with a chuckle.

"I'm glad we will be building our life together here."

Adam nodded, pulling away just enough to look into her eyes. "Speaking of beginning our life together—I think we should go do that now. What do you say, my darling?" He held out his hand to her.

"Yes. Let's go." She grabbed his hand, and together, they walked to the car, decorated with streamers and tin cans and words in the back window that said *Just Married*, which had been a sharp contrast to the black buggies that had filled the parking lot earlier.

Hand in hand, they drove away down the winding country road. It was the same road where Freya had thought her life was going to end during that fateful blizzard, but God had used that same road to bring her a new life full of love and joy instead—and He would continue to do so for many years to come.

About the Author (Ashley Emma)

Visit www.AshleyEmmaAuthor.com to download free eBooks by Ashley Emma!

Ashley Emma wrote her first novel at age 12 and published it at 16. She was home schooled and knew since she was a child that she wanted to be a novelist. She's written over 20 books and is now an award-winning USA Today bestselling author of over 15 books, mostly Amish fiction. (Many more titles coming soon!)

Ashley has a deep respect and love for the Amish and wanted to make sure her Amish books were genuine. When she was 20, she stayed with three Amish families in a community in Maine where she made many friends and did her research for her Amish books. To read about what it was like to live among the Amish, check out her book Amish for a Week (a true story).

Ashley's novel Amish Alias was a Gold Medal Winner in the NYC Book Awards 2021. Her bestselling book Undercover Amish received 26 out of 27 points as a finalist in the Maine Romance Writers Strut Your Stuff novel writing competition in 2015. Its sequel Amish Under Fire was a semi-finalist in Harlequin's So You Think You Can Write novel writing competition also in 2015. Two of her short stories have been published online in writing contests and she co-wrote an article for ProofreadAnywhere.com in 2016. She judged the Fifth Anniversary Writing Contest for Becoming Writer in the summer of 2016.

Ashley owns Fearless Publishing House in Maine where she lives with her husband and four children. She is passionate about helping her clients self-publish their own books so they can build their businesses or achieve their dream of becoming an author.

Download some of Ashley's free Amish books at www.AshleyEmmaAuthor.com.

ashley@ashleyemmaauthor.com

>>>>Check out Ashley's TV interview with News Center 6 Maine! https://www.newscentermaine.com/article/news/local/207/207-interview/what-led-a-writer-to-the-amish/97-5d22729f-9cd0-4358-809d-305e7324f8f1

GET 4 OF ASHLEY EMMA'S AMISH EBOOKS FOR FREE

www.AshleyEmmaAuthor.com

Your free ebook novellas and printable coloring pages

   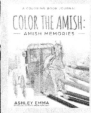

All of Ashley Emma's Books on Amazon

(This series can be read out of order or as standalone novels.)

Detective Olivia Mast would rather run through gunfire than return to her former Amish community in Unity, Maine, where she killed her abusive husband in self-defense.

Olivia covertly investigates a murder there while protecting the man she dated as a teen: Isaac Troyer, a potential target.

When Olivia tells Isaac she is a detective, will he be willing to break Amish rules to help her arrest the killer?

Undercover Amish was a finalist in Maine Romance Writers Strut Your Stuff Competition 2015 where it received 26 out of 27 points and has 455+ Amazon reviews!

Buy here: https://www.amazon.com/Ashley-Emma/e/B00IYTZTQE/

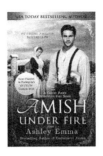

After Maria Mast's abusive ex-boyfriend is arrested for being involved in sex trafficking and modern-day slavery, she thinks that she and her son Carter can safely return to her Amish community.

But the danger has only just begun.

Someone begins stalking her, and they want blood and revenge.

Agent Derek Turner of Covert Police Detectives Unit is assigned as her bodyguard and goes with her to her Amish community in Unity, Maine.

Maria's secretive eyes, painful past, and cautious demeanor intrigue him.

As the human trafficking ring begins to target the Amish community, Derek wonders if the distraction of her will cost him his career…and Maria's life.

Buy on Amazon: https://www.amazon.com/Ashley-Emma/e/B00IYTZTQE/

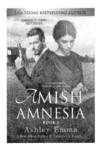

When Officer Jefferson Martin witnesses a young woman being hit by a car near his campsite, all thoughts of vacation vanish as the car speeds off.

When the malnourished, battered woman wakes up, she can't remember anything before the accident. They don't know her name, so they call her Jane.

When someone breaks into her hospital room and tries to kill her before getting away, Jefferson volunteers to protect Jane around the clock. He takes her back to their Kennebunkport beach house along with his upbeat sister Estella and his friend who served with him overseas in the Marine Corps, Ben Banks.

At first, Jane's stalker leaves strange notes, but then his attacks become bolder and more dangerous.

Buy on Amazon: https://www.amazon.com/Ashley-Emma/e/B00IYTZTQE/

Threatened. Orphaned. On the run.

With no one else to turn to, these two terrified sisters can only hope their Amish aunt will take them in. But the quaint Amish community of Unity, Maine, is not as safe as it seems.

After Charlotte Cooper's parents die and her abusive ex-fiancé threatens her, the only way to protect her younger sister Zoe is by faking their deaths and leaving town.

The sisters' only hope of a safe haven lies with their estranged Amish aunt in Unity, Maine, where their mother grew up before she left the Amish.

Elijah Hochstettler, the family's handsome farmhand, grows closer to Charlotte as she digs up dark family secrets that her mother kept from her.

Buy on Amazon here: https://www.amazon.com/Ashley-Emma/e/B00IYTZTQE/

When nurse Anna Hershberger finds a man with a bullet wound who begs her to help him without taking him to the hospital, she has a choice to make.

Going against his wishes, she takes him to the hospital to help him after he passes out. She thinks she made the right decision...until an assassin storms in with a gun. Anna has no choice but to go on the run with her patient.

This handsome stranger, who says his name is Connor, insists that they can't contact the police for help because there are moles leaking information. His mission is to shut down a local sex trafficking ring targeting Anna's former Amish community in Unity, Maine, and he needs her help most of all.

Since Anna was kidnapped by sex traffickers in her Amish community, she would love nothing more than to get justice and help put the criminals behind bars.

But can she trust Connor to not get her killed? And is he really who he says he is?

Buy on Amazon: https://www.amazon.com/Ashley-Emma/e/B00IYTZTQE/

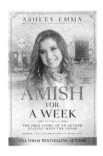

Ever wondered what it would be like to live in an Amish community? Now you can find out in this true story with photos.

Buy on Amazon: https://www.amazon.com/Ashley-Emma/e/B00IYTZTQE/

An heiress on the run.
A heartbroken Amish man, sleep-walking through life.
Can true love's kiss break the spell?
After his wife dies and he returns to his Amish community, Dominic feels numb and frozen, like he's under a spell.
When he rescues a woman from a car wreck in a snowstorm, he brings her home to his mother and six younger siblings. They care for her while she sleeps for several days, and when she wakes up in a panic, she pretends to have amnesia.
But waking up is only the beginning of Snow's story.

Buy on Amazon: https://www.amazon.com/Ashley-Emma/e/B00IYTZTQE/

She's an Amish beauty with a love of reading, hiding a painful secret. He's a reclusive, scarred military hero who won't let anyone in. Can true love really be enough?

On her way home from the bookstore, Belle's buggy crashes in front of the old mansion that everyone else avoids, of all places.

What she finds inside the mansion is not a monster, but a man. Scarred both physiologically and physically by the horrors of military combat, Cole's burned and disfigured face tells the story of all he lost to the war in a devastating explosion.

He's been hiding from the world ever since.

After Cole ends up hiring her as his housekeeper and caretaker for his firecracker of a grandmother, Belle can't help her curiosity as she wonders what exactly Cole does in his office all day.

Why is Cole's office so off-limits to Belle? What is he hiding in there?

https://www.amazon.com/Ashley-Emma/e/B00IYTZTQE/

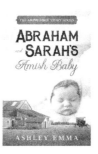

Abraham and Sarah know in their hearts that they are meant to have children, but what if they are wrong? And if they are meant to have children, how will God make it possible?

Just when all seems lost, God once again answers their prayers in a miraculous and unexpected way that begins a new chapter in their lives.

In this emotional family saga, experience hope and inspiration through this beloved Bible story retold.

https://www.amazon.com/Abraham-Sarahs-Amish-Baby-family-ebook/dp/B09DWCBD7M

**Gomer is not your typical Amish woman.
On the outside, Gomer seems like a lovely, sweet, young Amish woman, but she's hiding a scandalous secret.**

Gomer was created to sing. Most of all, she loves to sing on stage for the audience--she loves the applause, the lights, and the performance--**but her Amish community forbids it.**

How can Hosea find his wife, bring her home, and piece their family back together again when it seems impossible?

https://www.amazon.com/Hosea-Gomers-Amish-Secret-family-ebook/dp/B09GQVCBM9

When Ruth's husband Mahlon dies one morning on his way out the door, she thinks she will never find love again--but little does she know that God has a miraculous plan for her future.

In Unity, Ruth catches the eye of successful farmer Boaz Petersheim. He's drawn to her not only because of her beauty, but because of her loyalty and devotion to her mother-in-law, Naomi. When Ruth asks for a job harvesting wheat in his fields, he immediately hires her because he can see how much she wants to take care of her mother-in-law, even though she is the only female worker among his male employees.

When rumors sweep through the community after a near-death experience, who will Boaz believe?

https://www.amazon.com/gp/product/B09M7XV76C

Excerpt of Amish Alias (Book 5)

CHAPTER ONE

"Mom, are we there yet?" nine-year-old Charlotte Cooper asked from the back seat of her parents' van. Her legs pumped up and down in anticipation. Mom had said they were going to a farm where her aunt lived, and she couldn't wait to see the animals. The ride was taking forever.

"Just a few more minutes, honey," Mom said from the driver's seat.

Charlotte put her coloring book down and patted the lollipop in her pocket Mommy had given her for the trip. She was tempted to eat it now, but decided to save it for the ride home. She hoped it wouldn't melt in her pocket. The van was hot even though she was wearing shorts and her favorite pink princess T-shirt. Charlotte shoved her damp blonde curls out of her eyes.

The van passed a yellow diamond-shaped sign that had a black silhouette of a horse and carriage on it. "Mommy, what does that sign mean?"

"It's a warning to drive slowly because there are horses and buggies on the road here."

"What? Horses and bugs?"

"No." Mom smiled. "They're called buggies. They're like the carriages you've seen in your storybooks. Except they are not pumpkin-shaped. They are black and shaped more like a box."

Charlotte imagined a black box being pulled by a horse. If she were a princess, she would like a pumpkin carriage much better. "Why are there buggies here?"

"The folks who live in this area don't drive cars."

They don't drive cars? Charlotte thought. "Then what do they drive?"

"They only drive buggies," Mom said.

How fast do buggies go? Charlotte wondered. Not fast as a car, I bet. "Why would anyone not drive a car? They're so much faster than buggies."

"I know, honey. Some people are just …different." Mom glanced at Charlotte in the rear-view mirror. "But being different isn't a bad thing."

Charlotte gazed out the window. Even though they had just passed a pizza place a few minutes ago, all she could see now were huge fields and plain-looking houses.

There was nothing around. This looked like a boring place to live. What did people do to have fun here besides playing outside?

A horse and carriage rumbled past them on the unpaved road, going in the other direction. A girl wearing a blue dress and a white bonnet sat on the top seat, guiding a dark brown horse. She looked just like a picture Charlotte had seen in her history book at school. "Look, Mom." Charlotte pointed at the big black box on wheels.

"It's not polite to point, Charlie."

Charlotte dropped her hand to her side. "Why is that girl dressed like a pilgrim, Mom? She's wearing a bonnet. Are we near Plymouth Plantation?"

Mom didn't answer. Maybe she was too distracted. She seemed really focused on the mailbox up ahead.

"We're here," Mom said and turned onto a long driveway.

Charlotte gaped at the chocolate-colored horses in the fields and the clucking chickens congregating in the front yard. The van bounced over bumps on the gravel path leading to a huge tan house with bright blue curtains hanging in the windows. The dark red roof had a large metal pipe coming out of the top with smoke coming out of it, and behind the house stood a big red barn. Charlotte wondered how many animals were in there.

Mom parked the van and helped Charlotte out. "I'm going inside to talk to your Aunt Esther. I don't want to bring you inside because... Well... You should just wait here. I won't be long."

"Can I walk around?"

Before Mom could answer, a young boy about Charlotte's age walked out of the barn. He saw them and waved.

"Can I go play with him?" Charlotte asked.

"Hi!" The boy ran over. "I've never seen you around here before. Want to go see the animals in the barn?"

"Can I go in the barn with him?" Charlotte asked her mother.

"What's your name?" Mom asked the boy. "Is Esther your Maam?"

"I'm Elijah. No, she's not my mother. My Maam and Daed are out running errands, so I'm playing here until they get back. My parents are best friends with Esther and Irvin. I come here all the time. I know my way around the barn real well."

Mom crossed her arms and bit her lip, then looked at Charlotte. "I suppose you can go in. But stay away from the horses."

"We will, ma'am," said Elijah.

Charlotte and Elijah took off running toward the barn. They ran into the dim interior and she breathed in. It smelled like hay and animals, just like the county fair she had gone to last fall with her mom and dad. To the left, she heard pigs squealing. To the right, she heard sheep bleating.

Which animals should we go see first? Charlotte wondered, tapping her toes on the hay-covered floor.

Elijah leaned over the edge of the sheep pen, patting a lamb's nose. He was dressed in plain black-and-white clothing and a straw hat. His brown hair reached the collar of his white shirt. He even wore suspenders. Charlotte glanced down at her princess T-shirt and wondered why he didn't dress like other kids at her school. Every kid she knew wore cool T-shirts. Why are the people here dressed in such plain, old-fashioned clothes?

Charlotte stepped forward. He turned around, looked at her, and grinned. "So what's your name, anyway?"

"I'm Charlotte. Well, you can call me Charlie."

"Charlie? That's a boy's name."

"It's my nickname. I like it."

"Suit yourself. Where are you from?"

"Biddeford, Maine. Where are you from?"

"I live in Smyrna, Maine."

"Oh." Charlotte raised an eyebrow. Smyrna? Where was that?

Elijah smiled. "It's a bigger Amish community in northern Maine."

Charlotte shrugged. "Never heard of it."

Elijah shrugged. "Want to pet the sheep?"

"Yeah." They climbed up onto some boards stacked along the edge of the enclosure. Several of the animals sniffed their fingers and let out high-pitched noises. "They sound like people," Charlotte said, giggling. "The lambs sound like babies crying, and the big sheep sound like adults making sheep noises."

When the biggest sheep looked at them and cried baaa loudly, they laughed even harder.

Charlotte looked at the boy next to her, who was still watching the sheep. A small smear of dirt covered some of the freckles on his cheek, and his brown eyes sparkled when he laughed. The hands that gripped the wooden boards of the sheep pen looked strong. She wondered what it would be like if he held her hand. As she watched Elijah tenderly stroke the nose of a sheep, she smiled.

When one lamb made an especially loud, funny noise that sounded like a baby crying, Elijah threw his head back as he laughed, and his hat fell off. Charlotte snatched it up and turned it over in her hands. "Wow. I've never held a straw hat before. We don't have these where I live. I thought people only wore ones like these in the olden days."

Elijah shrugged. "What's wrong with that?"

"Nothing." Charlotte smiled shyly and offered it back to him. "Here you go."

Elijah held up his hand. "You can keep it if you want." He smiled at her with those dark eyes.

Charlotte got a funny feeling in her stomach. It was the same way she felt just before saying her lines on stage in the school play. She knew she should say, "Thank you," like Mom had taught her. But she couldn't speak the words. Instead, she took the lollipop out of her pocket and handed it to him.

"Thanks," Elijah said, eyes wide.

"You're welcome."

Elijah gestured to Charlie's ankle. "Hey, what happened to your ankle?"

Charlie looked down at the familiar sight of the zig-zagging surgical scars that marred her ankle. "I've had a lot of surgeries on my ankle. When I was born, it wasn't formed right, but now it's all better and I can run and jump like other kids."

"Does it hurt?"

"No, not anymore. But it hurt when I had the surgeries. I had, like, six surgeries."

"Wow, really?"

"Charlotte!" Mom called. "We have to leave. Right now."

"Thanks for the hat, Elijah." Charlotte turned to leave. Then she stopped, turned around, and kissed him on the cheek.

Embarrassment flushed Elijah's cheeks.

Uh oh. Her own face heated, Charlotte sprinted toward her mother's voice.

"Get in the car," Mom said. "Your aunt refused to speak with us. She wants us to leave."

Charlotte had never heard her mother sound so upset. She climbed into the van, and Mom hastily buckled her in.

"Why didn't she want to talk to us, Mom?" Charlotte said.

Mom sniffed and shook her head. "It's hard to explain, baby."

"Why are you crying, Mom?"

"I just wanted to talk to my sister. And she wanted us to go away."

"That's not very nice," Charlotte said.

"I know, Charlie. Some people aren't nice. Remember that."

The van sped down the driveway as Charlotte clutched the straw hat.

"Why are you going so fast?" Charlotte said and craned her neck, hoping to see Elijah. She saw him standing outside the barn with one hand holding the lollipop and the other hand on his cheek where she'd kissed him. He was smiling crookedly.

Mom looked in the rearview mirror at Charlotte.

"Sorry," Mom said and slowed down.

Charlotte settled in her seat. She hoped she'd see Elijah again, and maybe he'd be her very own prince charming, like in her fairytale books.

But Mom never took her to the farm again.

CHAPTER TWO
Fifteen years later

"Hi, Mom," twenty-four-year-old Charlie said, stepping into her mother's hospital room in the cancer ward. "I brought you Queen Anne's lace, your favorite." She set the vase of white flowers on her mom's bedside table.

"Oh, thank you, honey." Mom smiled, but her face looked thin and pale, a bright scarf covering her head. "Come sit with me." She patted the edge of the bed, and Charlie sat down, taking her mother's frail hand.

"You know why Queen Anne's lace are my favorite flowers?" Mom asked quietly.

Charlie shook her head.

"Growing up in the Amish community, we'd get tons of Queen Anne's lace in the fields every summer. My sister, Esther, and I would try to pick as much as we could before the grass was cut down for hay. At the end of every August, we'd also check all around for milkweed and look for monarch caterpillars before they were destroyed. We'd try to save as many of them as we could. We'd put them in jars and watch them make their chrysalises, then watch in amazement as they transformed into butterflies and escaped them. I used to promise myself that I'd get out into the world one day, just like the butterflies, and leave the Amish community behind. I knew it would be painful to leave everyone and everything I knew, but it would be worth it."

"And was it?" Charlie asked, leaning in close.

"Of course. It was both—painful and worth it. I don't regret leaving though. I never have. I miss my family, and I wish I could talk to them, but it was their choice to shun me. Not mine." Determination still shone in Mom's tired eyes. "I had already been baptized into the church when I left. That's why I was shunned. I still don't understand that rule. I still don't understand so many of their rules. I couldn't bear a life without music, and the Amish aren't allowed to play instruments. I wanted to go to college, but that's forbidden, too. Then there was your father, the Englisher, the outsider. It was too much for them, even for Esther. She swore she would never shun me. In the end, she turned her back on me, too."

Mom stared at the Queen Anne's lace, as if memories of her childhood were coming back to her. She wiped away a tear.

"And that's why she turned you away that day you took me to see her," Charlie concluded.

"Yes. Honestly, I've been so hurt, but I'm not angry with her. I don't want to hold a grudge. I can't decide if we should try to contact her or not to tell her I'm..." Mom's voice trailed off, and she blew out a lungful of air. She shook her head and looked down. "She wouldn't come to see me, anyway. There's no point."

"Really? Your own sister wouldn't come to see you, even under these circumstances?" Charlie gasped.

"I doubt it. She'd risk being shunned if she did." Mom patted Charlie's hand. "Don't get me wrong. I loved growing up Amish. There are so many wonderful things about it. They help each other in hard times, and they're the most tightly knit group of people I've ever met. Their faith is rock-solid most of the time. But most people only see their quaint, simple lifestyle and don't realize the Amish are human, too. They make mistakes just like the rest of us. Sometimes they gossip or say harsh things."

"Of course. Everyone does that," Charlie said.

Mom continued. "And they have such strict rules. Rules that were too confining for me. Once your father taught me how to play the piano at the old museum, I couldn't understand why they wouldn't allow such a beautiful instrument that can even be used to worship the Lord."

Mom shook her head. "I just had to leave. But I will always miss my family. I'll miss how God and family always came first, how it was their priority. Life was simpler, and people were close. We worked hard, but we had a lot of fun." Mom's face lit up. "We'd play so many games outside, and even all kinds of board games inside. Even work events were fun. And the food... Don't get me started on the delicious food. Pies, cakes, casseroles, homemade bread... I spent countless hours cooking and baking with my mother and sisters. There are many things I've missed. But I'm so glad I left because I married your father and had my two beautiful daughters. I wouldn't trade you two for anything. I wouldn't ever go back and do it differently."

Gratitude swelled in Charlie's chest, and she swallowed a lump in her throat. "But how could Aunt Esther do that to you? I just don't understand."

Mom shrugged her frail shoulders, and the hospital gown rustled with the movement. "She didn't want to end up like me—shunned. I don't blame her. It's not her fault, really. It's all their strict rules. I don't think God would want us to cut off friends and family when they do something wrong. And I didn't even do anything wrong by leaving. I'll never see it their way." Mom hiked her chin in defiance.

What had her mother been like at Charlie's age? Charlie smiled, imagining Mom as a determined, confident young woman. "Well, your community shouldn't have done that to you, Mom. Especially Aunt Esther, your own sister."

"I don't want that to paint you a negative picture of the Amish. They really are wonderful people, and it's beautiful there. You probably would have loved growing up there."

Charlie shook her head with so much emphasis that loose tendrils of hair fell from her ponytail. "No. I'm glad we live here. I wouldn't have liked those rules either. I'm glad you left, Mom. You made the right choice."

***

Elijah Hochstettler trudged into his small house after a long day of work in the community store with Irvin. He pulled off his boots, loosened his suspenders, and started washing his hands, getting ready to go to dinner at the Holts' house. He splashed water on his beardless face, the trademark of a single Amish man, thinking of his married friends who all had beards. Sometimes he felt like he was the last single man in the entire community.

He sat on his small bed with a sigh and looked around his tiny home. From this spot, he could see almost the entire structure. The community had built this house for him when he'd moved here when he was eighteen, just after his parents had died. The Holts had been looking out for him ever since.

His dining room and living room were one room, and the bathroom was in the corner. It was a small cabin, but he was grateful that Irvin and the other men in the community had helped him build it. Someday he wanted to build a real house, if he ever found a woman to settle down with.

Another night alone. He wished he had a wife. He was only in his early twenties, but he had dreamed of getting married ever since he was a young teenager. He knew a wife was a gift from God, and he had watched how much in love his parents had been growing up. He could hardly wait to have such a special bond with one person.

If only his parents were still alive. Even if Elijah did have children one day, they would only have one set of grandparents. How Elijah's parents would have loved to have grandchildren. At least he had Esther and Irvin Holt. They were almost like parents to him. But even with the Holts right next door, he still felt lonely sometimes.

"At least I have You, Lord," Elijah said quietly.

He opened his Bible to see his familiar bookmark. His fingers brushed the waxy paper of the lollipop wrapper he had saved from his childhood. He had eaten the little orange sucker right away, since it was such a rare treat. But even after all these years, he could still not part with the simple wrapper.

Maybe it was silly. Over a decade had passed since that blonde Englisher girl had given it to him. How long had it been? Twelve years? Fifteen years? Her name was Charlie, short for Charlotte. He knew he'd never forget it because it was such an odd nickname for a girl. He remembered her laughing eyes. And the strange, exciting feeling she had given him.

Over the years, Elijah had been interested in a few girls. But he'd never pursued any of them because he didn't feel God calling him to. He never felt the kind of connection with them that he'd experienced with that girl in the barn when he was ten years old. He longed to feel that way about a woman. Maybe it had just been feelings one only had during childhood, but whatever it was, it had felt so genuine.

All this time, he'd kept the wrapper as a reminder to pray for that girl. For over fifteen years, he'd asked God to bring Charlie back into his life.

As he turned the wrapper over in his calloused hands, he prayed, "Lord, please keep her safe, help her love you more every day, and help me also love you more than anything. And if you do bring her back to me, please help me not mess it up."

He set down his Bible and walked to the Holts' house for supper.

The aroma of beef stew warmed his insides as he stepped into the familiar kitchen. Esther was slicing her homemade bread at the table.

"Hello, Elijah."

"Hi, Esther. I was wondering, do you remember that young girl named Charlie and her mother who came here about fifteen years ago? She was blonde, and she and her mother were Englishers. Who were they?"

"I don't know what you're talking about." Esther cut into the bread with more force than necessary.

"It's hard to forget. Her mom was so upset when they left. In fact, she said you refused to speak to them and made them leave. What was that all about?" He knew he was prying, but the words had just tumbled out. He couldn't stop them. "And I remember her name was Charlie because it's such an odd name for a girl."

"It was no one, Elijah. It does not concern you," she said stiffly.

"What happened? Something must have happened for you to not want to talk to her. Will they come back?" he pressed, knowing he should stop talking, but he couldn't. "It's not like you at all to turn someone away at the door."

"It's a long story, one I don't care to revisit. I do not suspect they will ever come back. Now, do not ask me again," she said in such a firm voice that he jumped in surprise. Esther had always been a mild and sweet woman. What had made her so angry? Elijah had never seen her act like that before.

Elijah knew he was crossing the line by a mile, but he just had to know who the girl was. "Esther, please, I just want to know—"

Esther lifted her head slowly, looking him right in the eye, and set her knife down on the table with a thud.

"Elijah," she said in a pained, low voice. Her eyes narrowed, giving her an expression that was so unlike her usual smiling face. "The woman was my sister. I can't talk about what happened. I just can't.

It's more complicated and terrible than you'll ever know. She's shunned. Don't ask me about her again."

"My apologies, Esther." Stunned, Elijah turned away in confusion. Why didn't Esther want to talk about her sister?

***

The following night, Dad got a phone call from the hospital while they were having dinner at home. Since Dad was sitting close enough to her, Charlie overheard the voice on the phone.

"Come to the hospital now. I'm afraid this could possibly be Joanna's last night," the woman on the phone told them.

"What's going on?" Zoe, Charlie's eight-year-old sister asked, looking between Charlie and their father. "Dad? Charlie?"

Dad just hung his head.

Charlie's eyes stung with tears as she patted her younger sister's hand. "We have to leave right now, Zoe. We have to go see Mom."

As Dad sped them to the hospital, Charlie said, "Dad, if you're going to drive like this, you really should wear your seat belt. I mean, you always should, but especially right now."

"You know I hate seat belts. There shouldn't even be a law that we have to wear them. It should be our own choice. And I hate how constricting they are. Besides, that's the last thing on my mind right now. Let's not have this argument again tonight."

Charlie sighed. How many times had they argued about seat belts over the years? Even Mom had tried to get Dad to wear one, but he wouldn't budge.

They arrived at the hospital and rushed to Mom's room.

It all felt unreal as they entered the white room containing her frail mother. Charlie halted at the door.

She couldn't do this.

She felt her throat constrict, and for a moment her stomach felt sick. "No, Dad, I can't," she whispered, her hand on her stomach. "I can't say goodbye."

"Charlie, this is your last chance. If you don't, you'll regret it forever. I know you can do it. You are made of the same stuff as your mother," he said and pulled her close, stroking her hair.

Compliments were rare from her father, but she was too heartbroken to truly appreciate it.

He let out a sob, and Charlie's heart wrenched. She hated it when her dad cried, which Charlie had only seen once or twice in her life. Zoe came over and wrapped her arms around them, then they walked over to the bed together.

They held her hand and whispered comforting words. They cried and laughed a little at fond memories. Her father said his goodbyes, Zoe said her goodbyes, and then it was Charlie's turn.

She did not bother trying to stop the flow of her tears. Sorrow crushed her spirit, and no matter how hard she tried she could not see how any silver lining could come from this. Was God punishing her for something? Why was He taking her beautiful, wonderful mother?

"Charlie, I love you," her mother whispered and clutched her hand with little strength.

"I love you too, Mom," Charlie choked out.

"Please promise me, Charlie. Chase your dreams and become a teacher."

"Okay, Mom. I will."

"I just want you to be happy."

"Mom, I will be. I promise."

"Take care of them."

"I will, Mom." She barely got the words out before another round of tears came.

"Thank you. I'll be watching."

Charlie nodded, unable to speak, biting her lip to keep from crying out.

"One more thing. There's something I need to tell you. Please tell your Aunt Esther that I forgive her. Promise me you will. And tell her I'm sorry. I am so sorry." Mom sobbed, and Charlie saw the same pain in her eyes she'd seen all those years ago after they left the Amish farm.

"Why, Mom? Sorry for what?"

"I lied to you yesterday, Charlie, when I said I wasn't angry with her. I didn't want you to think I was a bitter person. Honestly, I have been angry at her for years for shunning me. It was so hard to talk about. I'm so sorry I didn't tell you the whole story."

"It's okay, Mom. I love you."

"I love you too. Tell Esther I love her and that I'm sorry. I forgive her. I hope she forgives me too..." Regret shone in Mom's eyes, then her eyes fluttered closed and the monitor next to her started beeping loudly.

"Forgive you for what? Why does she need to forgive you?" Charlie asked, panic rising in her voice as her eyes darted to the monitor. "What's wrong? What's happening?"

"Her heart rate is dropping," the nurse said and called the doctor into the room.

Charlie's heart wrenched at the sight of Zoe weeping, begging Mom not to die. Dad reached for Mom.

"Mom!" Zoe screamed.

"I'm sorry," the nurse said to Dad. "This could be it."

The doctor assessed her and slowly shook his head, frowning. "I'm so sorry. We tried everything we could. She knew she was terminal and signed a DNR. There's nothing more we can do. We will give you some privacy. Please call us if you need anything. We are right down the hall."

Charlie stood on shaky legs, feeling like they would give out at any moment. The doctor continued talking, but his words sounded like muffled gibberish in her ears. He turned and walked out of the room.

Charlie squeezed Mom's hand. "Mom? Mom? Please, tell me what you want Aunt Esther to forgive you for." It seemed so important to Mom, and Charlie wasn't sure if Dad would talk about it, so this could be her last chance to find out. If Mom's dying wish was to ask Aunt Esther's forgiveness for something, Charlie wanted to honor it.

Mom barely opened her eyes and mumbled something incoherent.

"Joanna, we are all here." Dad took Mom's other hand, and Zoe stood by Mom's bed.

Then Mom managed to whisper slowly, "I love you all." Her eyes opened for one fleeting moment, and she looked at each of them. She gave a small smile. "I'm going with Jesus." Her eyes closed.

The machine beside them made one long beeping sound.

She was gone.

Zoe cried out. They held each other as they wept.

Charlie's heart felt literally broken. She sucked in some air, feeling her chest ache, as if there was no air left to breathe.

When they finally left the hospital, she was in a haze as her feet moved on auto pilot. After they got to the apartment, hours passed before they finished drying their tears.

What would Mom say to make her feel better? That this was God's will? Charlie knew that was exactly what she'd say.

Why did God want this to happen?

Why didn't He take me instead? Mom was so...good, she thought glumly.

Her whole life she had been taught about the perfect love of Jesus and His wonderful plan for her life. Why was this part of His plan? This was not a wonderful plan.

She fell on her bed, put her head down on her pillow and sighed. "God, please just help me get through this. I don't know what to think right now. Please help me stop doubting you and just trust You."

Someone knocked on the apartment door. When neither her father nor Zoe got up to see who it was, Charlie dragged herself off her bed and went to the door, opening it.

"Alex!" she cried in surprise.

Her ex-fiancé stood in the doorway in his crisp police uniform. Alex worked at the Covert Police Detectives Unit in Kennebunk, a nearby town.

Dad and Zoe quickly came over to see what was going on.

"I need to talk to you, Charlie," he told her with determination. He glanced at Charlie's dad and sister. "Alone."

"Not going to happen, Alex," Dad said, stomping towards Alex. "In fact, you broke my daughter's heart. You cheated on her. If she doesn't want to talk to you, she doesn't have to."

"This is terrible timing, Alex. My mother just passed away," Charlie told him, tears constricting her voice. "You should go."

"I'm really sorry. But I've got to tell you something important, Charlie," Alex insisted, taking hold of Charlie's arm a little too roughly. "Come talk to me in the hallway for one minute."

"No." Charlie shoved him away.

"Charlie!" Alex yelled and pulled on her arm again, harder this time. "Come on. I wouldn't be here if it wasn't really important."

"Enough. Get out of here right now, Alex. And don't come back, you hear?" Dad's tall, daunting form seemed to take up the entire doorway. He loomed over Alex threateningly, who then backed away with his hands up and stormed down the stairs.

Charlie let out a sigh of relief. Alex was gone. For now.

She leaned against the door, remembering the morning after Alex had dumped her publicly in a restaurant. She'd woken up to find Zoe cuddled up next to her after comforting her the night before. Charlie stretched her arms above her head, then she saw the ring glistening in the morning sunlight. She'd been so overtaken by her emotions the night before that she hadn't even thought to remove it. She took it off and thrust it onto the nightstand like it was something poisonous.

As she stared at it, deep sorrow replaced her anger. No matter how angry she felt, she knew it wouldn't eclipse the heartbreak. That ring had meant too much to her. It represented their future together. All it represented was Alex's unfaithfulness, how he had cheated on her and dumped her. She pounded her pillow in frustration. "Oh, Lord, I can't believe I got in this situation," she muttered. "I never thought something like this would happen to me."

She continued to stare at the diamond, wondering how much Alex had paid for it.

I could sell it. We could really use the money...

"Hey," she whispered to herself. "That's not a bad idea."

Just to make sure it was legal, Charlie had checked what the law said. She learned that in Maine, engagement rings were conditional gifts. If the engagement was broken by the recipient, she must return the ring. However, if the engagement was broken by her fiancé or by mutual consent, the ring was hers to keep. Since Alex broke up with her, she could legally keep the ring.

She uploaded the photos she had already taken of the ring to an auction site, wrote a brief description, and considered an asking price. She decided to set the asking price a little lower than other ones like it to attract more prospective buyers.

Charlie clicked "publish listing". There. She had done it.

The ring had sold, and at first, Charlie had been excited to receive the money so that she could buy a used car. Now that she couldn't get the ring back, she was paying for it dearly, and so was her family.

She wished more than anything that she had never sold that ring.

****

If you enjoyed this sample, check out Amish Alias in ebook or paperback on Amazon: https://www.amazon.com/Amish-Alias-Romantic-Suspense-Detectives-ebook/dp/B07ZCJBWJL/ref=sr_1_3?keywords=amish+alias+by+ashley+emma&qid=1643143428&sprefix=amish+alias%2Caps%2C183&sr=8-3

Printed in Great Britain
by Amazon